VISION OF
DEATH

This Large Print Book carries the
Seal of Approval of N.A.V.H.

VISION OF DEATH

Patricia Matthews
with
Clayton Matthews

Thorndike Press • Thorndike, Maine

Library of Congress Cataloging in Publication Data:

Matthews, Patricia, 1927–
    Vision of death / Patricia Matthews with Clayton
Matthews.
        p. cm.
    ISBN 1-56054-333-7 (alk. paper : lg. print)
    1. Large type books. I. Matthews, Clayton. II. Title.
[PS3563.A853V57   1993]   93-21868
813'.54—dc20   CIP

This book is a novel. No resemblance to actual persons
living or dead is intended.

Thorndike Large Print® Basic Series edition published in
1993 by arrangement with Severn House Publishers, Ltd.

VISION OF DEATH

PROLOGUE

Consuela Torres knew about mirages; they were tricks played upon the eyes by desert heat, and she was in the middle of the Arizona desert.

Once again, she turned to look back: behind her, a huge black horse and rider were coming toward her. They appeared to be moving several feet above the desert floor on shimmering heat waves.

Consuela turned away from them, staggered on. Her throat was so parched that she could not swallow. She wore no hat, only a scarf tied around her thick black hair. It provided no protection from the scorching sun, and her skin felt like it was on fire.

She had no firm idea where she was. Her husband, Gaudencio, had told her last night that they were in a place called the Organ Pipe Cactus National Monument. The huge plants were all around her, like uncaring watchers, offering neither sympathy nor aid.

She stopped a moment to adjust her *huaraches*. Earlier, she had staggered into a barrel cactus, and several of the needle-sharp spikes had embedded themselves in her feet. She had pulled most of them out, but a few still remained, working themselves painfully deeper into her flesh.

Fighting fatigue, pain, and hopelessness, she stood erect, looking toward the range of jagged mountains toward which she was heading. Two vultures circled gracefully overhead, taking her measure.

As she forced herself to move forward, her thoughts returned to last night, and the agony and mystery of what had happened.

An eternity ago, it seemed, she, her husband, and her brother had left their home in their native village of Ahuacatlan, in Mexico. Every year for three years, Gaudencio, and her brother, Eduardo, had gone to *El Norte* to work in the fields and the orange orchards, staying there from six to nine months. There was no work in their village, and many of the men went to the States every year, returning with enough American dollars to be considered well-to-do men, in Ahuacatlan. Last year she and Gaudencio had been married, and only weeks after the wedding he had left and remained away for eight months. The money he had brought with him had been very nice to have, but to Consuela, it was insufficient to make up for the loss of her husband for all those long months when she had been alone.

This year she had begged and cried to be taken with him. She had heard about others who had found work as house-cleaners for rich American women. She could do such work. However, she had not told him that she thought she might be with child. If it was true, if she was so blessed, she wanted that child to be born in *El Norte* where he — she had no doubt it would be a son — could receive a good education. Besides, it would be months before she would begin to show.

And so she kept at Gaudencio until he at last agreed. Two days ago she, Gaudencio, and Eduardo had ridden a Yellow Arrow bus to the Mexican border town of Sonoita, across from Lukeville, Arizona. It had been a long, wearying journey, over fifteen hundred miles, but Consuela had not minded, for Gaudencio was by her side.

In Sonoita, Gaudencio had contacted two *coyotes,* Mexican-Americans who made their living guiding illegals across the border, then transporting them to Phoenix, where they hoped to find work. They paid the *coyotes* two hundred American dollars apiece, almost all the money they had left from the year before.

Last night the *coyotes* had taken them, along with two other illegals, across the border. Once across, they were loaded into an old van. Consuela had been frightened then; the *coyotes* were rough men, and treated their passengers like cattle; but she had controlled her fear, not wishing Gaudencio to regret that he had brought her.

They had been driving for about an hour when another vehicle loomed up behind them. The *coyotes* became very nervous as the vehicle continued to follow them. Then, suddenly, spotlights blazed, blinding everyone in the back of the van. The other vehicle then pulled up alongside the driver's side of the van, and an amplified voice boomed: "Pull over! Now!"

Consuela felt her heart leap. She understood little English, but the meaning was clear.

The van slowed and stopped by the side of the road. *"Vamous!"* one of the other passengers hissed. *"La Migra!"*

Consuela clutched her husband's arm. Immigration! She knew that feared word; they all did.

She felt Eduardo pushing her forward as someone opened the door of the van. Then they were out and running into the desert; she, her brother, and Gaudencio staying together; the others scattering like rabbits, into the darkness.

Consuela risked one glance back at the highway. She saw a dark figure alighting from a large pickup and horse trailer, which, spotlights blazing, was parked alongside the van.

Then Gaudencio pulled her into a shallow gully, and the two vehicles were lost from sight.

She could hear shouts behind them, followed by two loud popping sounds — gunshots! Icy terror raced through her. Gaudencio whispered in her ear, "We must hurry, Consuela!"

Consuela gasped for breath. "But . . . gunshots! Why would *La Migra* shoot us? Why would they kill?"

Eduardo answered, "They may not be *La Migra;* they may be bandits. There are many bandits along the border. They kill the *coyotes.* They kill our people. If it is bandits they will take the money from the *coyotes,* then they may come after us for the little we have. We must hurry, *hermana.*"

He tugged at her arm, and they ran on.

After what seemed a very long time, when Consuela was certain that she could not go another step, they stopped. Gasping for breath, Gaudencio said, "We have run far enough. They are not coming. We must rest."

They dropped to the ground. Consuela clung to her husband's hand. She was still trembling with cold and terror. The night air was chill, and they had left their belongings in the van — their packs, their blanket rolls.

Teeth chattering, Consuela said, "We must have a fire."

Eduardo said, "But is it safe?"

Gaudencio looked at his wife with concern. "We must risk it," he said.

The two men gathered up what wood they could find. When the fire was started, they gathered around it for warmth.

Weary beyond belief, Consuela went to sleep leaning against Gaudencio's shoulder. Much later, something awoke her. Momentarily confused, she thought for a moment that she was at home, in their room. Then the dying fire flared, and the events of the night returned painfully to her mind. She saw that she was now lying upon the ground, Gaudencio beside her. On the other side of the fire, she could see Eduardo's curled form.

Shifting her body, she became aware that she urgently needed to relieve herself. Leaving the two men asleep, she arose and walked away from the campfire. A large rock offered seclusion, and although there was no one to see her, she crept behind it. Lowering her trousers, she squatted. A faint smear of gray lightened the horizon. Soon it would be dawn. What would happen on this new day was now in God's hands.

As she began to rise, a terrible sound broke the night stillness, the same sound that she had heard behind them as they had fled into the desert. A gunshot. Then another. Each was like a blow, causing her to stagger.

Fastening her trousers with trembling fingers, she peered around the rock in the direction of the fire. She could see nothing but a dying glow and the rounded forms of her husband and brother. Heart hammering in her chest, bent low, she crept toward the fire. No one came to intercept her. The night was again quiet.

As she neared the fire, a terrible fear began growing inside her. Gaudencio and Eduardo were lying as she had left them, but she knew, in her stomach and heart, that something was wrong.

She went to Gaudencio first, and as she bent to touch him, she saw the blood soaking into the sandy soil. Pushing back his hat, she saw the dark hole between his eyes. Not even the fear of her own death could stop the keening cry that scorched her throat. Before she looked at her brother, she knew that he had suffered the same fate.

Until long after dawn, she sat with her husband's head in her lap, rocking and praying for his soul and for that of her brother. She did not wonder who had done this terrible thing, for what did that matter. Her husband and her brother were dead, and she did not even have the means to bury them. She was alone in a desert where she had not the slightest idea of where to look for human habitation. There was a highway, but it had disappeared somewhere among the swells and depressions of the rolling terrain, and she had no idea in which direction it lay.

Why was she not dead too? It would be easier to be dead than to face this pain. Reaching into Gaudencio's pocket she felt for his treasured Swiss Army knife, given him by one of his employers. Opening the longest blade, she stared at it. Two quick cuts, one on each wrist, and she would be with them.

Then she thought of the child she was now certain she was carrying. She placed her hand upon her belly, and looked up at the sky. Suicide was a sin, and to take her own life would be to murder the child.

Drying her tears, she kissed Gaudencio's cold cheek, arose, and put the knife and the small sum of money Gaudencio had been carrying into her pocket. Her brother's pockets yielded a further small sum and a packet of gum. Leaving them was very hard. She had placed their hands across their chests, and their hats over their faces, and tried not to think about the buzzards already circling overhead.

Turning her face toward the rising sun, she

began to walk in what she hoped was a northeast direction. Gaudencio had told her that was the direction in which the city of Phoenix lay.

That had been some time ago. The cool of the night had long ago turned to fiery heat. She had chewed the last of the gum, and her throat was parched and dry.

It was then that she had first turned to look behind her, and stopped to stare. Far behind her she could see something moving above the shimmering heat waves. She sheltered her burning eyes with her hand. It was difficult to tell for sure, but it seemed to be a horse and rider, dark against the golden desert floor, but seeming to float above the earth.

Stunned by heat and exhaustion, the sight filled her with dread. Once, years ago, Consuela had seen an old American movie, Spanish dubbed, about the four horsemen of the Apocalypse, war, famine, pestilence, and death. Surely this dark horse and rider must be death; she could almost see the grinning skull atop the rider's shoulders. A mirage. Surely it must be that.

Turning she resumed walking, her will alone keeping her moving. She was not certain how long she walked, but when she turned again the figure was nearer. And then she heard it, the sound of hoofbeats. Did a mirage produce sound?

She attempted to pick up her pace, but her strength was gone, and there was nowhere to run if she had been able. Slowly she turned to face her fate. The ghostly horse and rider were close now, and there was no doubt — a black horse and a black rider!

Consuela's fingers closed around the gold cross hanging on the chain around her neck, closed so tightly that the arms cut into the flesh of her palm. She muttered, "Mary, mother of Jesus, protect me!" Quickly, she made the sign of the cross.

But the black horse plunged on, the sound of its hooves growing louder and louder, like a terrible thunder. As the great horse came near, Consuela could see its eyes, white and wild, and hear the bellows of its breath. Suddenly her fear fell away, and a feeling of inevitability and a strange peace filled her. Whispering Gaudencio's name, she did not hear the sound of the bullet that pierced her brain, and sent her to join him.

CHAPTER ONE

The informal hearing was held in the chambers of Judge Nancy Pritchard.

Judge Pritchard, a rangy woman of fifty-some years, glanced up at the younger of the two women across from her desk, her sharp gray eyes assessing the trim figure, the short, thick black hair, the no-nonsense business suit. "You are Casey Farrel?"

Casey said, "Yes, Your Honor."

Judge Pritchard nodded, and turned to the other woman: fortyish, plump, too much make-up, dyed blonde hair. "And you are Edith Black?"

The other woman nodded, "Yes, ma'am . . . Yes, Your Honor."

"I gather from the information that you are related to Donnie Patterson?"

"Yes. His mother was my sister. I'm his aunt."

Casey, standing next to the woman, was sure she could smell gin on Edith's breath, although it was only ten o'clock in the morning.

The judge turned her attention again to Casey.

"And you, Miss Farrel . . . Are you related to Donnie in any way?"

"No, Your Honor, I'm not."

The judge's eyes narrowed, then she leaned back, relaxing slightly. "I hope that you both understand why I chose to hold this hearing in my chambers instead of in open court. I have found that it is far less traumatic for the child. Do either of you have any objections?"

"No objection, Your Honor," Casey said.

Edith Black shrugged. "It's fine with me, Judge. I just hope that we can get it all settled today."

"Good," Judge Pritchard said crisply, then frowned. "But don't get your hopes too high, Miss Black. These things have a tendency to drag on. It's important to the boy that I don't make a hasty decision. I trust the boy *is* here?"

Casey nodded. "He's waiting in the hall, Your Honor."

The judge looked down at her desk, shuffled papers for a moment. "Wasn't there a third party involved in these proceedings?"

"Yes, Your Honor. Joshua Whitney. He's supposed to be here . . ."

As if in answer to her statement, a knock sounded at the door.

Judge Pritchard raised her voice, "Come!"

The door opened, and a tall man stepped in. The room seemed immediately smaller, as the impact of his six-feet four-inch bulk and bustling energy had their impact.

He flashed a wide smile at Casey, said, "I apologize, Your Honor, for being late. I was out on a call and couldn't get away on time."

"I presume you are Joshua Whitney?" the judge said, glancing down at her papers.

"Yes, Your Honor." He slid into the third chair, beside Casey. "Detective Sergeant Josh Whitney. Homicide."

"Oh, yes." Judge Pritchard turned those gimlet eyes on him. "I must confess to being a little unclear as to your involvement in this affair . . ."

Edith Black broke in, "He took Donnie away from me, Judge. He and that woman!"

Judge Pritchard's dark eyebrows rose. "Took him away from you? Are you inferring a criminal action, Ms. Black?"

"There was nothing criminal about it, Your Honor," Josh said strongly. "Depend on it. There was a serial killer on the loose, and the boy was in danger. We — Miss Farrel and I, took him under our wing for his protection. In fact, Miss Black insisted on it."

Edith Black's voice was aggrieved. "But I didn't know that this woman" — she gestured at Casey — "would take off across the country with him. They were gone for weeks without me having the least idea where Donnie was!"

Judge Pritchard looked down at the papers on her desk. "Is this in reference to the case of the Dumpster Killer, so-called?"

"Yes, Your Honor," Josh said.

The judge nodded. "I thought your name was familiar, Miss Farrel. You are to be commended for your work there."

She paused a moment, reading from the papers on the desk. Then looked up at Casey. "The boy was with you when you apprehended the killer?"

"Yes," Casey said. "He was after both of us, because we were witness to his dumping the body of one of his victims."

"And you, Officer Whitney, how are you involved with Donnie?"

Josh shifted uncomfortably. "Well, Your Honor . . ."

Edith Black broke in hotly, "He and this woman were living together. That's how he was involved!"

Casey was sure that she saw Judge Pritchard's lips twitch ever so slightly in amusement.

Josh leaned across her to growl, "It wasn't like that, and you know it."

He turned to the judge. "Casey was simply staying at my house, Your Honor. We weren't *living* together: at least not in the way that Miss Black implies. Besides, *Miss* Black has her own live-in boyfriend, as I recall."

"We're going to get married," Edith Black said primly.

Josh's look spoke volumes. "You said that months ago. And how do you know Casey and I aren't going to be married?"

"And are you, Sergeant?" Judge Pritchard asked.

"Well," Josh squirmed, shooting a sidelong glance at Casey. "We've discussed it."

The judge turned her gaze on Casey, and Casey could swear she saw a twinkle there. "Miss Farrel?"

"I'm not quite ready to consider marriage yet, Your Honor," Casey said steadily.

"I see," the judge said noncommittally, looking down again at the papers on her desk. "I gather from the separate addresses I have for you that you are not living together at this time, and that you, Miss Farrel, are the one who is filing adoption papers on the boy."

She raised her eyes, and Josh squirmed again. "Well, you see, Your Honor, I would like to take Donnie, I love the kid; but as a homicide officer my hours are long, and I never know when I'll be called out. It just wouldn't work, my raising a kid by myself."

The cool, gray eyes turned to Casey. "And what about you, Miss Farrel? Isn't your situation somewhat the same? I understand that you are a member of the Governor's Task

Force on Crime. Wouldn't you have the same problems as Sergeant Whitney?"

Casey shook her head. "No, Your Honor, I don't believe so. My hours are regular, most of the time. Donnie will be in school during the day, and I will be home in the evenings, and, unless something unusual crops up, on weekends. In the event that I am called out when he's home, I've arranged for a very reliable family to take care of him, a middle-aged couple with no children of their own. He will be well cared for, Your Honor. You have my assurance on that."

"Hah!" Edith Black said contemptuously. "Getting someone else to take care of him, do you call that a good environment for a ten-year-old boy?"

Again, Josh leaned across Casey, his face hard. "It's certainly better than what you've been giving him, you and that no good lush you're living with. Donnie has told me that Karson whacks him around."

Edith Black flushed. "That's all a lie! You can't prove a word of it. And at least I don't work. I'd always be at home, always there for Donnie."

Josh snorted, and turned to the judge. "There for him? They leave him alone, Your Honor, while they go out drinking, till all hours of the night. That's how he happened

22

to be out on the street when the Dumpster Killer . . ."

Using the blunt end of her pen like a gavel, Judge Pritchard rapped sharply on her desk. "Silence! I will tolerate no squabbling in my chambers!"

Josh and Edith Black fell silent.

The judge sighed. "I'd like to talk to the boy now. Send him in, please. The three of you wait outside."

Head high, Edith Black went first. Out in the hall, a small, wiry, tow-headed boy waited for them on a bench.

He jumped up, pointedly ignoring his aunt. "Josh, Casey, what happened in there? Did the judge say I can live with you?"

"Not yet, kiddo," Casey said gruffly. "The judge wants to talk to you first."

"How come, Casey?"

"It's the usual thing in these cases." She ran her fingers through his hair. "After all, you're the subject under discussion. You should have a say in it."

"Yeah, sport," Josh said. "Go on inside and see the judge. She won't hurt you. She's nice."

Giving them a dubious look, Donnie opened the door to the judge's chambers. Josh and Casey sat on the bench he had vacated. Edith Black had already lit a cigarette, and was pacing back and forth at the end of the hall, as far away from them as she could get.

Josh said in a low voice, "I'm sorry, babe. I didn't mean to start an argument in there. And I'm sorry I was late."

Casey shrugged. "I don't think it matters all that much; you really weren't needed."

He drew back. "That's not fair! I'm as fond of the kid as you are."

Casey shook her head. "I'm sorry, I didn't mean it that way. I know how much you think of Donnie. But I'm the one who's filing for adoption."

"And whose fault is that? We could be married, living together. A married couple would have a much better shot at adopting a kid. Depend on it!"

Casey sighed. "Josh, you promised not to bring that up again, not until I'm ready."

He held a hand up before his face. "I know, I know; but the question is, when will you be ready?"

"When I'm ready, I'll let you know." She softened the words with a smile.

Judge Pritchard watched the thin, blonde child edge his way apprehensively into the room. "Donnie?"

"Yes, ma'am."

"There's nothing to be afraid of, young man. I just have a few questions I must ask

24

you." She smiled, tapping her pen on the desk. "Come on in. Shut the door."

The boy closed the door, and crossed the room to perch warily on the edge of the chair immediately in front of her desk.

"You know why you're here, don't you, Donnie?"

He bobbed his head. "Yeah. You're supposed to decide who I'm going to live with."

"That's right. I know this is painful for you, being passed back and forth; but sometimes these things are necessary. I gather that you did not like living with your aunt?"

Donnie said hesitantly, "No, ma'am. I didn't."

"Why is that? She is your closest relative, after all."

Donnie looked down at his hands. The judge could see that they were thin, brown, and bore the usual childhood scars, but that the nails were trimmed and clean. She waited patiently until he spoke. When he did, his voice was very soft.

"She don't like us very much, and he don't either."

"Us?"

Donnie looked up. His eyes were very blue. "Me and Spot. He's my dog. Well, he *was* my dog, till that man killed him. Aunt Edie and Mr. Karson wouldn't let me keep him.

But Josh and Casey did."

The judge nodded. It was all in the papers on her desk. The "he" the boy referred to was the Dumpster Killer.

"And that's why you say that your aunt and Mr. Karson don't like you, because they wouldn't let you keep the dog?"

The boy narrowed his eyes. "Yes. Casey and Josh let me keep him till he . . ." He paused a moment, then smiled. "But Josh got me another dog. Spot Two."

The judge found herself smiling back. "You know the reason your aunt and Mr. Karson would not let you keep the dog may have nothing to do with how much your aunt or Mr. Karson like you. Your aunt lives in an apartment building, and most apartment buildings do not allow pets. So it would not be your aunt's decision. Do you understand, Donnie?"

The boy nodded reluctantly. "But it wasn't just that. They *really* were glad not to let me keep Spot! They didn't *like* Spot. And they don't like me, either. I'm just a *bother*."

Judge Pritchard sighed. She had handled a lot of child custody cases; and it was always difficult to determine which childish complaints were legitimate, and which were momentary whims, formed from the child's own particular, and not always accurate, viewpoint. A child, for instance, might opt to go with the parent who showered them with toys and gifts, and let them do anything they wanted; rather than stay with a parent who set boundaries and expected them to get decent grades and become a worthwhile adult. It was never easy.

"And who would you prefer to live with, your aunt, or Miss Farrel?"

Donnie leaned forward, said eagerly, "Josh and Casey!"

"But that doesn't seem possible under the circumstances, since they do not live together, and Miss Farrel is the one who is filing for adoption. Perhaps you should consider giving your aunt another chance."

The boy's face fell. "Do I have to?"

She sighed again. "No, Donnie. At least not now. Would you ask the others to come in? Then, you wait outside again. And thank you, Donnie, for talking to me. It wasn't so frightening now, was it?"

"No, ma'am," he said dutifully. But he was glad to be escaping the room. The lady looked very serious, but she was nice enough; although the thought that she had the power to decide who he was to live with scared him.

In the hall, he ran up to Josh and Casey. "She wants to talk to you again."

Josh ruffled his hair, and Casey put a hand on his shoulder. He squirmed like a puppy under their touch, then turned away as his aunt came marching up, smelling of cigarette smoke and strong perfume, smiling a hard, forced smile. She too reached for him, but he managed to evade her touch, as her smile turned to a grimace.

He watched the adults as they filed into the judge's chambers. He was going to be in for some hard times if he had to live with his aunt again, but he wasn't going to pretend any more. If that judge said that he had to live with Edie, well, he and Spot would simply run away. He had made up his mind.

Inside the judge's chambers Edith Black said eagerly, "Well, what did Donnie say?"

Judge Pritchard shook her head. "That is between me and the boy, Miss Black. For the moment, I have decided to make Donnie a ward of the court, temporarily."

Casey's heart sank and Josh said, "In this case, what does that mean, Judge?"

"It means, Sergeant, that I shall need some time to decide the issue here. I need more information on the backgrounds of both Farrel and Black before I make a final decision. Until I do, the boy will continue to reside with you, Miss Farrel . . ."

"That's not fair!" Edith Black cried. "I'm the boy's aunt!"

"I shall decide what is and what is not fair." The judge softened her tone. "He has been living with Miss Farrel for some time now, and seems to be doing well there. I don't wish to uproot him again for the comparatively short time it will take me to make a decision."

"And just what is 'a comparatively short time'?" Edith Black's sarcasm was blunted by her mispronunciation of the word comparatively.

The judge's look was cool. "I can't say for certain. A few weeks perhaps. The decision I make will affect Donnie's life forever. I will not be rushed. Now, run along, all of you. I have to be in court in fifteen minutes."

Edith Black was already on her way out, and she was hurrying down the hall as Josh and Casey stopped before Donnie, who jumped up.

"What did the judge say? Do I get to stay with you?"

Casey knelt beside him. "She hasn't made up her mind, Donnie. But you get to stay with me for now, anyway. Don't worry. It'll turn out all right."

Josh grasped the boy's shoulder. "Depend on it, sport. Look, I arranged for the rest of the day off. What say we take in the Cardinals' practice session this afternoon? Regular football season starts next Sunday."

Donnie looked at Casey. "Can I, Casey? Huh?"

Casey hesitated. "It's a school day, you know."

"Aw, come on, Casey," Josh said. "He's already missed half a day, why not the rest?"

Casey shook her head in mock exasperation. "Well, I have to scoot to my office. Some of us have to work. You two run along and play."

"Yeah!" Donnie bounced on his toes, snatched at Josh's hand. "Let's go, Josh!"

Casey watched as they went down the hall, Donnie gazing up into Josh's face. He worshipped the big detective. Casey loved the big jerk too; but enough to marry him? She was far from sure. After her bitter experience with her boss in California, and the subsequent abortion, she wasn't sure she was prepared for a serious relationship with any man. And yet, how would Donnie react if she broke up with Josh? She didn't even want to think about it.

Shaking her head, she strode out of the building, bracing herself for leaving the air-conditioned comfort for the blazing heat of September in Phoenix.

CHAPTER TWO

Casey's small office barely had room for a desk, chair, and filing cabinet. The Governor's Task Force on Crime had only been formed six months ago, and promises had been made that they would soon occupy more comfortable quarters. So far, that promise had not been kept. The Governor of Arizona had set up the task force to investigate and oversee various crimes throughout the state. The genesis of this action had been the brutal murders of several Buddhists in a temple outside Phoenix. The investigation had been horribly botched, and the Governor thought that a task force, to oversee future investigations, might help prevent future fiascoes. The members of the task force had the authority to oversee and investigate, but not to make arrests and prosecute.

The light on Casey's answering machine was blinking. She punched the button, and Bob Wilson's reedy voice came at her like an accusation: "Where the hell are you, Farrel? I've been trying to get you all morning. Call me!"

Casey sighed. Wilson was the new head of

the task force — Burns having been transferred — and not an easy man to work for.

Venting a deep sigh, she punched out his office number. "Bob? This is Casey. I . . ."

He rode right over her: "In my office. *Tout de suite.* We have a nasty one, five dead already, more expected."

Wilson's office was just a few doors down from Casey's; but Casey took her time getting there. She needed to organize herself before facing him. Wilson was as slippery as a greased flagpole, and just about as skinny. He was also ambitious, and paranoid as hell. He had been chief of police in a small town in the northern part of the state, and had campaigned hard and vigorously for the new Governor. This job was his reward; but he considered it only a way-station on his own climb to the top.

Still, he wasn't totally unlikable. He had a certain fierce charm, and a keen, if devious mind: which made him a good cop — most of the time, although not easy to deal with.

Casey took a last deep breath before opening the door to his office. As the door opened, Wilson jumped up from behind his desk. "Farrel! It's about time."

Casey gave a slight nod in acknowledgment of his statement. "Sorry, Boss. What's this all about?"

Wilson began to pace back and forth behind his desk. "Early this morning a park policeman in the Organ Pipe National Monument found a deserted van on Highway 85. Two men were found in the front seat of the van, shot to death. There was evidence that a number of illegal aliens had been riding in the back. Later this morning a Papago Indian called the Pima County Sheriff's Department in Ajo and told them that he had found a dead woman in the desert east of the park. They sent out a chopper to pick her up, and after they had done so, they found two more bodies, male, a couple of miles south of the woman. They were all Hispanics, and all had been shot once, in the head, as had the two male Hispanics in the van. We're pretty sure that the killings are connected. Probably the three in the desert had been in the van."

Casey shook her head. "Do you think it was the *coyotes?* It happens fairly often: The *coyotes* smuggled them across the border from down around Lukeville; then something goes wrong, they think the border patrol is after them, or sometimes the *coyotes* simply kill them for their money."

Wilson impatiently shook his head, and suddenly plopped down into his chair, giving Casey the opportunity to seat herself opposite him. His glare told her what he thought of her suggestion.

"Just who do you think those two men in the front seat of the van were? No, this time somebody killed both the *coyotes* and the wetbacks. They were all killed with the same gun, a .45 Colt, and they were all shot very neatly in the forehead."

"Execution style," said Casey.

The clap of Wilson's hands made Casey jump. "Bingo! The Lady Detective is catching on."

Casey felt her cheeks grow hot, and took another deep breath. The only way to deal with Wilson when he was in this mood was to not let him get to you.

"So, obviously, it wasn't the *coyotes*. So have they found anything yet, anything that would give us something to go on?"

Wilson lifted his lips in the thin-lipped grimace that he thought was a smile. "So far just one thing. The bodies in the desert, the two men and the girl; there were no tire tracks near the bodies, but there were hoofprints."

Casey frowned. "A killer on horseback? Well, that's different, anyway. I assume the tracks were followed."

"Of course, but they led back to the highway, then disappeared — maybe into a horse trailer."

Casey shook her head. "It seems a rather

old-fashioned and complicated way to hunt them down; what with all the four-wheeled drives around."

Wilson nodded. "Exactly. It's very odd, and that may eventually be of help to us."

"You said that the evidence points to there being several illegals in the van; more than the three dead?"

Wilson nodded again. "They found the passengers' bed rolls and belongings in the rear of the van. They must have been scared shitless to leave them. There were five bed rolls."

Casey grimaced at his vulgarity. "Then, what about the other two?"

"Must have gotten away clean," Wilson said with a shrug. "Maybe three ran one way and two another. The killer could only follow one group."

"So you think two got away."

"That's the way I read it." Wilson looked up at the ceiling. "So what we've got so far is two dead *coyotes* and three dead wetbacks."

Casey shook her head and frowned. "You know, you're a bigoted bastard, Wilson! Since this group probably came through Lukeville, I don't think that they crossed any rivers. Why not just call them illegals?"

Wilson grinned. "I call them the way I see them: Wetbacks; greasers; illegals; Mexes; or

Meskins, as the Texans call them — what's the difference. They are in this country illegally."

Casey shook her head again. "If you feel that way, why all the concern about this case?"

"Because they're dead, that's why. If they were alive, I wouldn't give a damn."

"I still fail to see how that concerns you, or the task force. Let the Pima County Sheriff's Department handle it."

"That's where you're wrong, Farrel. The task force was set up to supervise just this type of crime. The same snafus that caused all the trouble in the Temple slayings could easily happen here. The Sheriff's Department, the Border Patrol, the Park Rangers, they all think they should be handling it. And, since the crime was committed within the limits of the Papago Indian Reservation, the Feds will also be involved. Somebody has to coordinate this mess, and that somebody is us."

"All right, I get the picture; but may I ask one more thing? I take it that this conversation means that you are assigning me to the case. Why me? I'm new to the group, and I have no experience in investigating homicide cases."

Wilson's smile turned wolfish. "Because since the Dumpster Killer, you're our resident hotshot, the darling of the media. With you on the case, we're sure to get good coverage; and the Governor is interested in having the public know that he is doing something to prevent a recurrence of the Temple fiasco. All right?

"Besides, there has to be a first time, and this is yours. Here are some names."

He shoved a piece of paper across the desk. "The man in the Sheriff's Department at Ajo; the Park Ranger who found the van; the name of the Border Patrol guy who was called in — he's located at the Border Patrol station in Why. I don't have the name of the Indian who found the woman, but I'm sure somebody down there will have it."

With resignation Casey stood up, folded the sheet of paper into her purse, and started out.

"Farrel?"

She stopped, and turned again to face Wilson, who was gazing at her cryptically. "Another reason. You're part Indian, and that's mostly reservation country down there."

"I'm part Hopi, not Papago!"

He grinned. "An Indian is an Indian, as far as I'm concerned."

Casey choked back a hot retort, and went down the hall to her office, experiencing mixed feelings of excitement and unease. This was her first real case, and as such it was exciting. If she handled it well, it could do much for her career; but it wasn't a case to which she was looking forward. She had envisioned wading into the waters gently. She had already been involved in a couple of small cases, both involving non-violent crimes; but this was too much responsibility, too soon. She could not help wonder if Wilson had told her all his motives for giving her the assignment. If she fell on her face, she might very well be out of a job.

Once again in her office, she sat down at her desk and stared at the list of names. It wasn't much to go on. She would be starting from near-scratch.

Casey enjoyed her work, and was happy with the opportunity to hone the investigative skills she had acquired while working for the private detective agency. But, there were elements of the job that she did not care for. The main problem, as she saw it, was that task force members, like Rodney Dangerfield, didn't get much respect from the regular law enforcement agencies. In some instances, they had run into open hostility; and this could easily happen in a case like this, where so many different agencies were involved.

Folding the sheet of paper, she put it into her purse, then looked at her watch — well past noon. Josh and Donnie should be watching the Cardinals practice session about now.

She pulled her phone to her, and punched out the number of the homicide detail. When the phone was answered she said, "Would you please page Detective Whitney and have him call Casey Farrel, at my office, please? I know he's off-duty this afternoon, but it is rather urgent."

She hung up the phone, and busied herself catching up with her paper work, in preparation for leaving this afternoon.

Josh called thirty minutes later. "Hi, Casey. What's up? Can't stand for Donnie and me having a good time by ourselves?"

"Not really. Watching large men butt heads in the middle of a field was never one of my favorite things to do," she said crisply. "Now if it was a civilized game, like baseball . . . Anyway, I figure that a little male bonding is good for you guys, which brings me to my reason for calling; how would you like to keep Donnie for a few days? Wilson has a job for me, and it necessitates my going out of town."

"Oh? What's the job?"

Tersely, she told him about the assignment. When she was finished, Josh was silent a moment before he spoke. A bad sign.

"Casey, are you sure you're ready for this? It seems to me that it's a little like throwing the baby into the water to teach it to swim. Maybe I should have a word with Wilson . . ."

Casey felt a surge of annoyance. "Now you just stay out of this, Detective Whitney. If I can't handle the cases assigned me, then I should look for another job. Just answer my question, can you take Donnie for a few days?"

"Well, sure. I'd be happy to take the kid. Look, you be careful, okay? By the sound of it, you're stepping into a mudhole."

Casey felt her annoyance fade. "I'll be careful, Josh," she said in a softer tone.

"Well, *Vaya con Dios*," he said with an atrocious accent, causing Casey to laugh aloud. Because she would often be working with the Hispanic community, Casey had been studying Spanish, and Josh, ostensibly, had been helping her. Unfortunately, he had absolutely no ear for language.

"Please, Josh," she said teasingly, "your accent could set Mexican-American relations back a hundred years."

"You're cruel, babe, but I love you anyway. Just be careful. Remember all I've taught you."

"Sure. That will be a *big* help. You guys take care, and tell Donnie good-bye for me. Don't let him eat too much junk. I'll call you as soon as I'm back."

After she had hung up, Casey sat for several moments, a musing smile on her lips. Josh was brash, full of bustling energy, often barging into a situation like the proverbial bull into a china shop. Yet, for all that, he was a good man, kind, loving, and able to separate his work from his private life. Another plus was that so far, at least, he had been able to avoid the bitter cynicism prevalent in so many homicide cops.

If only he could be content with their present situation; if only he wouldn't press so hard for a more permanent relationship. She was deeply fond of him, yet she wasn't ready for marriage.

She gestured sharply, pushing it all out of her mind, and went back to clearing her desk.

The old man stared at his offspring in utter shock and horror. Of all his children this one was his favorite. Over the years certain of his children, from time to time, had shocked him; yet this revelation was almost impossible to believe or accept!

"You are telling me that you have killed five people, shot them down in cold blood?"

"It had to be done, Father."

"What do you mean, it had to be done? Surely there must have been another way."

"No. The coyotes *filmed the meeting. I have seen the tape. If the media got hold of it, it could ruin us. Would you like to have the public laughing at us, mocking us? Haven't you always told*

us that we must protect the family? That's what I was doing."

"But the other three, those in the van, why was it necessary to kill them?"

"Because it was very possible that they saw me shoot the two coyotes. When I stopped the van, I didn't know that there was anyone inside, until I saw them jump from the back. There were two more, but they ran in the opposite direction, and I couldn't follow both groups. Maybe I can track them down . . ."

The old man threw up his hands. "No! For God's sake, no more killing! You've done too much!"

"I don't understand your concern, Father. They were only Mexican illegals and worthless coyotes. You've never shown much concern about them before."

The old man stared, dazed by the brutal coldness of the statement. Had he sired a monster?

He sighed, and felt his shoulders slump. If he had, it was his monster and, to him, family was everything.

He motioned tiredly. "Go. Leave me alone now. I must think."

CHAPTER THREE

It was after two-thirty before Casey finally got away from her office. She drove directly to her apartment in Glendale, shed her clothes, took a quick shower, and got into a comfortable blouse and pants. She packed two bags. She had no idea of how long she would have to be gone, but it could be a week or even longer, and she might not be able to find a place to do her laundry.

Once in the car, she drove down Interstate 17, then turned west on Interstate 8 toward Gila Bend, where she would head south for Ajo. The drive would take about three hours. From her office, she had called and made reservations at a bed-and-breakfast place that her Mobile Guide recommended. She would arrive too late to visit the local Sheriff's Office, but that was the first thing on her agenda for tomorrow. As for now, she might as well use her driving time to review what she knew about the illegal alien situation.

Historically, the poor of Mexico had been migrating to the United States since 1848, when the United States, through the Mexican

War, acquired nearly half of Mexico. However, it was only during the last twenty years, when economic conditions in Mexico had worsened, that the emigrations had reached flood tide. In 1986 the INS reported that 1.7 million Mexican nationals were caught trying to slip across the borders of Arizona, Texas, and California. There was no official estimate of the number who made it safely, but the number had to be in the millions.

One of the things that made the situation so difficult, was that for years these illegal border crossings had been pretty much overlooked, and the law haphazardly enforced. The massive emigration was a source of cheap labor for ranchers and farmers in the U.S. who needed a large supply of seasonal labor. As North American workers became increasingly reluctant to perform the ill-paid stoop labor, the need became even greater; and although the crossings were illegal, for thirty-five years, hiring the illegals was not.

Eventually, the situation changed. As the number of illegals grew, and showed no signs of lessening, the alarm went up. There were cries that the Mexican nationals were taking jobs from American citizens, and that those who could not find work were turning to crime. Something had to be done.

And something was done. Laws were

passed. All Mexican citizens wishing to work in the U.S. must have green cards; and those already illegally in the U.S. were granted a period of time in which to apply for them. In addition, it was made illegal for growers to hire alien workers who did not have such cards. Everyone breathed a sigh of relief, confident that this would reduce the flow.

It did not. What it did do was to encourage the black market sale of forged documents. The market for false Social Security cards and birth certificates had been strong for years; now it became a triad, with forged green cards added. Also, many of the growers and other employers ignored the new law and hired the illegals anyway.

Casey had recently read an article in the *New York Times,* which stated that the population of Mexico would double by the year 2025; that half of the Mexicans in Mexico were under sixteen, and that the country could not employ forty percent of its adult workers. Experts stated that the wages paid in the U.S. were so much higher than those in Mexico that increased emigration of workers into the States was inevitable.

Casey had talked to a number of migrant workers. In their minds, crossing the border was not a crime, although they knew that it was illegal in the eyes of the North Americans.

Casey was reminded of a motto that hung on the wall of her boss's office: "When you are up to your ass in alligators, it's hard to think about draining the swamp."

And that's the way it was for most of these people. When your children are hungry and you have no other way to provide for them, you do what you must. Most of them knew of the risk involved, but the alternative, starvation, was not acceptable.

And so they took the chance, running the risk of being caught by *La Migra,* or the Border Patrol, and the greater risk of being killed by bandits or the very *coyotes* they paid to get them safely into the U.S. Many of them were caught by Immigration time after time; but they simply waited their chance and crossed again. Since it cost up to three hundred dollars or more, per person, to be transported across the border by the *coyotes,* when they ran out of money they simply walked across the desert, risking death in the unrelenting heat. Many perished in this fashion. It was a sad problem with no easy solution. But that problem, *per se,* was not what she was concerned with just now. The Task Force had been instructed to recommend laws where needed, but that applied only to the laws of Arizona. All laws concerning illegal border crossings were in the purview of the Federal

Government. What she had to concern herself with was the murders.

Casey sighed and stretched her back against her seat, thinking how lucky she was. Although she had seen hunger and poverty on her visits to the Hopi Reservation of her ancestors, she had never had to experience them herself. Casey's parents were both gone now, lost to a car accident when Casey was in her teens; but Casey's mother, a full-blooded Hopi, had left the reservation to marry an Anglo airline pilot; and Casey had been raised in a comfortable upper-middle class section of Flagstaff. The closest she had come to experiencing real poverty was last year, when a combination of circumstances had caused her to lose her apartment, and she had been forced to live in her car for a few weeks. But, even then she had never gone hungry, and now that was all behind her.

She glanced at the clock on the dashboard. Five fifteen. She was coming into the outskirts of Ajo now; and she realized that she was dead tired. Beginning with Donnie's hearing this morning, it had been a long, trying day. She might as well go directly to the bed-and-breakfast place, then get herself a decent meal and a good night's sleep.

The bed-and-breakfast place, called The Mine Manager's House, was situated atop a hill overlooking the town, and after Casey had parked her car, she stood for a moment looking out at the view. You could see almost everything there was to see of the town from here. The mine manager, Casey thought with a smile, could survey all of his domain from this spot.

Ajo was, or had been, one of the many Arizona copper towns; the property of the company that owned the mines. When the mines were closed, a number of years ago, the town had begun to die. Beside the shock of the closure, and the fact that there were now no jobs, there had been another problem for the people of Ajo — their homes. Many of the families had spent several generations in the town, and knew no other homes than the houses which the company owned. But, after some unpleasantness, an agreement had finally been reached, and those who wished to had been able to buy the houses in which they lived. With this out of the way, a concerted effort had been made to turn Ajo into a retirement and tourist community.

Casey had not been in Ajo for a while, and she was glad to see that the effort seemed to be succeeding. The location was good — close to Organ Pipe Cactus National Monument; and the climate, because of the higher altitude, had lower summer temperatures than did the surrounding desert. Also, it was a rather attractive little town, with a pretty little plaza, surrounded by shops and stores. Driving through town, Casey had seen that many of the old houses had been painted and restored, and a number of new homes were visible. It all added up to a feeling of renewal, of hope; and it made Casey feel good.

After she had checked into her room, she unpacked, took a quick shower, then went out for an early dinner. She hadn't had much lunch, and she was ravenous. Thinking about a nice, juicy steak, she headed back out to town, to a restaurant that boasted "The Best Steak in the West," a claim backed up by a quote from an article in the *New York Times*. Casey had eaten there before, and while she thought the quote might be a bit of an exaggeration, she remembered being pleasantly impressed with the food, the atmosphere, and the friendly service. After a satisfying meal, served by a cheerful Indian waitress who looked a little like Marilyn Whirlwind, one of the characters on "Northern Exposure," she headed back to the bed-and-breakfast, and turned in. Tomorrow would be another long day, and she wanted to be rested and ready for whatever it might throw at her. She fell asleep immediately, and despite her nervousness over the new case, slept like a rock.

She awoke at 7:00 a.m. feeling rested and energetic. After an elegant breakfast at the Mine Manager's House — orange juice; strawberries; fresh-baked waffles, nut breads, and muffins; and three cups of excellent coffee; on real china, with cloth napkins — she felt almost ready to face anything.

By nine she was at the Sheriff's sub-station, just on time for her appointment with Sergeant Ron Malvern, the deputy in charge of the case.

Malvern was a very tall, heavy-shouldered man who looked to be in his late forties. His manner was courteous and his accent country. "I'm only temporarily in charge of the case," he explained in his deep voice, after introducing himself. "Unless there are some new developments within a day or two, the case will be transferred to the Sheriff's Office in Tucson."

Casey nodded. "I see. And has anything new come up since the bodies were found?"

He shook his head. "Not so's you'd notice. Of course it's early yet; but I have a strong hunch that we have about all we're going to get. The results of the autopsies aren't in yet; but I don't see how they can reveal anything new. All of the victims were shot to death, one bullet between the eyes, execution style. Damned good shot, whoever the perp was."

"Any shell casings at the scene?"

Malvern shook his head. "Nary a one."

"And the bullets, do you know what caliber?"

He brightened. "Yes, that we do know. I called the coroner's office in Tucson first thing this morning. The slugs they dug out were .45s, apparently from an old Colt six-shooter, the kind that the gunfighters used in the bad old days."

He gave her a wry grin. "You don't suppose what we've got here is the ghost of Billy the Kid?"

She returned his smile. "I'll have to admit that it conjures an odd picture; a man on horseback carrying an ancient .45. Doesn't exactly fit the profile of the typical contemporary killer, does it? Do you have any local eccentrics who might fit that picture, Sergeant Malvern?"

He lifted a hand. "Ron, please. We're not very formal around here. But to answer your question, we're working on that; but, as you know, this state swarms with gun nuts. Do you have any idea how many old Colt .45s are floating around in collections? And people who own horses are not exactly in short supply either. Checking all that out will take some leg-work, and some time. You know how it is?"

She nodded. "According to my information,

there were apparently others in the back of the van."

"Yes. Evidently they took off in such a hurry that they left their belongings behind. From the number of bedrolls, we figure that there were at least five people in the back of the van."

"Any sign of the two who escaped?"

"Nope. They're being looked for; but the likelihood of finding that particular pair among all the illegals running around out there is not very good. They may have gone back across the border."

Casey sighed. "Not much to go on, is it?"

He nodded. "Not much. The killer left nothing at the scene except the hoofprints of his horse. We made castings, and if we ever find the horse we can compare the prints, but . . ." He shrugged.

"Any identification on the two *coyotes?*"

"Yeah, they had I.D. Both had addresses in Phoenix. We're in the process of checking it out now. As for the other three, they all had papers on them, but we're pretty sure they were forged."

"I'd like copies of all the papers found, if I may." She shook her head. "It all looks pretty hopeless, doesn't it?"

Malvern leaned back in his chair. "About as hopeless as it gets. Unless we get a break, the case will eventually be filed away as un-solved. Do you have any idea how many illegals have been murdered in southwestern Arizona in the past few years? Most of the cases are never solved. The only times we get our perp is when we find him standing over the body with a smoking gun; and that doesn't happen very often."

"I know. I've read the statistics; but then most of those killings were the result of rob-beries, or quarrels among the illegals them-selves. This case seems to be very different. My God, Ron! Five people!"

"I know. It's terrible. We'll do all we can, but I have to warn you, it may not be enough."

"Well, I'm going to do some nosing around. Do you have the name of the park ranger who discovered the van, and of the Papago Indian who found the woman? Also, whoever in the Border Patrol is in charge of looking for the other Mexicans who were in the van."

"Sure." Malvern tore off a piece of paper from a scratch pad, and scribbled. "But I think you're wasting your time, Casey."

"Could be, but it has to be done."

Malvern handed her the slip of paper and Casey folded it into her purse.

"Thanks for cooperating, Ron. Tell me something . . ." She looked at him keenly. "Do you mind me being here, nosing around?"

He grinned. "Nope. The way I figure it, what can I lose?"

He leaned his elbows on the desk. "I suppose you know what some cops call the members of the task force?"

Casey's smile had a wry edge. "I've heard several names, all of them less than charming; to which do you refer?"

His grin widened. "Of course I would never use the phrase myself, but some people refer to your group as T.F.s."

Casey rolled her eyes. "T.F.s? I'm afraid to ask."

"Total Fuck-ups. But I must say that it doesn't seem to apply to you; and I wish you luck."

Casey held out her hand. "You're a real gentleman, Sergeant Malvern, and I appreciate your wish. I can use all the luck I can get."

CHAPTER FOUR

It was still early when Casey left the sub-station, so she drove south toward Organ Pipe National Monument.

Remembering Malvern's remark, she had to grin as she recalled Rodney Dangerfield's well-known line: "I don't get no respect!"

So far, that could also be the motto of the task force. When she had mentioned this fact to Josh, he had said, "Give it time, babe. It's brand new and needs some time and experience to work smoothly. Soon as the task force unravels a few thorny cases, you'll get your respect."

Maybe he was right, but from the looks of things, it didn't appear that this particular case would be the one to build the task force's reputation. Of course this didn't mean that she was about to give up; after all, she had only been on the case for a day. Something might turn up: new evidence, a witness . . . Anything was possible.

Outside the car, the desert seemed endless. Reaching into the divider storage between the front seats, she pulled out a tape at random, and inserted it into her cassette player. In a few seconds the idiosyncratic jazz of Bela Fleck and the Flecktones filled the car. Good travelling music.

The view outside was repetitive; but she decided that it had an understated beauty of its own. Suddenly a white cross appeared and vanished by the roadside. A quarter of a mile further on, another appeared, surrounded by jars of wilted flowers.

Casey knew that the crosses marked the locations of deaths by accident on the highway. As she drove, she tried to count them; but stopped after the first half-dozen. The highway was wide, there was not much traffic, and no obstacles; yet there were so many crosses! What was there about a straight, monotonous stretch of road that caused drivers to speed, drive while drunk or sleepy, and kill themselves by the hundreds. Maybe it was simple human impatience. There were many such sections of highway in the U.S.; they were often given names like Blood Alley, or Hell Highway.

Casey shook her head, wondering if anyone would erect crosses at the spots where the illegals had been killed.

Casey looked down at her speedometer, and saw that she was going somewhat faster than the speed limit. She let off on the gas pedal with a feeling of chagrin.

Just ahead was the little town of Why. Once, while driving through, Casey had stopped there for a cold drink. Curious, she had asked the store proprietor about the town's name. He had grinned and told her it was because "*Why* would anyone want to build a town in a God-forsaken place like this?"

As she drove into town, she had to agree. Actually, Why didn't deserve the label of "town"; being simply a tiny sprawl of box-like structures, looking like careless dice tossed by a godly hand. But, it was located near the junction where the highway heading east to Tucson branched, and the Border Patrol did have an office here, just off the highway, to her left.

She turned off, and parked before the structure. Before getting out of the car, she got out the list of names that Ron Malvern had given her, and found the name of the Border Patrol Officer in charge of the search for the two missing illegals — Jack Cunningham.

She was in luck; the officer was in. Cunningham was middle-aged, medium height, thin, and brown as a nut. The latter part of this description, Casey thought, would fit most law enforcement officers who spent much of their time in the desert, under the fierce sun.

After Casey had introduced herself, Cunningham asked bluntly, "Why is the task force interested in this case?"

"Because The-Powers-That-Be decided that it has all the ear-marks of a sensational case. It isn't every day that five people are killed."

"And you figure that we'll screw it up?"

"Of course not, Mr. Cunningham. It's that in a case like this, where so many agencies are involved, a little coordination would be in order. I am only here to get an overview of the situation. I promise not to interfere with your investigation . . ."

"You've damned sure got that right," he muttered.

Casey forced herself to relax the tension building in her jaws, and kept her tone polite. "As you know, as a member of the task force, I have no power to make arrests; and the investigation is already in the hands of the Sheriff's Department."

"Yes," he admitted reluctantly. "But why you?"

Casey translated the sentence in her mind: "Why you, a woman?" She knew, from experience, that it would do her no good to snarl at him, and that it would do even less good to play the role of subservient female. The only way to deal with this kind of man, was to adopt a calm, business-like façade, and never let him know if he got to you.

"I don't question my superiors," she lied. "I presume I was assigned to this case because it involves Mexican Nationals, and I speak some Spanish."

He grunted, and the sound managed to express his doubt. "Okay. But as you just said, the Sheriff's Office is handling the case, so why come to me?"

"Because, as I understand it, you are in charge of the search for the two missing illegals who were thought to be in the van with the three who were killed. Am I wrong?"

She was pleased to see that he appeared a bit discomfited. "Yeah, we're looking for them — not that we're getting anywhere."

"I'm sure it isn't easy."

He gave a snort. "You've got that right. You have any idea how many illegals are wandering around out there?"

"That's been mentioned, yes."

He gave her a sharp look. "We've picked up several men in the general area where the van was found; but they all deny being in the van; so what can we do?"

"Fingerprints?"

He snorted. "If you eliminate those belonging to the five that were killed, there are literally hundreds of others. Those *coyotes*, by the way, were well known to us. They've been smuggling aliens across the border for a year or more. Unfortunately for us, they don't wipe the van down after every trip; so even if we pick up someone whose prints are in the van, we have no way of proving that they were there last night. *Comprende?*"

She nodded, feeling let down. "So there's no chance that you'll find them?"

"I didn't say that. We might get lucky; anyway, we'll keep looking."

Casey got to her feet. "I want to thank you, Mr. Cunningham, for your cooperation and trouble."

He thawed a little, even exhibiting a sliver of a smile. "I'm just sorry that I can't be of more help to you. And I must say something . . . You're the first member of the task force I've come in actual contact with, and I have to admit that you're not what I expected. From the rumors I've heard, you people are nosy-parkers, always stepping on toes and getting in the way. You don't seem like that at all."

She had to laugh. "Well, you can't always believe rumors, Mr. Cunningham; but thanks for the compliment — if that's what it is. I'll be on my way."

He gave her a wave, and bent back over his desk.

Outside, the heat had been building. When

she opened the door of her car it flooded out at her, dry and searing. She left the car door open and rolled down all the windows to let the hot air escape; then started the car, turned the air-conditioning and the blower to maximum, and turned south.

As she entered Organ Pipe State Monument, she saw a balloon floating low in the sky. This area was called Gringo Pass by many, and was used regularly by smugglers who flew under the radar carrying plane-loads of drugs. For that reason, low-flying balloons were being used to detect them, and to alert authorities to any planes that had not logged in a flight plan.

There were quite a few cars on the road, many of them recreation vehicles and campers. The park was a popular tourist attraction, as it offered accessible pueblo Indian ruins, as well as the giant cacti. When she reached the park center, the parking lot was crowded.

At the reception desk, inside the building, she asked for Webb Banks, the Park Ranger who had found the van. She was told that he was patrolling the park.

Casey explained herself to the woman behind the reception desk. "I'm Casey Farrel, from the Governor's Task Force on Crime. I'm here concerning the murder of the illegals."

The woman nodded. "I'll call Webb. He should be here shortly."

Casey found a place to sit on a nearby bench, enjoying the flow of cool air. She leaned her head back, and mulled over what she had learned so far. Nothing really, but at least she was taking the first steps.

It took about fifteen minutes for the ranger to arrive, and Casey was almost dozing when she heard his voice speak her name. "Casey Farrel? I'm Webb Banks."

She looked up to see a bear of a man, shambling, and amiable as a puppy. His big hand swallowed hers. In a rumbling voice he said, "Pleased to meet you, Miss Farrel. Would you mind talking outside? Too many folks in here, and I hate the air-conditioning. If the good Lord had wanted us always to be cool he'd have made the climate different, I always say."

Casey, regretfully, said yes. Outside, they sat side by side on a low stone wall enclosing a bed of cacti typical of the area.

His twinkling brown eyes regarded her keenly. "Now, what can I do for you?"

"I'm here about the killings the other night."

"Figured as much. What else would bring a member of the Governor's special task force trotting down here?"

"Particularly a woman?" she asked dryly.

He shook his head. "Why, not at all. You see, I figure that the good Lord intended for women to share equally with men, and that equality should extend to the work place."

Casey could not help but smile. The big man was very likable. "Well, that's very politically correct of you, Mr. Banks."

"Webb, please." His eyes twinkled at her. "Betsy, that's my wife, may have something to do with that. She's just a little bit of a thing, but she does come on strong. She's raised my consciousness a great deal."

"Good for her."

Banks grew serious. "Don't know that there's much I can tell you. It's all right there in the reports." He made a face. "Nasty business!"

"Yes, it is. I understand that you were the first to find the van?"

"Yep. I live in Ajo. I was on my way to the center yesterday morning early, when I spotted the van pulled off to the side of the road. My first thought was that it was some tourist taking a snooze. But something about it didn't strike me right, so after I drove a mile or two down the road, I turned and went back. When I approached the van, I found the two dead men in the front seat."

"The Sheriff's Office told me that there was no evidence found at the scene, no ejected shells, nothing like that?"

"That's right. Not a thing."

"How about tire marks of a second vehicle? Another car must have forced the van off the road."

Banks shook his head. "That's a good assumption, but the van wasn't far off the road. Likely the second vehicle never left the highway."

"And nobody saw anything?"

He shrugged. "The murders took place some time after midnight; not much traffic at that hour. And it probably didn't take very long: drive up beside the van; force it to the side of the road; leave the motor running; get out; shoot the *coyotes;* get back in the pickup and drive off. Maybe take ten minutes in all."

Casey sat up alertly. "Pickup? There was nothing in the report about a pickup."

"Oh, yeah. That's a recent development." He looked somewhat sheepish. "A call came in this morning shortly after I came in to work. An unidentified male, saying that he had been driving along that stretch of highway at a little after twelve thirty on the night in question. He saw the van pulled off to the side of the road, and a pickup, pulling a horse trailer, parked next to the van, on the pavement. He said that he thought little of it at the time, except that he was a little pissed that the pickup and trailer should be blocking the right-hand lane, and he had to pull out to pass. He called in because in the morning he saw a report on TV news about the van, and the bodies being discovered."

"Did he get the license number, or the make of the pickup?"

"Nope. Said that at the time he had no reason to pay particular attention; just thought it was some jerk parked in the road talking to a friend in the van."

She slumped back. "I suppose it was too much to hope for. How about the color of the pickup?"

"He says that it was dark, but he wasn't sure of the color, maybe dark blue, or black."

"And of course he didn't see the driver of the pickup."

"He said he *thought* the cab was empty, but he wasn't sure. And to answer your next question, he didn't see anyone outside the pickup, either."

"And the caller left no name or address?"

"Nope. The minute I asked him, he hung up. A concerned citizen — but not concerned enough to want to get involved with maybe having to appear as a witness in court. He could have been a tourist returning from Mexico. Might be a couple of hundred miles away by now."

Casey pondered for a moment. "Then the perp forced the van off the road, shot the two men in the cab, and was probably startled to see five people hop out of the back like a covey of flushed quail; three going one way, and two another, into the desert. He thought they might be able to identify him, and decided to go after the larger group. That's where the horse comes in. But one thing: he wouldn't have wanted to stay parked there on the highway, not with two dead men in the van."

Banks nodded. "I figure that he drove off onto one of the side roads. There's several in the area, and took off on horseback from there." He shook his head.

"Sheriff's Office is checking the nearest, but lots of vehicles pull off the road out here, and we have our share of riders. Little chance of finding a hoofprint to match those around where the bodies were found."

He shook his head again. "Perp must have been a pretty good tracker though, 'cause he sure found them."

Casey sighed. "That means that it's vitally important that we find the other two illegals. Are you looking for them?"

Banks shook his head. "Nope. Not my job. It's all out of our hands now. The Sheriff's Department and the Border Patrol have it."

Casey thought for a moment. "Have you

been out at the site of the killings in the desert?"

"Nope again. That happened out of the park. Look, Miss Farrel, I'd like to be of more help to you, but . . ." He spread his hands. "We're only involved in a limited way in such investigations. I wish I *were* more involved; it would relieve the tedium."

He grinned. "Also, I'm an avid mystery fan, and I'd dearly love to be in on solving a murder case. It would make my day. But, I guess if the good Lord had wanted me to solve murders, he would have seen to it that I had another job."

Casey got to her feet. "Well, at least I learned one new thing, about the pickup and the horse trailer, so my trip down here isn't a total waste. I want to thank you for your cooperation, Mr. Banks."

She held out her hand, and it was swallowed by his huge paw.

"It's been a pleasure, Miss Farrel, a real pleasure."

Casey took two steps toward her car in the parking lot, then paused, turning back. "Mr. Banks, I presume you told the Sheriff's Office about the pickup?"

He nodded. "Called them right after I got the call from the witness."

She gave him a wide smile. "You're a good

man, Ranger Banks."

He grinned widely. "Why, thank you kindly, Miss Farrel. I'll have to report that to Betsy; it always pleases her to know that I act like a gentleman around other ladies."

CHAPTER FIVE

By the time Casey got back to Ajo, it was nearly dark. She ate a fast food supper, picked up the day's edition of the Arizona *Republic*, and drove up the hill to the bed-and-breakfast.

After a brisk shower, she brushed her teeth, and got into bed with the *Republic*. The murders had made the front page, the story continuing in depth on an inside page. She read the article thoroughly; but there was nothing there that she didn't already know. There was no mention of the pickup or the horse trailer; but then the *Republic* went to press during the night; or, perhaps, the Sheriff's Department wanted to keep that bit of information quiet for the time being.

Casey skimmed through the rest of the paper, getting a chuckle from her favorite comic strips, despite the fact that you really needed a magnifying glass to read some of them. As usual, she felt a surge of annoyance that the editors chose to cram so many strips on the page that the drawings had been reduced to minuscule size. After trying to read the print in the tiny squares, she always vowed to write a letter of complaint, but she hadn't yet gotten to it.

Still not sleepy, she found the puzzle page and removed it from the rest of the paper. She enjoyed the puzzles, particularly the crossword, but did them all, even the rather childish Hocus Focus puzzle, which she always left to last. This puzzle consisted of two almost identical panels that challenged you to find the differences between the drawings.

Sometimes it was difficult to find all the changes, but tonight it was an easy one, and after finishing it, Casey put the page aside, wishing that she could so easily solve the puzzle of what she was beginning to think of as the Desert Murders.

Struck by a sudden idea, she delved into her attaché case for a yellow-sheeted pad and pencil. Propped up against the head-board, she began a rough sketch of the broad scene of the killings — the van and a pickup and horse trailer on the side of the highway in the park, two dead figures beside a blackened campfire in the desert just outside the boundaries of the park, and the figure of a dead woman several miles north of the campfire.

Holding it out in front of her eyes, the length of her arm, she studied it ruefully. She was never going to win any prizes for artistic talent, but the chief elements of the crime scenes were there. There was but one item missing, the figure of the killer.

She tore the sheet off the pad, started to crumple it, then hesitated. Perhaps she should keep it, add more detail from time to time. She put it into her attaché case.

Yawning, she turned out the light and settled down to sleep.

After another sumptuous breakfast the next morning, Casey paid her bill and checked out. She drove south again, but this time at the little town of Why she turned east on Highway 86, heading toward Tucson.

The name of the Papago Indian who had found the body of the woman in the desert was Jose Segundo. Segundo lived in Sells, where the tribal headquarters was located. The town had once been called Indian Oasis; but was re-named Sells in 1918, after Cato Sells, then Commissioner of Indian Affairs in Washington.

Sells was a town of less than three thousand people, but it was the center of most reservation activities. It had a modern hospital; a municipal center, which housed the tribal court, and the offices of the tribal police department; and the tribal government offices and assembly hall.

The Papago Indian Reservation covered almost three million acres, and had a population of around nine thousand. The principal economic activities on the reservation were mining; cattle raising; farming; and native arts and crafts.

There were many differences between the Papago and Casey's people, the Hopi. Casey had found that most non-Indians seemed to think of all Indian peoples as one group, not realizing the sometimes vast differences in language, culture, and appearance.

Some of the differences were caused by the land. The Hopi land, dry and ungenerous, gave sustenance reluctantly. Here, on the other hand, although rainfall was meager, water from wells and irrigation brought at least some nourishment to the dry soil, and one could see healthy farmlands, and herds of cattle grazing.

Since the Papago also received income from mining on the reservation, this meant that the Papago, while not affluent, were better off economically than the Hopi. But, in some ways, Casey thought, the poverty of the Hopis had protected them. Keeping themselves isolated, many Hopis had clung to their old gods and the ancient ceremonies. The Papago, Casey understood, as their old men died, had few left who could pass on the old ways, and most of the young men were not interested.

Many of the Papago were Roman Catholics, and most spoke English and Spanish, many preferring these languages to their native dialect.

Casey slowed the car as she entered the outskirts of Sells, and began looking for the street on which Jose Segundo lived. She finally found it — a dirt road meandering out of town. Many of the houses along the road were constructed of adobe, with a few stone houses here and there, and many wattle houses constructed of saguaro ribs or ocotillo branches plastered with adobe mud. The type of housing was usually a sign of the occupant's economic status. A wattle house was the easiest and the cheapest; adobe brick and stone houses were more expensive and more difficult to construct.

Jose Segundo lived in a small wattle house, the front of which was sheltered by an awning made of branches. Casey found him seated in a tilted-back chair, in the shade of the awning.

He did not stir, as she got out of the car. The day was hot and still, and beads of sweat popped out on Casey's forehead as she approached him. She could feel the dampness collecting at the base of her spine and between her breasts.

It was only a few degrees cooler in the shade of the awning.

"Mr. Jose Segundo?" she said.

"That's me."

He got to his feet slowly — a short, stocky man of some fifty years, wearing worn jeans and a plaid cotton shirt. The natural coloration of his broad face had been further darkened by the desert sun. His dark eyes regarded her incuriously.

"My name is Casey Farrel. I work for the Governor's Task Force on Crime. I'm down here investigating the murders that took place three nights ago. I understand that you found the woman's body?"

"I did, yes." He indicated that she should take the chair he'd just vacated; and seated himself on the low step in front of the door. "I've already told everything I know to a man from the Sheriff's Department. Why don't you cops get your act together?" he said in a growling voice.

She smiled placatingly. "I know it's a bother; but I would appreciate it if you would run through it again. Sometimes, when a little time has passed, people remember things that slipped their minds at the first telling. So if you'd humor me?"

He grunted. "At least you don't come on as strong as the Sheriff's guy did." He took out a pack of cigarettes, lit one, and smoked for a moment, gazing off into the distance.

"I really don't have all that much to tell."

"Why don't you start with your finding the body?"

"Well, I'd driven my old Jeep out into the desert, on a dirt road going south off Highway 86, when I saw buzzards circling off the road to the west. I knew something was dead or dying out there, so I left the road to see what it was. Then I saw the woman's body. It wasn't a good thing to see, I can tell you. Poor little thing."

"Did you see anyone else?"

He shook his head. "Nope. But then whoever shot her wouldn't have still been around. The guy that took my statement said she'd been dead for hours. If she had only been dead for a little while, I'd probably be in jail right now, instead of talking to you."

Casey nodded sympathetically. "Did you notice anything at the scene, anything out of the ordinary?"

His lips twitched in what might have been a smile. "Any clues, you mean?"

She smiled back. "Something like that, yes."

He shrugged. "Only the woman's footprints, and the hoofprints of a horse. When the rider left the area, he headed southwest. I'm a good tracker, so you can take my word on that. After seeing what somebody had done to her, believe me, I looked hard."

Again he shook his head. "She was young. Only about twenty. The bastard!"

"And you had never seen this woman before?"

His dark eyes squinted, as if evaluating her reasons for asking. "No. She was a stranger."

Casey looked at him steadily. "And what were you doing out there in the desert, Mr. Segundo?"

His eyes slid away, and for the first time he looked evasive. "I was hunting rabbits."

Casey didn't believe him, but went on: "Mr. Segundo, you know that two other bodies were found several miles southwest of where the woman was found?"

"Yes. I was told that."

"And on Highway 85, in Organ Pipe, two other bodies were found in a van."

"I heard about that on the news." His tone was cautious.

"The two men in the van were purportedly *coyotes*." She took her notes out of her purse. "Their names were Victor Sanchez and Pedro Castelar." She looked up. "Did you know either of these men? They lived on this side of the border."

Segundo's eyes were fixed on something above Casey's head. "Why should I know these men?" he asked with a shrug.

She leaned forward. "Mr. Segundo, look at me!"

He looked at her, his dark eyes flat.

"I want to make something clear. I have no interest in the smuggling of illegal workers; I am investigating five brutal, senseless murders, and nothing else."

"I understand," he said in a neutral voice.

"Do you? I know that many people of your tribe help smuggle aliens into the States by transporting them to the Phoenix area. Nothing you tell me here will go beyond me. You have my word on it."

She paused for a moment, and then said softly, "You have helped the illegals, haven't you, Mr. Segundo? That's the reason you were out in the desert, isn't it?"

His shoulders slumped, and he sighed. "I admit nothing."

"I know you had nothing to do with the murders. All I want to know is did you know the two *coyotes?*"

He sighed again. "I knew Pedro and Victor, yes. They were bad men. They sometimes robbed the Mexicans they brought over and left them out in the desert to die. For that reason I sometimes saw to it that the workers got to Phoenix safely."

"Did this Pedro and Victor usually take the workers to certain growers?"

"Not always, but most of the time. Often, the same workers come in every season to work the crops for the same growers."

"And were these five to be taken to places they had worked before?"

"That was my understanding, yes."

She leaned forward. "And just who were these employers?"

Segundo hesitated.

Casey leaned forward. "I need to know, Mr. Segundo. No one will ever know the information came from you."

Segundo sighed. "Three of the workers were to go to one rancho, two to another."

"What ranchos, Mr. Segundo?"

He threw up his hands. "They are rich, powerful people. They have much influence."

"Their names, please."

Segundo lowered his head, and Casey was afraid that she had lost him. When he looked at her again there was a flicker of fear in his eyes, but he spoke slowly: "The owners of the ranchos are Wager Halleck, and Alexander Dessaline. But you must remember your promise. They must never know that I have given you their names."

Slowly the old man hung up the phone and leaned back in his desk chair, his thoughts bleak. At the sound of the door opening he looked up to see his favorite progeny coming toward him.

Without preamble he said, "I have just called

the Governor's Office and found out that the Governor's new task force is looking into the murders of the Mexicans."

"So? That's nothing to be unduly concerned about. That task force is the laughing-stock of the state."

"The more people who investigate this matter, the more chances there are you will be found out. Even the incompetent get lucky now and then."

"There's nothing to find out. I'm not stupid, Father; I left no evidence behind."

"I have never judged you stupid, that's true; but perhaps I was in error. This was a stupid thing to do."

"It was something that had to be done, Father. Believe me, there is no evidence, and certainly no apparent motive to connect the family with these murders."

The man shook his head sadly. "Don't you feel any remorse for what you've done?"

"None at all. It was necessary. Haven't you always told us, Father, that when something has to be done, do it, never hesitate?"

The man lowered his eyes. "May God forgive me. I never meant for what I said to be taken in that way!"

"Didn't you? I found it very applicable."

When the man raised his eyes they were dark with pain.

CHAPTER SIX

That afternoon, Casey drove to Tucson, where she spent the night, before going to the coroner's office.

The autopsies on the bodies of the five victims had been completed. The two *coyotes* had traces of cocaine in their systems; but with the use of coke so prevalent, that, in Casey's opinion, was not enough to peg the killer's motive as drug-related.

The saddest thing in the coroner's report was the fact that the young woman had been six weeks pregnant. Had she known? Had her husband known? Reading this, Casey found herself fighting tears. Whoever killed these people deserved no mercy. As her father used to say, "He should be hung up by the yarbells!" And that would be too good for him.

After leaving the coroner's office, Casey checked in at the Sheriff's Department, and passed on, without naming her informant, the information that Jose Segundo had given her concerning the Halleck and Dessaline families.

Then, feeling her duty done, she headed for home, thinking warmly of Josh and Donnie;

and feeling guilty at the realization that this was the first time she had thought of them since reaching Ajo.

She smiled wryly, remembering how her mother used to scold her, and her father compliment her, when she became so immersed in what she was doing that she completely blocked out everything else. It was only later that she had understood their biases; but whether it was a feminine or a masculine trait, it certainly was an asset for a law officer. But now she had accomplished her mission, and for the moment could think of other things, and one of the things she thought about was how much she missed the physical presence of Josh's warm, well-muscled body.

When she reached Phoenix, she drove straight to her office — mentally cursing the heavy traffic — where the first thing she did was call Josh at the station. Amazingly, she caught him in.

"Casey! I was beginning to think you had run off to Mexico."

His warm, husky voice gave her a rush. Some of the accumulated tension of the last few days began to ease.

"And hello to you, too, Josh. I just this minute got into the office."

"And I'm the first one you called," he chuckled. "How about that?"

"Don't read too much into it, Detective," she said dryly.

His voice became serious. "What did you find out?"

"Not as much as I hoped. But there are some people I want to ask you about. Someone once told me that you know all the dirt there is to know on important people."

"A canard, babe, a canard," he said lightly. "Just who are these important people, and what do they have to do with your case?"

"Maybe nothing, but I'd rather not discuss it over the phone. I'm going to be a little late here, catching up; then I have to pick up Donnie. Is he okay?"

"Donnie's just fine. He's at school now, of course."

"Then why don't I take us all to dinner tonight, and we can talk."

"I have a better idea, Casey. Why don't I pick up Donnie, and some steaks and salad fixings, and we'll do a little barbecuing at my place? We can talk more freely there. Besides, you haven't been out to the house in ages."

"Sounds like a plan, Josh. I should make it out around seven."

Actually, she made it a little early — a few minutes after six-thirty. She felt tired, but excited. During the afternoon she had made a few calls, and had gotten some information she thought might be important. She couldn't wait to tell Josh.

Josh's car sat in the open garage. She thumbed the doorbell. Josh had given her a key to his house, and although he had protested, she had returned it after she got an apartment of her own. He was still pressing her to take it back.

Donnie answered the door. At his feet was the spotted dog, Spot II, that Josh had bought to replace the original Spot, who had been killed by the Dumpster Killer.

Donnie's face was all smiles, and Spot's tail beat a welcoming tattoo on the floor of the entryway. "Hi, Casey!" Donnie said in his husky little voice. "Josh said you'd be early. He says that you can depend on you always being early."

"Oh, he does, does he?" Casey stooped to give the boy a hug. He smelled of soap, and Casey felt a sharp pang as she thought of the child killed in the womb of its mother in the desert.

"And so, how have you been. Did you miss me?"

He nodded, suddenly very much a boy, afraid to admit to anything that smacked of sentiment. "But Josh and I had a good time batching it."

Casey smiled, recognizing Josh's phrase. She ruffled Donnie's hair, and stooped to scratch Spot behind the ears. The little dog wriggled ecstatically. *He* wasn't afraid to show his feelings. "I'm sure you did," she said. "Now, where's the lord of the manor?"

"Out on the deck." Donnie grabbed her hand and led her through the kitchen to the deck outside, which overlooked the ravine below.

It was a beautiful evening; the high Arizona sky was still blue, the sun just beginning to grow low in the west; the air clear, and growing cooler with the help of a fresh breeze.

On the serving cart sat a large bowl of salad; a bottle of ranch-style dressing; a package of brown-crusted rolls from the bakery; and three steaks, two large, and one small. On the large gas grill were three potatoes wrapped in foil, steaming merrily. They smelled delicious, and Casey realized that she was starving.

Josh was in a deck chair, feet propped up on the railing, a martini glass in one hand. On the table beside him was a frosty container, which held, Casey knew, more martinis.

"Well, you look comfortable," she said with a smile. God, he looked good!

"Depend on it." He raised his glass in a toast. "Hi, babe. Hard day?"

She sighed. "Hard enough." She wanted to kiss him, but she was darned if she was going to do it with him sitting in that chair. If he wanted to kiss her, he could get up!

Something batted against her leg, and she looked down to see Spot looking up at her eagerly. Suddenly she felt tired and stressed. "Go away, Dog," she said crossly. "Stop pestering me."

"He's just glad to see you, Casey," Donnie said in an injured tone.

Josh chuckled. "Yeah, he's just glad to see you, Casey."

"Well, I'm glad to see somebody is," Casey said, realizing that she sounded cranky and aggrieved, and feeling annoyed with herself for sounding so.

Josh looked at her sharply, then turned to Donnie. "Donnie, why don't you take Spot outside and let him chase a ball or something? Don't go too far from the house; I'll be calling you for supper before too long."

Donnie snapped his fingers, and the dog scampered after him into the kitchen. A moment later Casey heard the front door slam.

Casey sighed. "I'm sorry, I didn't mean to snap; but I'm a little tired."

"I know." He stood up, moved to her, and took her in his arms. It felt so good that she never wanted to leave; but she didn't want him to know that. She stayed there for a long moment, absorbing his calm and the reassurance of his strength.

She then pulled away, but not before he had kissed her tenderly on the cheek. For a man, and a cop, he often showed surprising sensitivity. "How about a martini?" he said. "It will relax you."

She nodded gratefully, and sank into the deck chair next to Josh's, while he filled a chilled glass to the brim and handed it to her.

"Hungry?"

"I am." She took a sip of the martini. It was icy and faintly bitter — a typical Josh Whitney martini.

"Then I'll start the steaks."

"Want me to help?"

He shook his head. "You take your shoes off and relax. I had an easy day today, no homicides, can you imagine? Must be some kind of record."

Feeling better, Casey did so. As Josh turned his attention to the steaks, Casey put her feet up on the deck railing, glad that she had worn pants instead of a skirt. It was nice here on the deck; the mountains were clear in the distance, a smoky blue, and the sun was now low on the horizon. Birds chirped and sang in the ravine, but otherwise it was quiet; the nearest house was a hundred yards away, and the street which ran before Josh's house had very little traffic.

Casey stretched. She could get used to this. But then, she had stayed here for several weeks before running from the Dumpster Killer, and it hadn't worked out. Josh had kept pushing for a more permanent relationship, and she just wasn't ready for . . .

The coals hissed, as Josh laid the seasoned steaks on the grill, then crossed over to pick up his drink.

"So, tell me about it, babe."

She did. It didn't take long. When she had finished, he turned the steaks, and asked: "And what did your boss have to say?"

She shook her head. "I haven't talked to him yet."

Josh raised his eyebrows, and she answered his unspoken question with a smile. "I figure that I deserve a peaceful evening before bearding The Wilson, and I intend to do that by telling him, tomorrow morning, that I got in late tonight. Do you dare to contradict me, Detective?"

Josh laughed, tossed back the remains of his martini, and shook his head. "Not me, lady. If you can live with the guilt . . ."

Casey sipped her drink and sighed, "I can live with it very well, thank you. How is that steak coming. I'm starved!"

In answer, he leaned over the deck rail and called for Donnie. By the time the boy appeared, Josh had the salad, steak, and potatoes on the table between the two deck chairs. Donnie, he served inside, in front of the TV

For a while conversation lagged, while the inner man and woman were fed. By the time Josh brought out the pot of fresh brewed Columbia Supremo, Casey felt that she just might survive.

While they sat sipping the aromatic coffee, Josh returned to the subject of her trip. "It does look like a cold case. You know what they say: If a homicide isn't solved within forty-eight hours of commission, it probably never will be."

Casey sighed. "I know that, Josh; but what am I supposed to do, just declare it hopeless and give up?"

Josh touched her hand gently. "Of course not, babe. I just meant that you shouldn't feel bad if this case bogs down. Sometimes there is simply not enough to go on. I don't expect you to do anything less than your best. Now, what intrigues me is the information you got concerning the Hallecks and the Dessalines. Are you going to follow that up?"

Casey nodded. "Of course. It seems pretty certain that they dealt with those *coyotes,* and it is entirely possible that the two missing illegals worked for them as well."

Josh frowned. "You know that you may be getting into some heavy stuff? The Dessalines and the Hallecks have a long history in the valley, and they've got lots of clout, as well as money. I'm afraid that you may find that you won't get much support if you start to investigate them. I hate to say it, but with their connections they can pull a lot of powerful strings, some that go right to the top."

Casey set down her cup. "God! I hate that. Nobody should be above the law!"

Josh refilled her cup. "You're right, no one should be, but the fact remains that some people are just more equal than others, and it takes a lot of nerve to challenge them. Are you sure you're up to it? You could make some powerful enemies, and it might all be for nothing."

Casey scowled. "I'm going to do my job — or at least try to — and that means following up on any information that I can get. It's little enough, God knows."

Josh nodded. "I'm not trying to discourage you. Just wanted to be certain that you know what you're getting into. Do you know much about the families?"

"Not really. Their names crop up in the news now and again. I know they're rich. I know that Wager Halleck served two terms as a U.S. Senator from Arizona, and was once considered a presidential candidate although he wasn't able to swing the nomination."

Josh grinned. "Yeah, the old boy was once a contender. Now, of course, he must be in his seventies; but I understand that he's still a pistol. He's been a widower for years, but I hear that he's still quite the ladies' man."

"What about Dessaline? I know less about him."

Josh leaned back in his chair. "Let's see, the Dessalines are also one of the old, founding families. Alexander Dessaline must be in his late seventies now, but still active. He, like Halleck, is one of the famous forty, the power brokers in Arizona. No one gets elected to public office in Arizona without their sanction.

"Both families have a lot in common; their lineage goes way back. Both men had grand-parents who settled around Phoenix in the eighteen hundreds. Now, both families have wealth, power, and prestige. Also, both men have fairly large families. I think Halleck has five kids, three boys and two girls, if I'm not mistaken; and Dessaline has four, two of each."

Casey hugged her arms. A breeze had come up, and the air was growing cool. "You make them sound formidable."

"Depend on it. Another thing they have in

common is ruthlessness. All that wealth and power has made them used to having their own way. And, like I said, they aren't going to take kindly to having you ask questions about their business."

Casey was silent for a moment, and then told him what she had found out that afternoon: "That may well be, but I'm afraid I've already started. While I was in the office this afternoon I did some checking, and I found that both men have horse trailers registered in their names."

Josh snorted. "Come on, Casey. That doesn't mean doodly-squat. This is Arizona, remember? Probably half the population — those who have the money — has horses, and trailers to haul them. And, while we're at it, I'll bet that both men, or someone in their families, has a gun collection. It would be par for the course."

"I know that this doesn't mean that they were involved in the deaths; but I can't help but feel that there is a connection." Her tone was defensive. "After all, they do hire illegals."

"Whoa, there, woman!" he laughed. "You haven't exactly proved that yet. All you have is the word of an informant."

She shook her head. "I've learned to trust my instincts, Josh, and my instinct tells me that there's something there. I just have to find it."

Josh put down his cup and reached for her hand. "I thought that gut feelings were supposed to be my department. Every time we have a homicide, some other cop always asks me if I have one of my famous hunches about it."

"Well, maybe it's catching, Josh. Or maybe it's that famous women's intuition, but I can feel that I'm right. It may be indirectly, but in some way or another one of those families is involved in this thing."

He shrugged. "Maybe you're right. So what's your first move?"

"Well," she said thoughtfully, "first I need to learn a lot more about the two families. What else can you tell me?"

"Well, there is one thing, despite all these things they have in common, they are bitter enemies."

"Oh! Why?"

"Well, the story I've heard is that forty years ago, when they were both young, Wager took Alexander's girl away from him and married her. The word is that Alexander did not take it at all well. And when Bess Halleck, the girl in question, died about ten years later — right after bearing the last of five children, a girl — Alexander blamed Wager for her death.

She was supposed to be delicate, you see; and Alexander claimed that Wager had worked her too hard, and had given her too many kids."

"And that's it, a little name calling in the heat of passion?"

"Well, not entirely. You know how these things are, they develop a life of their own; somebody does something to somebody else, they retaliate; it keeps growing. Dessaline, because of his jealousy of Halleck, wanted to get to him. Halleck got himself elected to the Senate — he sort of slipped that by before Dessaline knew what was going on — but Alexander was able to prevent him from grabbing the big one. He put his money, power, and influence into seeing that Wager didn't get the presidential nomination. This, of course, made Wager hate Alexander, and so on."

Casey shook her head. "Such a waste. Think of what they could have done with all that money and energy."

Josh shrugged. "Well, that's human nature, babe; and not the best side of it."

"Do you think that either of them is capable of killing? Of course I don't mean that they would do it themselves, but would either of them be the type to hire someone to do it, if it would solve a problem for them?"

Josh held up his hands. "Who knows? From

what I have seen and read, I would say that they can both be ruthless, but that's not quite the same thing."

"What about their kids? Family feuds usually extend themselves to following generations."

"I don't know much about them. The only one who's been much in the news is Mark Halleck, Wager's eldest. He's a lawyer with one of the most prestigious law firms in Arizona, and the word is that he's planning on running for governor in the next election. I do remember reading something to the effect that all of the children of both families still live in Arizona."

He grinned briefly. "I guess they don't want to get too far away from all that money they stand to inherit."

"And what about the wives. Did Halleck ever marry again?"

"Nope. He claimed he could never find another woman as good as Bess."

"What about Dessaline's wife? I wonder how she feels about her husband carrying on a life-long feud over a woman who married another man? Is she still living?"

"Oh, yes, very much so. Catherine Dessaline is heavily into the social scene in the Phoenix area, and there isn't a worthwhile charity drive or function that she isn't involved in."

Casey was silent for a moment, and then: "Tomorrow I think that I'll do a computer search and see what I get on the other members of the families."

Josh put his hand on hers. "Well, just be careful and don't stir up any hornets' nests. And if and when you get to the stage where you're asking questions, take it very easy. Okay?"

Casey smiled, but it was a bit forced. "I know I haven't been with the task force very long, Josh, but they trained me well at the detective agency. I do know my job."

Josh looked embarrassed. "I know, babe, it's just that I'm a worrier, particularly when someone I care about is involved. I just can't stop myself. So . . ." He paused. "I'll say one more thing: Be careful around your boss. He may not be too happy when he learns that you intend to investigate the Hallecks and the Dessalines."

Casey frowned. "What are you saying? You know that I don't care a lot for the guy, but I think he's straight enough. I don't figure him to back down under pressure."

"He's a bureaucrat, Casey. It's been my experience that all bureaucrats walk gentle around wealth and power."

"Well, tomorrow I'll bring him up to date. Gently."

She yawned suddenly. "God, I'm pooped. I'll help you clean up, then scoop up Donnie and head home."

He stood, taking her hand. "Stay, Casey," he said in a soft voice. "It's been a while."

She tensed, but did not take her hand from his. "But Donnie . . . ?"

"He'll be in the guest room. And, he was here before. That didn't stop us then."

Casey hesitated. "I wasn't trying to adopt him then, and didn't have to be careful of my reputation. By the way, there was no message from Judge Pritchard. Have you heard anything?"

He put his hands on her shoulders and gently drew her nearer. "No. And don't try to change the subject. Haven't you missed me, just a little?"

He lowered his head to hers, and as she felt the heat of his mouth against her lips, all resistance drained from her.

"All right," she said. "But after Donnie is asleep."

He gave her a squeeze that compressed her ribs. "Great. And I think it's about time he went to bed, don't you?"

CHAPTER SEVEN

The next morning, when she briefed Bob Wilson on what she had discovered, Casey felt herself proven right concerning her evaluation of his probable reaction.

At the mention of the Halleck and Dessaline names, Wilson leaned across his desk, his face alight, his eyes showing the delight of a greedy man gazing at a pile of money. "You think one of those high-and-mighty bastards may be involved? God! That would be too much to hope for!"

Casey replied cautiously, "I'm not sure at this stage, Bob. It might just be coincidence; but I think I should check it out."

"Well, you go after them." He sat back and put his hands behind his head. "It would sure be a feather in our caps if the task force nailed the killer while the Pima County cops run around with their heads up their asses. And, if the Dessalines or the Hallecks are involved, it would mean *mucho* publicity."

Casey shook her head. "You put things so beautifully, Bob," she said dryly.

"I call 'em the way I see 'em," he said cheerfully.

"And it doesn't bother you that the Hallecks and the Dessalines may raise a stink if I start asking questions? I'm told they have a lot of power and influence."

He glowered at her. "We're above influence; that's why the Governor formed the task force, he wanted a body that wouldn't be vulnerable to pressure." He held up a hand. "But that doesn't mean that you are to go stirring up things, unless you have something dirty on the stick you use to stir with."

Casey raised her eyebrows. "That's a rather twisted metaphor; but I get the point. Don't worry, I'll be careful."

She got to her feet. "I just wanted to be sure that I had your support."

"You've got it, Farrel. I'm behind you all the way."

The rest of that day and all the next, Casey spent at the library in research on the Hallecks and the Dessalines; scrolling through the microfilms of old newspapers and digging back through old issues of magazines, until her eyes burned.

The next day she hit the Hall of Records, where she dug through birth records, death records, land records, census records, looking

for anything that had to do with the two families, dry statistics, vital or otherwise.

The third day she spent at the computer,
putting in the data she had collected, and using
certain techniques that she had learned at the
agency, none of which were legal, but which
were effective, to access financial and tax records.

By late afternoon, she had all the chaff sifted
out, and she settled back to scan several sheets
of printout.

*WAGER HALLECK: 77; widower;
semi-retired; net worth approx. 30 million;
severe heart attack five years ago, resulting
in heart transplant (health still not the best,
limiting physical activity); no criminal record, not even a traffic violation; subjected
to three tax audits over past ten years (all
three audits resulted in substantial addi-
tional tax levies, contested all three, won
one, lost two).*

*MARK HALLECK: Eldest son; 38, un-
married; net worth, approx. two million;
Harvard Law school; Junior partner,
Mateson, Cartier Law Firm in Phoenix,
specializing in corporate law; active in civic
affairs; active in Republican Party, but has
never held office; no criminal record; drives
a BMW; has apartment Phoenix, but lives*

much of the time at family home, with fa-
ther.

ALLEN HALLECK: 36; Married to Margaret Larson Halleck, 1981; two children; net worth, approx. three million; graduate Asu, major Economics; manager of Arizona Frontier Bank (one of two banks owned by Wager Halleck); owns house in Paradise Valley; drives gray Porsche 911; no criminal record; children attend private schools.

ANN MARIE HALLECK CULSHAW: 35; married to James Culshaw, 1978; net worth less than one-hundred thousand; three children; attended ASU, received degree in music; husband a golf pro; owns a condo in Scottsdale; no criminal record.

STEVEN HALLECK: 32; married and divorced; no children; approx. net worth zero; attended UCLA where he was All-American football player, a half-back, tried out for Denver Broncos, but did not survive first cut; worked as backfield coach for two years at UCLA but was fired in middle of second season when involved in a sex and drug scandal involving a teenage girl, charges dropped and hushed up; returned to Phoenix and became stockbroker, working for two local firms over a period of four years, fired from both jobs, reportedly for convincing clients to invest in bad stocks; presently unemployed, living at home with father.

THERESA HALLECK: 30; Married and divorced; no children; financial worth not available; but bank account is often overdrawn, father pays her bills and makes deposits to her account; ex-husband is movie actor whose career went down the tubes four years ago because of cocaine use, marriage lasted two years which Theresa spent in Beverly Hills with her husband; after divorce Theresa returned to Phoenix and her father's house, taking back her maiden name; attended USC majoring in Fine Arts; periodically active in amateur theater in Phoenix; several traffic violations including one for driving while under the influence; like brother, Allen, she drives a gray Porsche 911.

Casey rubbed her burning eyes, and leaned back in her chair, trying to ease the headache beginning to throb behind her eyes.

Reaching into her top drawer, she took out a bottle of aspirin, poured two into the palm of her hand, and went out into the hall for a paper cup of water.

After downing the aspirin, she returned to

her office, deep in thought.

Wager Halleck's wife had indeed been busy for the ten years of her marriage; there was not more than two years between the births of any of her children. Still, that was hardly enough reason to accuse a man of being responsible for his wife's death.

At any rate, despite the money and the power, it seemed that all wasn't perfect in the Halleck family. Certainly Steven didn't sound like a prize. His past had been pretty shady, and he was now unemployed, living at home on his father's sufferance. Wager couldn't be too happy about that. And it would appear that Theresa was a little on the wild side, if not downright unstable. The past of both Steven and Theresa would bear some looking into.

Stretching again, Casey picked up the printout on the Dessalines and began to read:

ALEXANDER DESSALINE: 79; in good health; resides in a ranch-style mansion west of Phoenix; four children, two boys, two girls; owns Dessaline Construction Company and Dessaline Real Estate Development Corp.; although retired, still keeps his hand in; net worth, approx. fifty million; no criminal record; wife Catherine, 72, very active in community affairs, well known for giving charity functions.

JARVIS DESSALINE: 41; married to Carol Dunston Dessaline; net worth approx. three million; three children, all boys; president of Dessaline Construction; from all accounts a dynamo, a shrewd businessman who has been even more successful than his father in running the company; attended Arizona State University, degree in business administration; lives in half-million dollar home in Fountain Hills.

GLENN DESSALINE: 39; married and divorced twice; one child by first wife; ran through the million dollar trust established by his father for all his children at age twenty-five, in three years; left college in second year; has never held a job for long; lives on Dessaline Ranch and manages the orange groves; numerous traffic tickets; twice arrested for drunk driving, six years ago license suspended for a year; arrested once for assault in a bar, drunk and disorderly; has reputation as a womanizer; only financial assets a two-year-old Caddy, not yet paid for; often overdrawn at bank.

SANDRA DESSALINE: 36; unmarried; graduated ASU with a degree in Business Administration; took over as president of Dessaline Real Estate Development when Alexander retired; has increased the size and profits of the company since; has made shrewd investments and is well off financially; approx. net worth, five million; is often seen in the company of Phoenix's most eligible bachelors, but apparently has never become permanently attached; often helps her mother with charity and social functions; no criminal record aside from a couple of minor traffic violations.

HELEN DESSALINE MONROE: wife of Earl Monroe; two children; married immediately after graduating high school, no college; net worth, approx. three million; husband owns and manages several apartment buildings; active in civic affairs; both Monroes active in politics in Republican party, husband has run twice, unsuccessfully, for city council in Tempe, is rumored to be running again this year; no criminal record.

Casey sighed and leaned back. Her headache had faded to a dull ache, but was still annoying.

So, both families had two black sheep, but there was nothing in the material she had so far collected to indicate that any member of either family was involved in anything that might lead to murder. Still, now she had a handle on the background of each family, and a general feel for the separate members. Was she wrong in her feeling that somehow they were connected with the deaths in the desert? There was really awfully little to go on, only the fact that both families owned ranches that hired illegals, and that three of the dead illegals were *probably* on their way to one rancho, where they had worked before. At any rate, that connection had to be checked out; then she would decide how much further she would go with individual family members.

She looked at her watch, 5:30 p.m. She should have left a half hour ago. Donnie would have been home now for more than two hours. She sighed. The phrase "latch key child" had such a disparaging sound. Of course he was old enough now to take care of himself for an hour or so; but she always felt a pang of guilt if she was later than usual.

He was no doubt on his belly before the TV, his head propped on Spot II. She felt some guilt about that, too. She was going to have to set her foot down about the amount of time he spent watching, despite the temptation to use the TV as a convenient baby sitter.

She grinned to herself wryly; being a working mother was hard, but she had asked for this.

Still, she didn't move for a bit. The offices were mostly empty now, and she savored the quiet of the building. The morning edition of the Arizona *Republic* was on her desk; she had not had time to read it as yet. She decided to take a few minutes to look through it. If she left now, she would be caught in the mad surge of rush-hour traffic; if she waited a bit, it would have thinned out.

Picking up the paper, she glanced through it. Already the story of the five murders was reduced to a few paragraphs on a back page. The Pima County Sheriff's Department stated that they had no active suspects as yet, but were following up some promising leads.

She sighed. That was usually police-speak for "no new developments." Within a week, there would be so many new murders that these five would be put on the back burner. Of course, the file would never be closed, but in effect, it might as well be.

Well, the case was her baby, and she had no intention of giving up on it.

Since this was Friday, the paper included a weekend section, mentioning all of the weekend events in and around Phoenix.

Looking through this section, she came across an item that immediately caught her attention: Tomorrow, Saturday night, there was to be a charity banquet for the homeless children of Phoenix, to be held at the Biltmore Hotel. Catherine Dessaline, chairperson for the drive, would preside over the banquet. There would be dancing. The Governor was going to be present. Tickets were two hundred and fifty dollars per person.

Casey lowered the paper. Probably several members of the Dessaline family would be in attendance. But two hundred and fifty dollars! She pursed her mouth in a silent whistle, trying to remember her bank balance; two hundred and fifty dollars would take about half of it.

But why should she even consider paying it out of her own pocket? It was an expense involving an ongoing investigation.

She wondered if Bob Wilson was still in his office. She knew that he had been having trouble with his wife and often avoided going home as long as possible.

She punched out his number. He answered on the first ring, growling, "Yeah?"

"It's me, Casey."

"What are you still doing here? Don't you know that all government workers flee promptly at five?"

"I could ask you the same, but then I know why you're still around." She smiled at his grunt.

"I just have a quick question; can the expense account stand a two hundred and fifty dollar tab? Catherine Dessaline is giving a charity banquet tomorrow night, a benefit for homeless children."

He grunted again. "Farrel, you well know that we can't spend state funds on charity donations! Especially not in these days of tight budgets."

"Come on, Bob, you can squeeze it in somewhere. It would be a great chance for me to meet the Dessalines. We've already agreed that it would be unwise for me to question them head on, at least at this stage of the investigation; and you can hardly expect me to foot the bill out of my own pocket."

There was a moment's silence, then: "Okay, Farrel, I'll see what I can do. But something had better come of this, or I'll have your head!" His disconnect hurt her ear.

Smiling softly, Casey dialed the number listed in the paper. As late as it was, the affair might be sold out, but she doubted it. The recession was having its effect on everything. She soon found that this assumption was correct; there were still tickets available. She made a reservation, promising to have her check with her the next evening.

Hanging up, she hoped that Wilson would come through for her. The rent on her apartment was due next week.

Her earlier surmise was correct also — when

she got home, Donnie was lying on the floor in front of the TV, Spot II asleep under his arm.

Donnie bounded to his feet. "Hi, Casey!" He ran to her and she hugged him against her.

"Hi, kiddo." She ruffled his hair. "Have a good day?"

"It was okay, I guess." He wrinkled up his face, then grinned. "What's for supper. I'm hungry!"

She headed for her room. "You're always hungry. We're having hot turkey sandwiches and gravy, carrot and celery sticks with baby tomatoes, and milk."

At the door to her room, she turned back to look at him. He pondered thoughtfully for a moment, then grinned. "Alllll-right!"

She waited for the inevitable question. "And what's for dessert?"

"Frozen yogurt and oatmeal cookies. Okay?"

He dropped back down in front of the TV. "Okay!"

Casey continued on into her room, smiling to herself. She was becoming an expert in limited truth. When Donnie had first come to live with her, she had made the mistake of letting him know that the food she served him was nutritious, low fat, and good for him. It soon became apparent that to Donnie, healthy food translated to dull food, sissy food, stuff that no respectable red-blooded American boy would willingly eat. Now, Casey made no mention of such facts as: turkey breast is low in fat; the bread was whole wheat; the "gravy" was great tasting, but had almost no fat; the raw carrot and celery sticks and the "baby" tomatoes were a lure to get Donnie to eat his veggies — somehow they were not so repugnant raw. Maybe it was because of the picnic connotation — and the frozen yogurt and the oatmeal cookies came from the health food store.

When she came out, in her running clothes, Donnie looked up. "I thought you said we were going to eat?"

Reaching down, she pulled him to his feet. "Yes, but dinner won't take but a minute to fix, and I need a run. We won't be gone long. Are you up for it?"

He groaned melodramatically, putting his hands to his stomach. "But I'm starving."

"You can have an apple while I set out the things for supper and lock up the house. Come on. If we don't get some exercise, we're going to turn into couch potatoes. Don't you want Arnold to respect you? You know what he says about physical fitness."

Donnie gave her a baleful glare, clearly unable to tell if she was kidding or not.

"Okay. But not a long one. An apple isn't very big!"

The sky was still light, and a slight breeze moved the dry air so that it felt like hot silk against the skin.

Casey started out at an easy lope, looking down at Donnie's blonde head bobbing beside her. Spot II was already far ahead of them. Donnie and Spot sure didn't need to worry about gaining weight; they both had the metabolism of race horses; ate everything in sight, and never gained a pound. However, the exercise was good for them; helped them get rid of some of their excess energy, and it was something they could all do together.

Casey had not been running very long. She had started shortly after moving into the apartment, soon after she realized that she was gaining weight and losing stamina.

She enjoyed her runs, but had yet to develop the dedication, the unbridled enthusiasm, of the dedicated runners. Running was hard work, and sometimes painful. She listened to other runners speak of the ecstasy they experienced when they broke the famous "barrier" and made it through into euphoria; but she had never experienced this, and had begun to believe she never would.

What kept her at it, was the fact that it worked; she had lost the gained pounds, and now felt physically fit and energetic. It was a good way to feel, and worth the price.

Her apartment building was located on the edge of an area of vacant lots. Construction had been planned for more apartment buildings and condos on the vacant land, but overbuilding in the eighties and the current recession had caused a delay in construction. At one time the land here had all been farmland, and a canal, which once brought water from the Salt River for irrigation, now stretched, dry and weed-grown like an ancient river bed, across the area.

A well-worn path followed the canal bed, and it made a good running track. The only traffic hazards were other runners; but most of them seemed to prefer the comparative cool of early morning. Tonight she saw only a few people, a mixture of joggers, walkers and runners.

She settled into an easy pace, Donnie pumping to keep up with her. Knowledgeable runners had told her with barely concealed condescension that the trick was to find your natural rhythm and fall into it. If done properly, you wouldn't notice the jolts at all.

"But then, I never did have a sense of rhythm," she said aloud.

Donnie, now a few steps ahead of her —
a matter of pride — glanced back at her.
"What did you say, Casey?"

"Nothing," Casey panted. "Just talking to
myself."

Donnie matched his words to his stride.
"Josh says that when a person starts talking
to themselves, they're losing it."

"Losing what?"

"I dunno. I didn't ask." He shot her a sly
look. "I thought maybe it was something that
a kid shouldn't know."

Casey didn't have enough breath to laugh,
but she grinned. Sometimes Donnie exhibited
a vein of dry humor that surprised her. She
slowed her pace a little, watching as the boy
ran on ahead, chasing Spot II and being chased
in return; and feeling a welling of love so
strong that it was almost pain. It would really
hurt her if Judge Pritchard refused to let her
adopt him.

Again, she wondered if the reason she
wanted to adopt Donnie was because of the
baby she had aborted in California. She had
felt it was necessary, under the circumstances;
but the memory of the experience still haunted
her, still lay like a weight somewhere in the
dark depths of her unconscious.

She had told Josh most of the secrets of her
life, feeling that she should be honest with

113

him; but even he did not know about that. She firmly believed that a woman had the right to choose what she did with her body, and that, in many cases, the choice to have an abortion was the logical and proper thing to do; but that was before she faced her own personal decision. Casey had always prided herself on being clearheaded and logical, but it was plain to her that her response, in this case, had nothing to do with either process; it was strictly gut level. And, it was equally clear to her, that she had not yet made her peace with the decision she had made.

But, nothing would be solved by thinking about it now. Now she had better get Donnie home, get him fed, check out his homework, and get him to bed. Tomorrow morning would arrive all too early; and tomorrow night she was scheduled to beard the matriarch of the Dessaline family in her natural haunts. She found the idea both exhilarating and frightening.

CHAPTER EIGHT

As Casey parked her car in the lot before the Biltmore she smiled. She had expected to feel like a poor relation in her just-washed Mustang — she hadn't wanted to drive her State car because of the plates — but it wasn't as bad as she had feared. Of course there were a great many of the usual assortment of vanity cars; but among the Mercedes, BMWs, Rolls, and fancy sports cars with exotic names, there was a goodly sprinkling of sturdy Jeep Cherokees, Ford Explorers, and other respectable middle-class cars. It sure wouldn't be this way if this was in Hollywood. There, they hid anything but the most expensive vehicles somewhere out of sight, pretending that no one but the super-rich, or those who spent like they were super-rich, existed.

Phoenix, thank God, was a little more realistic. Here a man might have millions, and prefer to drive a sturdy ranch wagon, or a four-wheel drive vehicle, proving both his practicality and his desire to keep a low profile.

At any rate, she obviously didn't need to

start feeling inferior just yet. Cheerfully, she handed the Mustang over to the attendant, and feeling a rush of excitement, prepared to enter the hotel.

She knew that she looked well, for she was wearing her one expensive dress. It was basic. It was black. And it had the elegance and simplicity of a garment that would never go out of style — at least that was what the saleslady had told her when she bought it two months ago, on sale, but still costing much more than Casey was used to paying. Now, however, she was glad that she had taken the plunge. The dress was sleeveless, with a matching stole; and the soft, flowing silk set off her dark cap of hair, and her dark eyes, and made her skin look like ivory — at least that was what Josh had told her when she dropped Donnie off at his house. "I wish I was going with you, babe," he had said wistfully. "You should have an escort, and I don't know that I like the idea of your looking so desirable around all of those wealthy wolves. They'll be on you like butter on toast."

Casey, flattered despite herself, kissed his cheek. "You can't afford it, Detective. I can't either, but the Force is paying. It's a dirty job but . . ."

He had released her reluctantly. "Yeah, yeah. I know. Rub it in, why don't you?"

And so now here she was, handing the woman at the table her check, and picking up her ticket — feeling an urge to break into "What Do the Simple Folk Do" from *Camelot*.

As she entered the banquet room, she could see that it was filling rapidly, most of the people congregating at the two bars on opposite sides of the large room.

Now, where was her table. Since she wasn't anyone important, she figured that it must be in the back of the room, and it was.

She looked at her watch. There was an hour yet before dinner, so she might as well get herself a drink, and mingle. Maybe she'd get lucky.

It took a while for Casey to make her way to the crowded bar and order a vodka tonic, at five bucks a pop. Drink in hand, she made her way across to the end of the room that had the fewest people, and to a position where she could get a good view of the room. The noise level was high, and climbing with each drink consumed.

Slowly, she scanned the room. There were a few faces she recognized — social and political notables — from newspaper and TV coverage; but no one she knew to talk to. She tensed as the Governor strode in through the entrance, his wife on his arm. People began clustering around him as he worked the crowd. Although Casey worked for the man, she had never met him, and had never seen him in the flesh; so she watched him curiously. He was a personable man, with considerable charisma, a successful businessman who had come to the office with much personal wealth, but very little political experience. His popularity had started out high, but had been steadily falling ever since his election.

Personally, Casey thought that he had done some good things, including the establishment of the task force.

Her attention sharpened as she saw the Governor being approached by a slender, silver-haired woman in an evening dress. Catherine Dessaline. Casey knew that the woman was seventy-two, but it was hard to believe; she looked a good ten or fifteen years younger. She was beautifully gowned and coifed, and projected an aura of pampered privilege.

Casey wondered if the woman was, like herself, unescorted. She could see no husband or children in attendance; but in this crowd, who could tell. Mrs. Dessaline was talking with the Governor now, their heads close together, and Casey wondered how she could get to meet the woman, without appearing gauche. Obviously, she would have to wait until the Governor moved on, but when he did, Mrs. Dessaline moved along with him, still talking.

Casey shrugged, took the last swallow of liquid in her glass, decided that given the weakness of the drink another wouldn't hurt, and started toward the bar.

After another lengthy wait, she got her drink, started away from the bar, and collided with someone. Stumbling backward, her drink flew out of her hand. Fortunately, none of it spilled on her.

"Dammit!" she muttered reflexively, before looking up at the chest of a well-tailored tux. Looking higher, she found herself staring into a pair of quizzical hazel eyes set in a ruggedly handsome face which bore an expression of dismay.

Casey, embarrassed by her unladylike outburst, was prepared to apologize, but he beat her to it. "I'm sorry," he said. "It was my fault. I wasn't watching where I was going."

Completely disarmed, Casey found herself, uncharacteristically, at a loss for words. He really was very attractive. He was perhaps a little taller than Josh, with a well-styled head of thick, wavy chestnut hair, an expensive looking tan, and a killer smile.

With a start, she realized that he was speaking again.

"Did any of it get on you?"

She glanced down at herself, glad for the

excuse to look away for a moment. "Doesn't seem so."

"Well, you must let me buy you another. It's the least I can do, considering."

Casey nodded, and he took her arm with an easy familiarity that Casey would have resented in any other man, and led her back to the bar. Casey could not help noticing that while she had found it necessary to fight her way through to get a drink, the throng parted for him like the waters of the Red Sea parted for Moses. How did he do that?

"What are you drinking."

"Vodka tonic."

He placed the order, then turned back to Casey with a quick smile. "I'm Mark Halleck. And you are?"

Casey, despite a feeling of shock, managed to get out her name. "Casey Farrel." Her mind was going a mile a minute.

He smiled again, ruefully, and handed her her drink. "You looked surprised. No, shocked is a better word. I wonder why?"

Casey grasped her drink, determined to get out of this gracefully. She smiled back. "It's just that I'm surprised to see you here. This is a Dessaline affair, and I have heard that the Hallecks and the Dessalines are . . ." Shit! She was putting her foot in it again.

He laughed softly. "Like the fabled Hatfields and the McCoys, I know. But that old feud is mostly between our daddies. Few of the children in either family pay any attention to it. Besides, this is a charity function, and as far as Catherine is concerned, Halleck money is as welcome as any."

Casey nodded, feeling a little less awkward and more than a little daring. "And you're thinking of running for governor, and you're here to shake a few political hands."

He looked momentarily startled, then threw back his head and laughed lustily. "Right! You're not hesitant to speak your mind, are you, Miss Farrel? Well, I like that. What do you say we move out of this crush and talk a bit. By the way, may I call you Casey?"

She nodded, and he took her arm again and steered her out of the crowd to a quiet spot against one wall.

Casey, feeling high on success, took a sip of her drink. This was more than she had hoped for. She had gone fishing for a Dessaline, and caught a Halleck. A large one.

As she lowered her glass, she became aware that Halleck's hands were empty. He saw her glance and interpreted it correctly. "I don't drink," he said unapologetically, then raised his hand. "No. I'm not alcoholic, it's just that I like to be well aware of what I am doing at all times."

Casey nodded sagely. "A wise decision for a politician, I'm sure, and one which more of them should follow."

She filed away the mental note that this man liked to be in control. A not unusual trait for a politician.

He gave her his easy smile, but his eyes were sharp. "You're a perceptive young woman, Ms. Casey Farrel."

She lifted her glass. "Likewise, I'm sure. Or, as my father used to say, 'It takes one to know one.' "

She was, she found, enjoying this exchange, perhaps too much. There was an edge of flirtatiousness to the conversation that gave it excitement; and she had to remind herself forcibly that she was here on business, and that she might not have long in his company.

She took another sip of her drink. "Tell me, did you really want to go into politics, or was there . . . family pressure?"

"You mean, did my father influence me? You might find this hard to believe, but no. Just the opposite, in fact." He leaned against the wall, gazing off over the crowd. "Father always said that politics is a dirty business. Of course, that may have been just sour grapes. As I remember it, he enjoyed being a U.S. Senator; it was when he failed to get the party nomination for President that disillusionment set in."

"And you don't fear that happening to you?"

He shrugged. "Maybe, maybe not. Anyway, I'd like to make a try for it; and I intend to win."

"And you are used to winning, right?"

He looked at her steadily. "Yes, I am. Does that put you off?"

This time it was her turn to shrug. "I'm not sure. Confidence is a good thing; it helps you get where you want to go. But overconfidence can trip you up. A balance is nice."

He shook his head. "You're a funny girl, Casey Farrel. You make me laugh. But now it's your turn. What do you do?"

Casey hesitated. "I'm in police work," she said, finally.

His eyes narrowed briefly, but it was only a second's lapse, then he was again jovial. "Police work. I wouldn't have guessed. You don't seem the type. What kind of police work, the Phoenix force, Sheriff's Office, private eye?"

Casey again hesitated. She had gone to some effort to keep her interest in the Dessaline and Halleck family members *sub rosa,* but she had not considered that she might get involved in such a personal conversation with any of them this soon. Asked a direct question, she could not lie. If her investigation went on, they would eventually know anyway.

Reluctantly, she said, "I'm a member of the Governor's Task Force on Crime."

This time his expression did not change, but he tilted his head. "It must be interesting work."

Casey took a sip of her drink. "I'm hoping it will turn out to be," she replied. "I haven't been at it long enough to tell. So far, it's been dull, rather routine."

His eyes lit up and he snapped his fingers. "I knew your name sounded familiar. You're the young woman who caught the Dumpster Killer. I'm impressed."

Casey felt herself flush. "Well, I helped, yes."

"Well, I'm sure *that* wasn't dull."

"You're right, it wasn't, it was terrifying; but that was before I joined the task force. Maybe I should be grateful for the change."

He grinned, apparently at ease. "Well, once the force really gets operating, I'm sure it will be involved in many important cases. You know, the establishment of the task force is one of the few good things the Governor has done. It should serve a useful, and much needed, function."

Casey nodded, her mind busy. Since it had been necessary to admit to this man what she did for a living, why not go all the way? He was apparently being open with her, and if her investigation of the families grew serious, she might not have another opportunity like this.

"I am involved in a rather interesting case at the moment," she said casually, her eyes on his face, "the killing of five Mexican citizens in Organ Pipe National Monument."

Did she see a brief flash of something in his eyes? Or was it her imagination?

He frowned. "A terrible thing, terrible. Are you making any progress?"

She shook her head. "It's only been a couple of days. However, there are no witnesses and no clues, and the experts tell me there is little chance of solving the case. What do you think?"

"I think that it's a little out of the area of my expertise; but I suppose they may be right. At any rate, I know that the Sheriff's Office will do everything it can; and you too, of course."

Casey gave him what she hoped was an enigmatic smile. "Of course. You're not the only one who likes to win, you know."

He began to laugh, cut it short, and touched her arm. "Casey, brace yourself," he said softly, looking over her shoulder.

Before Casey could turn around a blurred voice said, "Well, look who's here."

"Hello, Glenn," Halleck said softly.

By now, Casey had completed her turn. The man behind her was tall, going to plump, with a round, bloated face and blue eyes almost hidden by drooping lids. His hair — what there was of it — was a faded blond, and needed a combing. He was wearing a rumpled tux, and he swayed slightly as if he could not quite get her in focus.

"And who have we here?"

"Glenn Dessaline, Casey Farrel," Mark said with a weary gesture.

Glenn Dessaline's bleary glance raked Casey from face to toe, and then back up again, with a drunken insolence that made her skin crawl.

"A pretty one, Mark," he finally said with a leer. "Heeding the savvy politico's advice and finding a spouse to help you garner votes?"

"Glenn, you're smashed," Mark said with disgust.

"So what's new, old buddy? It's my usual condition. Ask anybody."

"Is my wayward son bothering you, Mark?" asked a soft, deep voice with lingering traces of a Southern drawl.

Casey turned and saw Catherine Dessaline just behind her. Up close you could see the age, but she still was magnificent. She carried with her such an aura of power and command, that Casey had to struggle not to revert to a shy school girl in her presence.

Mrs. Dessaline's disapproving glance rested on her son. "Why don't you go to our table, Glenn? They are about to serve the salads. You need something in your stomach."

Glenn Dessaline's glance became sullen, but his voice was appeasing when he answered. "Of course, Mother." Raising a hand in mock salute to Mark, he wove erratically away.

"I must apologize, Mark, for Glenn's behavior," Catherine said, her curious gaze on Casey. "When he's had too much to drink, which unfortunately is too often, he has a tendency to speak rashly."

Mark shrugged. "I've long since become immune to insults from Glenn, Catherine."

He turned to Casey. "Casey, this is Catherine Dessaline. Catherine, Casey Farrel."

As he finished the introduction, his gaze went past the two women to a man coming toward them, and he became distant.

"Hello, Jarvis."

Casey looked curiously at Jarvis Dessaline: tall; balding; with an ascetic appearance, heightened by rimless glasses; aristocratic nose; a haughty air; and prim lips.

The newcomer ignored Mark and Casey, his chilly gray eyes fixed on Catherine. In a high voice he said disapprovingly, "Mother, I don't think you should be disparaging a member of our family before others, particularly a Halleck. ❦

Catherine Dessaline's nostrils flared. "Really, Jarvis," she said coolly, "I don't think I was telling Mark anything that he, and the rest of the city, don't already know."

Jarvis's face pinked at her rebuke, but he said firmly: "Nevertheless." He took his mother by the arm. "Dinner is being served, and we should be at our table."

Catherine sighed. "All right, Jarvis."

She looked directly at Casey, who found the gaze of those gray eyes unsettling. "I am pleased to have met you, Miss Farrel. Thank you for attending our banquet. It is, as you know, for a good cause . . ."

Anything else she might have said was not audible, as Jarvis hurried her away through the thinning crowd, the members of which were now taking their seats at the tables.

"Sorry, Casey," Mark said ruefully. "There are a couple of the Dessalines who still carry on the old feud, and Jarvis is one of them. I've always suspected it's because it adds a tinge of excitement to an otherwise dull life. Also, he doesn't agree with my politics."

"He's a Democrat?" Casey asked amusedly.

Mark shook his head. "No, we're both registered Republicans; but Jarvis is about as conservative as you can get. He regards my political beliefs as dangerously close to Communism."

Casey looked at him thoughtfully. "But I understand that your father, Senator Halleck, is strongly conservative."

"Oh, he is. Or rather was. Father has mellowed some over the years, not a whole lot, but some, at least enough to be tolerant of my middle-of-the-road views . . ." He broke off, a smile spreading across his face. "Here's someone I want you to meet, Casey."

Casey, wondering what it was about this man that attracted people to the point that she wasn't left alone for more than a few minutes at a time, faced around again. Approaching was a tall, well-built woman of perhaps thirty. She had short, straight hair as black as Casey's own, a narrow face, and cool green eyes. In Casey's hasty estimate the emerald evening gown, which showed her strong figure to advantage, must have cost several thousand dollars. Her only jewelry was a magnificent emerald in a heavy gold setting, which sparkled against the smooth, tanned skin just above her cleavage.

Mark said, "This is my sister, Theresa. Theresa, this is Casey Farrel."

Although there wasn't a marked family resemblance, Casey's mind had already performed an intuitive leap; she had known that this woman was Theresa Halleck before Mark had made the introduction. She murmured, "I'm pleased to meet you, Miss Halleck."

"And I you, Miss Farrel," Theresa said in a remote voice, linking her arm with that of her brother.

"Casey is an investigator with the Governor's Task Force on Crime," Mark said.

Theresa showed little reaction. "Oh? That must be interesting work, Miss Farrel."

Casey felt herself bristle. This woman's calm, almost arrogant self-assurance was insulting. She was making it clear that she had no interest in Casey, and her body language said that she and her brother were on one side, and Casey on another.

Slowly, Casey said, "It can be, yes."

But Theresa's attention had already wandered. "Mark, everybody's sitting down to dinner. Hadn't we better . . ."

"Of course, Theresa." He turned to Casey, a trace of an apologetic smile on his lips. "I guess duty calls. Perhaps we can talk later."

Casey said nothing. Theresa was already pulling her brother away. Casey watched them move toward the front table, thinking that, even though they were brother and sister, and although there was no physical resemblance, they reminded her of Jack and Jackie Kennedy

— gilded with charisma, touched by the magic of Camelot for one brief and shining moment.

She shook her head, laughing ruefully at her fancy, and went to her own table. Despite the rather unpleasant meeting with Theresa Halleck, she felt a surge of excitement; for the evening had, so far, brought her more than she had hoped for. She didn't expect more such luck — usually, at these affairs the guests disappeared right after the speeches — but she had already met three Dessalines, and two Hallecks, and although she had not found out much that would help her in her investigation, she hadn't really expected to at this first contact. At any rate, she *had* made contact, and, hopefully, this would make things easier if and when it came down to questioning them.

Smiling at her seven table-mates, she attacked the inevitable banquet chicken with something like enthusiasm.

CHAPTER NINE

When Casey entered her office early Monday morning, there was a terse memo on her desk: "Meeting at nine sharp, main meeting room. Bring all pertinent material on Organ Pipe murders. Robert Wilson."

She stared at the memo bemusedly, feeling a pulse of irritation. Wilson could have informed her Friday about the meeting. Was he trying to put her, unprepared, on the hot seat?

The file she had put together so far was thin, consisting mainly of her notes on the Dessalines and the Hallecks. She briefly debated the wisdom of revealing this material, but the connection, however tenuous, was there; and she had already told the Pima County Sheriff's Department about the tie-in with the two *coyotes*.

Picking up the file, she went down the hall to the meeting room. She was surprised to find Wilson, and five other men, all strangers, already gathered. At one end of the room was a table with a coffee urn, and a plate piled high with pastry. The men seated at the long table were drinking coffee, and several of them were smoking, filling the room with noxious fumes.

When she entered, Wilson rose from where he sat at the end of the table. "Farrel, come on in. We were waiting for you."

Casey stopped behind an empty chair, but did not sit down, her glance ranged questioningly around at the strange faces.

Wilson gave her a false smile. "You're probably wondering just who these guys are, Farrel. Over the weekend the Governor and I had a little talk. He thought it would be a good idea to have a meeting of all the different law enforcement agencies involved in this case. Gentlemen, this is Casey Farrel, who is overseeing the investigation for us. Farrel, the man on your immediate right is Ben Thornton, Pima County Sheriff's Office. Going around the table, Jerry Russell, Immigration; Chuck Dunlap, State Department of Public Safety; Walt Edwards, Maricopa County Sheriff's Office; and last, Paul Storey, Homicide, Phoenix Police Department."

Casey studied the men. None were in uniform, but all had the fit look and sharp eyes that seemed to stamp law enforcement people everywhere.

Wilson continued, "Walt, why don't you go first."

Walt Edwards, a slim man of fifty with thinning brown hair and long fingers stained yellow from nicotine, drew on his cigarette, expelled smoke, and nodded. "Yeah. Last Friday, Ben here drove up from Tucson, saying he wanted to talk to some local residents about the case. I went along with him. You want to take it from there, Ben?"

Ben Thornton was fortyish, heavy-set, with a shock of black hair prematurely streaked with white, and a broad face that looked perpetually angry. That angry face turned Casey's way now as Thornton leaned forward.

He said harshly, "I came up here to investigate a lead that I understand came from you, Ms. Farrel, concerning a connection between the two dead *coyotes* and the Halleck and Dessaline ranches. Is that correct?"

Casey looked at him levelly. "Yes, Mr. Thornton, that is correct. Did you question the families?"

"I did, along with Walt."

Casey frowned. She had been with Mark Halleck Saturday night. Why hadn't he mentioned that these two men had been around asking questions? It would have been the natural thing to do, when she had told him that she was working on the case. She said, "And did you find any connection?"

"Yes, for all the good it does us."

"What, exactly, does that mean?"

Thornton put his meaty hands on the table. "I'll tell you what it means, Ms. Farrel. We talked to Alexander Dessaline and to Halleck's foreman, a man named Raskin, and both admitted that in the past they had done business with the *coyotes,* who delivered Mexican workers for their groves. Now, however, due to the new laws, they no longer do so. They both stated, emphatically, that there had been no contact this year; and that the three dead workers must have been destined for some other employer."

"They could be lying," said Casey calmly.

Thornton snorted. "Of course they could, but there's no way to prove it. And even if they are, what does that mean? It sure as hell doesn't provide them with a motive for murder."

Thornton's attitude was beginning to annoy Casey; but the only way to deal with hotheads like this was to keep your cool.

"Were the workers they hired in prior years undocumented?"

"They say that any Mexican Nationals they used always had green cards. What the hell difference does that make, anyway? If they had been caught using undocumented workers — which seldom happens — the most they would have gotten was a fine, and these people were killed in the desert, nowhere near either the Dessaline or the Halleck Ranchos. Come on, Farrel. What the hell do you think you're doing here?"

"What about the other members of the families, the children? Did you question any of them?"

Thornton stared. "What the hell for? Most of them live away from home, and they own nothing that would require seasonal labor. Look, these families are influential in Phoenix. Why should they be in any way involved with the murder of three Mexican illegals and two *coyotes*?"

"If we knew that, we might have a motive for the killings, mightn't we?"

He gestured in disgust. "Aw, you're reaching, Farrel, really reaching. And in that regard, just how did you find out these two *coyotes* had done business in the past with the Hallecks and the Dessalines?"

"I can't tell you that," Casey said with a shake of her head. "I promised that I wouldn't reveal the name of my informant."

"But he, or she might be involved. Did you ever think of that?"

Casey shook her head again. "I'm convinced otherwise."

Thornton's face clenched like a threatening fist as he leaned over the table. "I don't give a rat's ass what you're convinced of. This case can only grow nastier, and if this informant of yours has any information, it has to be shared with the rest of us."

Casey's pulse was pounding, but she said steadily, "I've already shared it with you, for all the good it did."

Thornton slapped the table. "Goddammit, I want to question this guy!"

"I won't break my word. I have a right to protect my informant."

Thornton slumped back in his chair. "Shit. What the hell do you know about law enforcement? Just because you helped nail that Dumpster Killer, and that was inadvertent . . ."

Bob Wilson interjected smoothly, "This isn't getting us anywhere. Let's all calm down. If Ms. Farrel says there's nothing to be gained from revealing her source, we must respect that. She's a more than competent investigator."

"Yeah, sure," Thornton muttered, but he subsided.

Casey glanced quickly at the others. Aside from Thornton, none of the men showed any overt hostility, but most of them wore amused, tolerant expressions. Smug bastards, she thought angrily, but I guess I should be grateful for small favors.

She turned toward Russell, the man from Immigration. "Mr. Russell, can you tell me if there has been any progress in finding the other two illegals who were in the van?"

The man from Immigration shook his head. "Not even a smell of them. We've picked up and questioned every illegal we could find in the area. Although we promised them immunity, each and every one denied being in that van, or knowing the pair of dead *coyotes*. And none of their fingerprints matched those we found in the van."

"If you want my opinion," Thornton growled, "it's a case of another *coyote*, or *coyotes*, killing that pair. It happens, a falling out among thieves."

Chuck Dunlap of the DPS spoke up, "Or a drug deal gone sour. It's not unusual for these *coyotes* to smuggle drugs as well as workers."

"And the three illegals were killed because they were witnesses," Casey said.

"Of course. It was just their bad luck to be in the wrong place at the wrong time. The killer, or killers, probably didn't even know they were in the van, until they jumped out of the back."

Casey shook her head. "I just find that hard to believe. If they had been killed at the scene, yes; but to go after them, track them down in the desert. . . . Another *coyote,* or even a dope dealer, would know that illegals wouldn't go to the law. They couldn't afford to. It would be like them to kill witnesses if they had a chance at the scene; but not like them to take time that could have been used for getting away, to track those people into the desert. And what about the horse?"

Dunlap shrugged. "The dealers are very creative. They use whatever they can get their hands on, whatever works. It's quite possible that some of them use horses. Who knows?"

"I understand that castings were made of the horse's hoofprints; any progress on that?"

It was Ben Thornton who answered. "Not much. It was a big sucker, and shod with round nails. Right now I'm talking with black-smiths, but it's going to be a hell of a job, unless we get lucky."

Casey shook her head. "It still doesn't fit. Anyway, what about the two *coyotes,*" she looked down at her notes, "Pedro Castelar and Victor Sanchez? They have addresses in Phoenix, have their relatives been questioned?"

Paul Storey of the Phoenix PD lifted his hand. "Yes. Ben called me and gave me their names, but I came up with zilch. Sanchez had an apartment in the barrio. I talked to the building manager, who told me that Sanchez had lived there for two years, and hadn't been seen since the day before the killings. He let me into the apartment. Nothing there. And no trace of any relatives in this country."

"And Castelar?" Casey said. "He was the registered owner of the van."

"He lived with his mother only a few blocks from Sanchez's apartment building. The old woman speaks nothing but Spanish — at least that's what she says. But she also says that her son worked at a convenience store, and she became very angry when I asked her if she knew about his activities as a *coyote*. She said that he was a hardworking boy, who took good care of his old mother. The names, Halleck and Dessaline, rang no bells. I couldn't press her too much, seeing as how her son had just died. She said that she had not seen Pedro since the day before the murders." Storey smiled slightly. "Of course Pedro had no job with the convenience store. He'd been fired over a year ago."

Casey nodded at the too familiar story. You could write a book about the classic denial of mothers of bad boys — "He was a good boy. He wouldn't hurt anybody!" And the kid, or man, caught with the victim's blood on his hands. You would think that sometime over the years the parent would have gotten a clue. It was sad.

She turned to Storey. "What have you found on the van?"

"New. Purchased a couple of months ago for cash, twenty thousand."

Casey frowned. "Is there that much money in running illegals?"

Storey shrugged. "I shouldn't think so, not after paying expenses and supporting himself and his mother. But, like Chuck said, they could have been running drugs, a lot of them do."

Casey nodded, and wrote down the information on her pad. It wasn't much, but it was another piece of the puzzle.

The rest of the meeting consisted mainly of a re-hash of the few facts she was already aware of. Finally Bob Wilson dismissed them. "You guys go ahead with your investigations, and Casey will continue on this end. If you come up with anything please contact her right away so she can get an overview of what is going on. I want to reassure you again, that we don't want to interfere with your investigations; and that while Ms. Farrel will be doing some investigation of her own, she is mainly here to coordinate your efforts, so be cooperative. Savvy?"

The men nodded, some of them giving Casey a wary glance. She smiled back sweetly, and stood at the door with Bob Wilson, as he shook hands with each man as they left.

When the last of them had gone, he laughed shortly. "Those assholes!"

Casey gave him a level look. "You put it delicately, as usual, Bob; however, this time I couldn't agree more."

Bob ran his hands through his hair and let his breath out in an explosive sigh. "Look, Farrel, I want you to continue full speed ahead. I know what I said to them, but I want *you* to solve this case. If we get the credit, it will make people sit up and take notice of the task force."

"And the Governor will be pleased," Casey said with a smile.

"The Governor will be pleased." He grinned. "And if the Governor is happy . . . ?"

"We're all happy. Right?"

"Right! I'll be behind you all the way, even if you step on some Halleck or Dessaline toes. You understand?"

"Sure." Privately, Casey wondered how *far* behind. Resisting the impulse to stand at attention and salute, she said, "And how about if I come up with something, should I share it with those guys?"

He hesitated, rolling his eyes upward. "When you come across something you think is important, see me. We'll have a head session, and then decide."

★ ★ ★

Casey left the conference room, walking back to her office in deep thought.

Was she wrong in aiming the thrust of her investigation at the Hallecks and the Dessalines? Was she becoming obsessed? Could Thornton be right; was the whole affair as simple as a falling out among drug smugglers?

Josh had told her, many times, that when investigating a homicide, it was a mistake to become fixated on any one theory to the point where you neglected other theories, other suspects. He said that even when he had one of his famous hunches, he was careful not to overlook other areas of investigation.

Was her conviction that either the Halleck family or the Dessaline family was involved nothing but a hunch? She certainly had very little in the way of proof to hang her theory on; yet, there was the connection, and it was one of the few hard facts she had.

Back in her office, she called Josh's station and caught him just as he was leaving.

"Hi, Casey. You caught me at a bad time. I'm on my way to question a suspect on these pizza delivery men killings."

"Just a quick question, Josh. We had a meeting here this morning, with representatives from the different law enforcement agencies. One of the men was Detective Paul Storey, Phoenix Homicide. I was wondering what you could tell me about him."

"Storey? Sure. What do you want to know?"

"Well, for starters, what kind of an investigator is he?"

Josh chuckled. "Paul is what I think of as a nine-to-fiver. He puts in his shift, does what is required of him, but not much more. He seems to be one of those guys who can go home to his wife and family and put everything out of his mind until he goes to work again. I'm not saying that that's a bad thing; probably just the opposite. I'm sure that it helps stave off burn-out, and I know it has to be better for his family. In fact, I wish that I could do it."

"No, you don't," said Casey, smiling to herself. "So Storey is conscientious, but not gung-ho. Do you think he's thorough? I mean if he questioned someone, do you think he would have gotten everything that he could, everything that was there?"

Josh hesitated. "Well, it would depend. I can't see him really pushing anyone, and if the person questioned was a hard case, I can think of people who could probably get more out of him, or her — gotta remember equal opportunity. Now, I gotta go, babe. Call me later, okay?"

She had scarcely hung up the phone when it rang. She picked it up, hoping that it was nothing that would keep her from leaving the office. "Hello?"

A warm masculine voice said, "Casey Farrel?"

"Yes, this is Casey."

"Mark Halleck, Casey. How are you?"

Casey experienced a surge of surprise and pleasure. "Mark! I'm fine."

"You know, I've been thinking of you off and on since the other night, and I can't remember when a woman I just met had that effect on me."

Casey felt her face grow hot, and she suddenly felt embarrassed and shy. "Well, I'm flattered," she said, attempting to sound casual, and certain that she sounded as awkward as she felt.

Mark paused, and she felt a moment's panic, wondering why he had called. When he spoke again, he sounded oddly hesitant. "Casey, the reason I called, my father is giving a party this Wednesday for my sister, Theresa, barbecue, the whole nine yards. It's going to be held at Castle Rock . . ."

"Castle Rock, what's that?"

"It's a house that Dad built a couple of years ago in Carefree. It's a fabulous place — if I may be excused a little family immodesty —

and well worth seeing. Will you?"

"Will I what?"

"Come to the party. I'm inviting you to be my guest. It's on Wednesday afternoon, and will go on until who knows. I realize that it's short notice, and my only excuse for that is that I didn't meet you until Saturday. How about it. You'll have fun, I promise."

Casey was silent for a moment, her mind busy. She was attracted to Mark Halleck, she couldn't deny it, and flattered that he was seeking her out. It would also be another opportunity to meet the members of his family, in an informal setting. That thought made her feel more than a little guilty. Was it cricket to use a friendship, even a budding one, to investigate these people?

She was roused from her thoughts by Mark's voice, "Casey, are you still there?"

She gave a start. "Yes, I'm here, and I'd be delighted to come, but I won't be able to get away too early."

He sounded relieved. "Great. I can't get off early either. It's Zonie informal, of course, so be casual. Give me your address, and I'll pick you up at six. Will that be all right?"

"Six will be fine." She gave him her address.

Then he surprised her again. "By the way, Casey, Father told me that some detectives have been around asking about the two dead *coyotes* you're investigating. Father knew them, since they used to bring him seasonal workers for the groves; but he hasn't been in contact with them since he moved into Castle Rock. Bart Raskin, the ranch foreman, has been handling the grove hiring since then. I just thought you might like to know."

Casey felt another surge of guilt, but it didn't stop her from using the opening he had given her. "Did you know the men, Mark?"

He answered without hesitation. "Never met them; but then I'd have no reason to, I never have had anything to do with the operation of the ranch."

Casey cleared her throat. "Well, thanks for telling me. This is all just routine, you know. We have to follow up every lead. I expect that they have been questioning all growers who were known to have contact with Sanchez and Castelar."

He laughed lightly. "It's always nice to be reassured that one is not a murder suspect. I'll see you at six on Wednesday, Casey."

"I'll be looking forward to it."

But, as she hung up the phone, she was foreseeing at least two problems. One was Josh — he wasn't going to be happy about her going out with another man, even under the guise of business. The other was the birthday girl, Theresa Halleck. If her attitude last Saturday night was any yardstick, Theresa was not going to be too thrilled to see Casey walk into her father's house on her brother's arm.

CHAPTER TEN

Most of the frame houses on the street where the Castelar residence was located were old and shabby. Here and there Casey could see one recently painted, standing out like a symbol of hope. Even more touching were those which, though unpainted and worn, looked clean, and had well-tended yards. It was easy to tell which families were on their way up, those who were poor, but kept trying, and those who had given up.

The Castelar house declared itself to belong to one of the latter group. Looking worn and sad, it sat well back from the street in an overgrown lot, seeming to shimmer slightly in the heat waves rising from the street and sidewalk.

Casey put her hand on the door handle of her car, reluctant to leave its air-conditioned comfort for the bake-oven outside.

Forcing herself, she opened the door and stepped out into the heat. In the skimpy shade of a stumpy palm tree next door, two Hispanic children sat on a sagging couch, two little girls of about five and seven, playing with raggedy dolls. Upon seeing her, they stopped their play and sat perfectly still, staring at her with round, dark eyes.

Casey smiled at them, and walked up the cracked walk to the house, watching that she did not trip on the broken concrete.

Hoping that the rotting wood would hold, she stepped up onto the wooden porch, where a torn screen made a half-hearted attempt to shield the inner front door. She tried the battered doorbell, but could hear no ring. She had to knock twice before she heard the sound of footsteps inside.

The footsteps paused, and the door opened a crack to disclose the face of a young woman. At the sight of Casey, the woman's eyes narrowed.

"We are not accepting company. There has been a death in the family," she said tightly.

"I know," Casey said, holding out her card. "That's the reason I'm here. Casey Farrel, from the Governor's Task Force on Crime. I am investigating Pedro Castelar's murder."

The woman frowned at the card. A woman's voice behind her spoke in Spanish. Casey could only catch a word or two.

The young woman turned her head. "Someone investigating Pedro's death, *Mamacita*," she said in Spanish.

The voice spoke again, angry and querulous.

"My mother says that a man has already been here, asking questions about Pedro."

Casey nodded. "I know that; however, I have a few questions of my own."

"The funeral was just yesterday." Anger flashed in the woman's dark eyes.

"My sincere condolences, and I apologize for intruding on your time of sorrow, but I'm sure your mother wants her son's murderer caught and punished. You are . . ."

"Dolores Chavez. Pedro was my brother."

"Again, I'm sorry, Mrs. Chavez; but I do really need to talk to your mother. Only a few questions, and then I'll be gone and won't bother you again," Casey said with her fingers crossed behind her back.

Dolores Chavez turned to the woman in the room behind her. "She says that she must speak with you. It is important if she is to find Pedro's killer," she said in Spanish.

There was a pause, and then a soft *"Si."*

Dolores Chavez stepped back reluctantly, and Casey stepped inside. The small living room was dim, and smelled of incense. Candles flickered in a small shrine on a table against the back wall, from the wind from an electric fan. Despite the fan, the room was very hot.

As Casey's eyes became accustomed to the gloom, she saw Mrs. Castelar sitting erect in a small straight chair before the shrine. Her long, black dress covered her from neck to ankle, and all that was visible of her was a pale, wrinkled face and two gnarled hands, busy telling the beads of the rosary in her lap.

"*Mamacita*, this is Miss Casey Farrel."

To Casey the young woman said: "My mother speaks very little English. I'll interpret."

Casey hesitated. Her own Spanish was quite good; however, she might learn more if they thought that she did not understand. She nodded. "Thank you."

She turned to the older woman. "Mrs. Castelar, I apologize for intruding at this time, but if we want to catch the person who did this to your son, I must ask you a few questions."

After Dolores had translated Casey's statement, the old woman turned her face toward Casey, her eyes blazing with hatred.

The hatred was so naked, so intense, that Casey almost drew back. Instead, she attempted to keep her tone calm, and her question as non-inflammatory as possible.

"Mrs. Castelar, do you know the names of any growers or ranchers that your son did business with?"

The woman's narrow face seemed to close in on itself, as she gave an answer in rapid Spanish.

"She says that Pedro did not smuggle in illegal workers like the man said. She says that he worked in a convenience store. He was a good boy!"

Casey nodded. That was what she had heard the old woman say. Looking at Dolores she saw a flicker of something in the young woman's eyes that indicated that her assessment of her brother might be different, but this was not the time to push it.

Casey said, as gently as she could, "Tell your mother that the owner of the convenience store says that Pedro had not worked there in over a year."

This time Mrs. Castelar did not wait for an interpretation. "That is a lie!" She spat out the words.

Casey shook her head. "The owner would have no reason to lie, and there are ways of checking. I'm sorry. Does the name Halleck, or Dessaline mean anything to you?"

The old woman shook her head, and spoke to her daughter in Spanish.

"She says that those names mean nothing to her, and that the other policeman already asked that."

"Yes," said Casey, "I'm sure he did. Did your son have anything to do with drugs, Mrs. Castelar?"

Again the old woman spoke directly to

Casey: "That is a lie!"

"Mrs. Castelar," Casey said softly, "they did tests on the bodies of Pedro, and Victor Sanchez. There were traces of cocaine in both."

Again there was a flicker in the eyes of Dolores before she turned to her mother to interpret.

Mrs. Castelar got to her feet slowly. "The police are stupid," she said in clear but accented English. "My son did not use drugs!"

She turned away, hobbling toward the door in the back of the room.

Casey called out after her, "Señora Castelar, please, one more question. The new van belonging to your son. Where did he get it?"

The old woman hunched her shoulders, and walked on, disappearing into the darkness of the doorway.

Dolores said, "He bought it, lady. You think Chicanos drive nothing but old wrecks or heavy Chevys?"

Casey could see the anger in the young woman's eyes, but there was simply no way to ask these questions without offending the family, and they had to be asked.

"No, I don't think that, Mrs. Chavez. I know that he bought the van . . . with cash."

She let the words hang there, and saw the anger in Dolores's eyes change to evasiveness. "The thing is, if your brother worked in a convenience store, where they pay minimum wages, how was he able to accumulate twenty thousand dollars in cash? It's an honest question, and the answer may have something to do with your brother's murder."

She took a deep breath. "There is also the matter of your brother being there on the highway with five illegal aliens in the back of his van. If he wasn't smuggling them into the U.S., what was he doing with them?"

Dolores Chavez looked down at the floor. When she looked up again, Casey felt a surge of sympathy for the pain in her eyes.

"It may be as you say," Dolores said slowly. "I don't really know, one way or another. Pedro and I haven't been very close these last few years. As you seem to have figured out, he wasn't exactly a model citizen; but I was never really sure what he was involved in. I have my own family, a good man and two cute kids. I didn't *want* to know what Pedro was doing. I tried to stay away from him. It wasn't hard; he used Mom's house as an address, but he wasn't home much, and when he was, I stayed away. So you see, I can't really tell you anything. All I *can* do is to try to protect my mother. If it helps her pain to think he was a good, hardworking son, I'm going to try to let her keep thinking that."

Casey, chastened, nodded her head. "You're

right," she said softly, touching the other woman on the arm. "Your mother is lucky to have you. You're a good daughter. It's just that I want to see this murderer put away, and to do this, I need information. Here's my card. If you, or your mother think of anything, anything at all, please call me. Sometimes something that seems irrelevant can be important. Will you do that?"

Dolores nodded. "They say that one of the Mexican Nationals killed was a woman; is that true?"

Casey nodded.

"She was somebody's daughter too," said Dolores. "I'll keep the card."

The apartment building where Victor Sanchez had lived was only a half-dozen blocks away from the Castelar home. The building was a rambling, three-story structure, built in the shape of a U, with a swimming pool in the center. Leaves floated in the pool, which appeared not to have been cleaned in some time. The building, about twenty-five years old, had a scruffy, run-down look. The nameplates on the row of mailboxes in the entryway placed Victor Sanchez in Apartment 208.

Casey, standing just inside the U, at the near end of the pool, was wondering just what she was doing here. Paul Storey, the Phoenix

Homicide Detective, had already conducted a search of the place, and there were no relatives to question. What did she expect to find?

The apartment entrances all faced the pool and courtyard, so she walked around the pool, looking at the numbers. When she found 208, she stepped back and looked upward, to the second landing. As she did so, the curtain covering the window beside the door moved.

Casey felt her pulse leap. Someone was there. Maybe it was just the apartment manager; but with any luck at all, it would be a friend or relative of Victor Sanchez, someone she could talk to.

Hurriedly she found the stairs, and took them two at a time; when she reached the door of 208, she was out of breath. She knocked at the flimsy door. There was no answer. Pressing her thumb to the door bell, she pressed it, holding it down. The buzzer was noisy, and easy to hear through the thin walls. Still no answer. Finally, she knocked again, then called out. "I know someone's in there. I saw you. I want to talk to you."

There was silence for a moment, and then the sound of soft footsteps. At last the door opened — slowly and narrowly, just the width of the chain — a slice of pale, narrow face appeared in the aperture, and a girlish voice said softly: "Victor isn't here."

"I know that," Casey said gently. "I want to talk with you. My name is Casey Farrel, and I'm from the Governor's Task Force on Crime."

She flipped open her wallet so that the other woman could see her ID. "I am trying to find out who killed Victor. I need to ask you some questions. Please let me in."

The woman hesitated, and Casey could feel her ambivalence. She had the natural distrust of the law that went with this territory; but Casey sensed that she also wanted to talk to someone. Casey concentrated on trying to look kind and disarming. She smiled. That seemed to weigh the balance, and the woman nodded slightly, unfastened the chain, and opened the door.

Releasing the breath that she had not realized she had been holding, Casey stepped into the apartment, her eyes quickly scanning the interior.

The apartment itself was pretty much what she had expected; but the furnishings were something of a surprise. The furniture was of good quality, and looked comfortable. There were several very nice prints on the walls, landscapes, and a bouquet of fresh flowers on the table in the dining area. Either Victor Sanchez had good taste, or someone else was responsible. An air-conditioner hummed in the window, and the room was comfortably cool. A large and fancy entertainment center took up a good portion of one wall.

Casey turned her gaze to the young woman standing nervously before her. Small-boned, plump, fair-skinned, with black hair and eyes, pretty, and well dressed, but timid. And young. Very young.

Casey smiled again. "Nice apartment. Did you decorate it?"

The young woman nodded and blushed attractively. "Victor let me pick it out," she said; and then her eyes filled with tears. "I can't believe he's dead."

Casey touched her arm. "I know. I'm sorry. Look, can we sit down?"

Wiping her eyes, the young woman nodded, and gestured to the comfortable looking sofa set against one wall. Casey settled herself, and the young woman sat down at the opposite end of the sofa.

"Like I said, my name is Casey Farrel." Casey waited expectantly, and the young woman nodded. "Yes. I'm Rita. Rita Valera, I'm . . . I was . . . Victor's girl."

This time it was Casey's turn to nod. "I thought you might be. Did you live here with Victor?"

Rita shook her head. "I stay here some times, but I live with my parents."

She looked down at her hands and Casey noticed the long, manicured nails, painted with pale polish. "My dad is . . . well, he's pretty strict. He wants me to live at home until Victor and I are married. I'm . . ." she hesitated, and then said proudly, "I'm younger than I look."

Casey repressed a smile. The girl looked all of sixteen. "And your dad would make trouble for Victor if you disobeyed and moved in with him. Right?"

Rita nodded. She seemed grateful for Casey's perceptiveness. "I keep a few things here. I came today to get them, and to say good-bye . . . You know."

Casey nodded sympathetically. She couldn't help liking the girl; and whatever Victor had been, this kid had evidently cared for him.

Tears were again welling in Rita's eyes. "But now . . ." She sniffed. "Now Victor's dead . . ."

Casey moved next to the girl, and put her arm around her narrow shoulders. "I know. I'm sorry. I know this is a bad time, but I need to ask you some questions. I'm sure you want us to catch Victor's killer. I know it won't bring Victor back; but there has to be some satisfaction in knowing that the killer will pay for what he did? Right?"

Tearfully, Rita nodded. "I guess so. What

do you want to know?"

Casey took a deep breath. "Some of this is going to be difficult to ask; but I have to do it. First, did you know that Victor was involved, together with Pedro Castelar, in smuggling Mexican Nationals across the border?"

Rita looked down again at her hands. When she spoke, it was only a little above a whisper. "Yes."

She looked up pleadingly. "I know you think that's bad; but Victor explained it to me. The people in Mexico are starving, and there is no work. Here, in Phoenix and other places, the big ranchos need workers. Victor was helping all of them."

Casey nodded and kept her expression neutral. "Yes, I know. It's not an easy problem to solve. Do you know if Victor was also smuggling drugs?"

Rita looked shocked, then angry. "No. Victor, he'd never do anything like that."

Casey said gently, "There were traces of cocaine in his blood."

Rita squirmed uncomfortably. "Victor used to use a little once in a while, but he wasn't hooked. He could take it or leave it. But that doesn't mean he was smuggling, or dealing."

Casey kept her voice calm. "No, you're right. It doesn't. It's just that his friend, Pedro, recently bought a new van, and paid cash for it, and I was wondering where he got so much money. I thought that since you knew Pedro so well, he might have told you?"

A look of relief suffused Rita's face. "Oh, yes, I can tell you that. Victor told me that he and Pedro had come into some money together, quite a lot of money. Pedro used his share to buy the van, and Victor bought the television and stuff. We were going to use the rest for our wedding."

Casey tried to act calm in the face of her rising excitement. At last, maybe she was getting somewhere.

"And did Victor tell you where this windfall, this money, came from? Did he tell you how he got it?"

Rita's face fell. "Well, no. He wouldn't tell me that; but he did say that there was plenty more where that came from, and that he could get more whenever he wanted it."

Casey leaned forward. "Did he ever mention the names Dessaline and Halleck?"

Rita shook her head. "No. I'm pretty sure he didn't."

"How about the names of the ranchers that he brought in the workers for?"

Rita shook her head again. "No. He said he didn't want me to know too much about what he was doing, it would be safer that way.

So I didn't ask him any questions. I figured he knew best."

"Did Victor ever speak of any enemies that he or Pedro might have, someone who would want to get even, or hurt them?"

Rita was still a moment in thought. "Not that I remember. Oh, he said that sometimes the illegals got mad about the money they had to pay. Sometimes they claimed they were being robbed; but Victor said that they didn't realize all the expenses he had. Besides, he didn't charge any more than any other *coyotes*. And it couldn't have been the illegals, the paper said that they were killed too, three of them anyway."

Casey nodded. "There is that." She saw no reason to explain why she thought the three passengers were murdered.

"Well, I want to thank you for cooperating with me, Rita. Here, I want you to have my card. If you think of anything else, please call me. In fact, if you just need someone to talk to, call me. I know this is hard on you; but I can tell that you're a strong woman. You'll survive it."

Rita's narrow back straightened. "I know that I have to try to be brave. The priest tells me that it's God's will."

Casey nodded. It was cold, but she couldn't help thinking that the killer, whoever he was, might have done this girl a big favor. It was dangerous to generalize, but from what she had learned of Victor Sanchez, it was very probable that he had been leading this inexperienced girl down the well-known garden path, and that Rita would have found only unhappiness and disillusionment at the end of it. Now it was possible that she might find some decent, hardworking man with whom she could have a good life.

"I'll need your address," she said. "I won't bother you unless I have to, but I need it for the record."

She handed the girl another one of her own cards and her pen, and Rita, in a round, schoolgirlish hand, put down the asked for information.

As she left the apartment Casey evaluated what she had learned. Again, it wasn't much, but it did pretty much establish the fact that the money to buy the van had not come from a legitimate source. Large sums of money that one could easily acquire at any time were few and far between. If the two men had not been running dope, what *had* they been doing? Could they have been involved in blackmail?

CHAPTER ELEVEN

After a late and quick lunch, Casey headed west out of Phoenix, through Peoria and Glendale. It was midafternoon now, and she was tired, sweaty, and badly in need of a shower; but she wanted to conduct one more interview before the day was over. If she was very lucky, she might learn something that would validate the conclusion that was forming in her mind.

Victor Sanchez and Pedro Castelar had found a money tree, one large enough to supply them with a large sum of cash, and which, Victor had said, could be picked again.

This type of payoff had the unmistakable earmarks of a certain type of crime, blackmail. And, considering the *coyotes'* connection with at least two important families, this made sense. The Hallecks and the Dessalines both had money. They also both had large families complete with black sheep. The sticker was, what could two lowly *coyotes* have learned that would allow them to blackmail anyone from such an illustrious family?

She knew what Josh would say about her supposition: "Where's the evidence, babe?

Hunches are fine, but in the end you've got to have the evidence!"

Well, that was what she was trying to get, in the only way she knew how. You had to start with what you had, and all she had was a thin connection between the *coyotes* and the Dessaline and Halleck families. She was headed now toward the Dessaline Rancho. Wednesday night's visit to Castle Rock with Mark should provide her an unofficial chance to talk to members of that family.

She was out of the heavily populated area now. On each side of the road she could see orange and grapefruit groves interspersed with fields of lettuce and other vegetable crops. Everywhere she looked it was green and bountiful. The houses that flashed past were neat and comfortable looking. Norman Rockwell would have been proud.

She rolled down the driver's window. Most of the fruit in the groves had already been picked, but the hot air was still redolent with the tangy odor of citrus. Then she spotted a private road on her right. The road was spanned by a large wooden arch bearing the name DESSALINE RANCH.

She was almost past it before she saw it, and had to brake too sharply. Luckily, there were no cars directly behind her, and she turned onto the well-kept macadamized road.

As she drove slowly into the midst of the grove, she saw, with surprise, that the trees here had not yet been harvested. Much of the fruit had fallen and lay rotting on the ground. The smell of over-ripe oranges was almost overpowering. She rolled her window back up, wondering why they were letting the fruit go to waste.

She drove for at least a half mile before she came to the house, first entering a huge plaza-like square, which the road circled. This square was bordered by an ornamental garden that framed a large, grassy central area, in the center of which was a rock pool fed by the water dripping down the pile of stone at one end.

The house itself, on the opposite side of the square, was large, white-stucco, Mexican ranch style, and surrounded by huge oaks, cottonwoods, and several towering palms.

As Casey progressed around the drive she glimpsed several barns and outbuildings further back, including what looked like a horse barn and corrals.

As Casey looked at the well-kept oasis of greenery, she could not help thinking that the Dessaline water bill must be out of sight. But then they could afford it.

Casey parked in the drive in front of the house. There were no other cars in evidence.

Climbing the flagstone steps, she approached the huge, double doors, which were beautifully carved, and ornamented with ornate brass door knockers. There was also a bell, and she pressed that and waited for an answer. It came almost immediately, as the door on the right opened, and Casey saw, to her surprise, Catherine Dessaline. She was wearing stained pants and carried a pair of pruning shears. Her face was shaded by a wide-brimmed hat.

Casey, who had been expecting a maid, found that she had to concentrate to avoid stammering. She held out her card. "Mrs. Dessaline, I'm Casey Farrel, investigator with the Governor's Task Force on Crime."

Catherine took the card, blinked down at it, then up again, at Casey. She frowned. "Haven't we met before?"

Casey nodded. "Yes. We met at your charity banquet last week."

The woman's face cleared. "Oh, yes. Mark Halleck introduced you. You'll have to forgive my appearance, I've been pruning roses in the patio."

She stepped back from the door. "Well, come in, my dear. It's much cooler inside."

Casey stepped into the blessed coolness that only excellent air-conditioning can bring, and Catherine shut the door behind her.

Casey looked around quickly. The huge room was beautifully, but casually furnished, fine woods, good fabrics, glowing colors. The far wall consisted entirely of handsome French doors, through which Casey could see the patio to which Catherine had evidently been referring. The patio was very large, and the flowerbeds and hanging pots were a riot of color. In the center of the patio was a swimming pool bordered with colorful Mexican tiles. The water was brilliantly blue, and serene; and Casey looked at it longingly.

Casey said, "I noticed your flowers out front. They're lovely."

Catherine's face took on a look of pride. "It's a hobby of mine, even an avocation, one might say. My roses have won many prizes."

"That must be gratifying."

"It is, my dear, but I'm sure that you didn't come out all this way just to hear about my roses. You announced yourself in your official capacity, so I assume that you are here on official business." She smiled at Casey questioningly.

Casey nodded rather sheepishly. There was something about this woman that made her feel like a gauche school girl. She was incredibly poised and gracious; but it was clear that she was nobody's fool. Deciding that directness would best serve her purpose Casey smiled and said, "I'm afraid so. It concerns the five murders last week at Organ Pipe National Monument. You've heard about them?"

Catherine's patrician face assumed an expression of distaste. "Of course. A terrible thing. The world has become an awful place, hasn't it? But what can that have to do with us?"

"Two of the victims have, in the past, apparently supplied your grove with workers, and we have a witness who says that three of the other victims were destined for your rancho." She smiled apologetically, thinking that this small stretching of the truth was excusable. "We have to investigate every lead, no matter how tenuous."

Catherine nodded, her expression noncommittal. "Yes. I can understand that. Well, you had better talk to Alexander. I'm afraid that I know nothing about the operation of the grove. Alexander is in his study. We can go across the patio. It's quicker."

She motioned, and struck off at a brisk pace. Casey hurried to catch up with her. It wasn't until they were in the patio that Casey saw the man in swim shorts, supine in one of the lounge chairs, in the partial shade of the sheltered walkway that extended from the walls of the house. On the table next to him was an empty glass. The man seemed to be asleep, or passed out.

Catherine walked past the sleeping man without a word or a glance, but as Casey came abreast of the man she recognized him. It was Glenn Dessaline, the drunk who had been insulting to Mark Halleck at the charity dinner.

On the other side of the patio was another set of French doors, at which Catherine paused and knocked. The interior of the room was hidden by narrow-slatted blinds.

A grumbling voice called out: "Yes?"

Catherine opened the door. "Alexander, there is someone here to see you."

Casey followed her into the room, a large, book-lined office or study. At the far side of the room was an old-fashioned roll-top desk. Sitting in front of it was an elderly man wearing a dove-colored western shirt and breeches. The pants were tucked into scuffed western boots.

Alexander Dessaline stood to greet them. Casey quickly took in the craggy, sternly lined face, and the shock of white hair. Blue eyes, apparently undimmed by age, looked down at her sharply. It was plain to see that this was a man used to power and position. He might be old, but he still stood strong, like some old tree that had weathered countless storms and years.

"This is Miss Casey Farrel," Catherine said. "She's with the Governor's Task Force on

Crime, and she wants to ask you some questions about the illegals that were murdered in Organ Pipe."

The old man frowned and fixed Casey with his stern, blue stare. "You know that the Sheriff's man has already been out here?"

Casey nodded. "Yes, I do, and I'm sorry to bother you again, but the Governor has asked me to coordinate the efforts of the various agencies involved in this, and I have some questions of my own. I will try to be brief."

Catherine Dessaline put her hand on Casey's arm. "Well," she said brightly, "I'd best get back to my roses. I'll leave you two to talk."

Casey and Alexander Dessaline turned to watch Catherine, gracefully, leave the room. When she had exited, Dessaline turned his sharp blue gaze again to Casey.

"Well, have a seat, Miss Farrel. I don't stand as well as I used to."

He eased himself down into the chair in front of the desk, and motioned Casey to a leather chair nearby.

"Very well, let's get on with it. What do you want to know?"

Casey sat back against the smooth leather. It felt cool against her back. "I need to know if you have ever employed any of these people." She held out to him a slip of paper upon which she had written the names of the five murdered Mexicans.

Dessaline took the slip, and reached for the glasses that lay on the desk top. Behind the lenses, his blue eyes looked huge and rather eerie. He read the list, then handed it back to her.

"None of the names are familiar to me, but then it's been some time since I've actively handled the grove. Excuse me."

Rising somewhat stiffly, he went to the door, opened it, and called out: "Glenn. Get in here!"

As Dessaline stood in the doorway, looking out into the patio, Casey looked around the room. Through the window opposite the patio door, she could see the horse barn, and she felt her pulse leap. Parked in front of the barn was a dark blue pickup, attached to a single-stall horse trailer, fitting exactly the description of the truck and trailer seen parked by the victim's van.

She took a deep breath. Slow down, she told herself. Like Josh says, half the population of Arizona own horses and horse trailers, and there must be hundreds of dark pickups. Still her pulse wouldn't slow.

Afraid that Dessaline would wonder at her stare, she turned away from the window and looked straight at the glass-walled gun rack that took up most of one wall. She knew enough about guns to know that it was a good collection. There were rifles, shotguns, and a large selection of hand guns of all types, styles and ages, including a beautiful matched pair of Frontier Colt .45s. Another coincidence? Maybe, but she suddenly itched to get her hands on those Colts for testing. Of course there was no chance of that without a warrant, and she couldn't get a warrant without proof that would convince a judge he should grant one.

She realized that she was still staring at the cabinet, when she heard Dessaline's voice, "Are you interested in guns, Miss Farrel?"

She jumped, and cursed herself for doing so. "It's a beautiful collection," she said, hoping that he wouldn't hear the nervousness in her voice.

He nodded, and, for the first time, smiled. Casey noticed that the smile softened his face only minimally. "Yes, and I say so with no undue modesty. Many of the pieces go way back in my family. Those two Frontier Colts, for example, belonged to my great-grandfather, Clyde Dessaline. He served a number of years as U.S. Marshal in the Territory. The story has it that he once faced down Wyatt Earp wearing those same two Colts."

A sudden slap-slap of rubber thongs sounded at the door, and Glenn Dessaline entered the room.

"Please, Father, not that old story again," he said with a nasty laugh.

The older man's face tightened as he turned toward his son. It was obvious from his expression that he was not pleased with what he saw.

"Some of us," he said, "take pride in our heritage, our forefathers. But then some of us *have* pride."

He gestured toward Casey. "This is Miss Farrel, from the Governor's Task Force, she wants to ask you some questions about the running of the grove."

Glenn Dessaline took a step toward Casey, and she instinctively drew back from the effluvia of old booze and cigarettes that enveloped her.

His bloodshot eyes squinted at her in suspicion. "Say, didn't I see you at Mother's charity bash last Friday?"

Casey, surprised that he was able to remember, nodded coolly. "Yes, you did."

His unfriendly expression did not change. "Why are you asking questions about the grove? What does that have to do with you?"

Casey, trying not to make her distaste too obvious, took another step backward. "As your father told you, I'm with the Governor's Task Force on Crime, and I am investigating the deaths of two *coyotes* and three Mexican

Nationals, that occurred recently in Organ Pipe State Park. We have a witness who says that the two *coyotes* used to supply your ranch with grove workers, and that three others were on their way to your ranch when they were murdered."

A measure of sobriety returned to Glenn's eyes, and his manner lost something of its truculence, as Casey went on:

"The names of the two men who supposedly brought in workers for you are Pedro Castelar, and Victor Sanchez. Did you know them?"

Glenn blinked. "Sure, I know that pair, and they did haul in pickers for us, or at least they used to. But I haven't seen them in over a year at least. And they couldn't have been bringing us any workers this year. This year we didn't pick. You must have noticed when you drove in, the oranges are still on the trees."

Casey nodded, feeling let down. If the *coyotes* hadn't been bringing the workers here, what happened to her theory? When she had seen the truck and the gun cabinet she had been sure it was all going to fall into place. Shit!

To keep the conversation going, she asked, "Why is that? Why didn't you pick this year? It seems a shame for all those oranges to go to waste."

The sneer came back to Glenn's face. "The

price of oranges is down, and the cost of growing and picking them is up. If we paid pickers to get in this crop, we'd lose money, so I decided not to pick this year. Raising horses is more profitable. I've been trying to talk the old man here into taking out the trees, and turning the whole place into a horse ranch."

The old man's face darkened. "We have plenty of horses around here already. My father planted those trees. He'd turn over in his grave if we destroyed them."

"What can a man do?" Glenn spread his hands, grinning; but bitterness burned in his eyes. "Father turned the place over to me to run, but he won't let me do it."

Obviously they had had this discussion before, and Casey could see what direction it was taking. "Speaking of horses," she said to Glenn, "I see there's a horse trailer and pickup out by the barn. Do you drive it, Mr. Dessaline?"

He frowned. "Yes. I drive it around the ranch, it's just a work vehicle. We also use it to haul a horse trailer now and then. Why?"

"Did you happen to be hauling a horse trailer around last Tuesday evening, some time around midnight, down on Highway 85, through Organ Pipe?"

Glenn stared. "Hell, no! I haven't been

down there in years; why would I be down there?"

Casey returned his stare unflinchingly. "That's what I'm trying to find out, Mr. Dessaline. A dark pickup, pulling a single horse trailer was spotted alongside the van where the two murdered *coyotes* were found."

All traces of intoxication were now gone from Glenn Dessaline's face. "Well, it damned sure wasn't me. What are you trying to pull?"

Casey shook her head. "Nothing, Mr. Dessaline. But I have to ask these questions. It's part of my job."

Glenn turned to his father. "Does she have a right to ask me this shit? Do I have to answer?"

The older Dessaline's face was unreadable. Casey, beginning to feel the tension of a possible confrontation, met his sharp gaze; but had no idea of what he was thinking. Cravenly, she hoped that there was not going to be a scene.

But the older man's tone was calm as he said: "You don't have to answer, Glenn. But I'd advise you to."

Glenn, his face red, shook his head. "Shit. If I don't then I look guilty. I know the drill. Hell, what does it matter, I have nothing to hide. I was here at the ranch all evening."

Casey felt herself relax, he wasn't going to

stonewall. "Did you have dinner here, with the family?"

Glenn's glance slid sideways toward his father. "Well, no. I wasn't feeling well, so I just fixed a snack and ate in my room."

Casey looked at the elder Dessaline. "Can you verify that, Mr. Dessaline."

Dessaline's mouth thinned and his glance at his son was cold. "No, Miss Farrel, I'm afraid I can't. The last time I saw Glenn that evening was around five o'clock. He was drinking, and if I know my son, and I believe I do, he very probably spent the rest of the night drunk and passed out in his room."

Glenn flushed darkly and looked down at his feet.

Casey said quickly, "Did you notice if the truck and trailer were parked out there all night?"

The old man shook his head. "I'm afraid I couldn't say. I didn't notice them; but then they are often parked behind the barn, out of direct sight of the house."

Glenn said hastily, "The trailer and pickup weren't here that night. A bearing was shot in the trailer wheel, and the pickup was due for servicing. I . . ." He flushed. "Father is right, I did spend the afternoon drinking, and I was . . . a little muddled concerning the time. I got to the garage too late, it was closed.

So I left the pickup and trailer, put the key and a note in the letter slot, and walked home. It's just a couple of miles, and I needed to clear my head. You can check with Wesley, the garage owner. He'll tell you that he found the truck and trailer there the next morning."

Casey looked at his eyes. He seemed to be telling the truth, but . . . "It doesn't prove that the vehicles were left there that evening. They could have been left at anytime during the night."

Glenn's face turned white, then red. "You're implying that I could have driven to Organ Pipe and back again before morning, and left the truck and trailer there then." His voice was thin.

Casey kept her tone unaccusing. "Did anyone in the family, or any of your help see you that night? Did anyone see you come or go?"

Mutely he shook his head.

She turned to Alexander Dessaline. "How many people were in the house that night?"

The old man's eyes remained frosty. "Only my wife and myself, and the cook and housekeeper. At the time Glenn refers to, the cook was preparing our dinner, and the housekeeper was probably in her room. She retires early to her own quarters in the west wing. She's quite deaf, and keeps the TV blaring until she goes to sleep."

"So it's unlikely that either of them would have seen or heard Glenn leave?"

"Very unlikely."

"How about the ranch workers?"

It was Glenn who answered. He sounded aggrieved. "There's only two of them who live on the place; and the bunkhouse is separated from the main house and corrals by the grove."

"I may want to talk to them anyway." Casey had her notebook and pen out. Moving to the big window, she jotted down the license number of the truck and trailer.

As she was doing so, a harsh voice behind her said loudly, "What the devil's going on here?"

Casey turned in time to see Jarvis Dessaline stride through the doorway, his angry gaze finding her immediately.

"Mother called me at the bank, and said that some investigator was here asking questions. I presume that's you?"

Casey, her face growing hot, nodded curtly. "Casey Farrel, the Governor's Task Force on Crime."

Jarvis kept his eyes on Casey's face. She could feel the anger coming off him in waves. A pretty excitable family, she thought.

"And just what do you suppose this family

has to do with five dead Mexicans?" Jarvis asked, his voice dripping sarcasm.

Casey kept her glance steady. "And how do you know that's what I'm here about?" she asked softly.

For just a second, Jarvis lost his composure, then, smoothly, "Mother told me when she called."

Casey let her disbelief show. "And would you mind telling me where *you* were last Tuesday night, Mr. Dessaline?"

His look was scornful. "I don't have to answer your questions, Miss Farrel. I happen to know that your powers are very limited. You don't have the power of subpoena, you don't have the power of arrest; in fact you can do very little. However, since you ask, I will tell you: I was at home all evening last Tuesday. My wife and children can corroborate that, and that is my last word on the subject."

Casey felt herself stand a little straighter — this son-of-a-bitch really chapped her hide. "I am quite aware of my limitations, Mr. Dessaline. But I *am* empowered to investigate, and I can always bring in an officer who *does* have the powers you mention."

"Then perhaps you should do just that," Jarvis snapped.

"Very well, if you want it that way."

Casey turned to the elder Dessaline. "Mr. Dessaline, I want to thank you for your co-operation. I'm sorry if I have caused you any distress or inconvenience."

Alexander Dessaline nodded, but did not answer, his expression still inscrutable.

Casey said nothing to either of the younger Dessalines, but turned to go. As she did so, she could not resist a last look at the gun cabinet, and she noted that all three Dessalines followed her gaze.

Cursing herself for an idiot, Casey left the study, closing the door behind her.

In the patio, she saw Catherine Dessaline still busy pruning her roses. She wasn't alone; another, much younger woman was with her. The young woman was brown-haired, with a good figure. She was attired in a stylishly cut business suit. Her curious gaze followed Casey's progress, and she said something in a low voice to Catherine, who looked up and saw Casey.

"Oh, are you leaving, Miss Farrel?" she said.

Casey nodded. She raised her voice. "Yes, Mrs. Dessaline. I'm finished for now. Don't bother to see me out; I can find my own way."

She could feel the other woman's gaze on her back. She was almost certain that the younger woman was Sandra Dessaline. She

183

wanted to talk to her, too; but considering Jarvis Dessaline's reaction to her presence here, now did not seem the time. Feeling hot, tired, sweaty and out-of-sorts, Casey marched out to her hot car and got in. What sustained her during the drive back home was the feeling that she was getting somewhere at last — she wasn't sure where, but something was beginning to happen.

The old man stared in mounting dismay at his offspring, who paced restlessly back and forth in front of him.

"This woman, Casey Farrel, Father, something must be done about her. She is rapidly becoming a nuisance, and my feeling is that she does not discourage easily."

The old man shook his head. "As I promised, I have made some inquiries into her background. She is far from being an experienced investigator. I seriously doubt that she will uncover anything harmful; and you have assured me that there are no witnesses, and no damning evidence. So what harm can she do?"

"Even an idiot may stumble across something. I told you everything was clean, no witnesses, no evidence; but there is always a chance that she could come across something I haven't thought of, some thread that would unravel the whole affair. I don't want to take that chance.

"And speaking of assurances, you assured me that you would bring pressure to bear to derail this entire investigation."

The old man stirred uneasily. "I have tried, but it's not that simple. My influence can only extend so far. The slaughter of five people can arouse a great deal of indignation, and the Governor is determined to prove the worth of this new task force. Bob Wilson, the head of the task force, is extremely ambitious, and hopes to use his position on it to advance to higher things. He won't let this be swept under the rug."

"Then I must do something about this woman on my own."

The old man felt his heart tremble, as he gazed at the icy smile on the face of his favorite child. "Please," he said, "no more killing!"

The smile grew colder still. "I will do what is necessary, Father."

CHAPTER TWELVE

The water was cool and refreshing, and Casey let it beat against her tense neck and back.

This was Donnie's day for Little League practice — one of her neighbors whose son was also on the pee-wee team picked up both boys — and so he wouldn't be home for another hour, at least.

She had, she decided, just about enough time for a good run to clear her mind and body after sitting most of the day in a stuffy car.

As she got into clean running clothes, she tried to empty her mind, but she could not stop thinking of the Dessalines. After leaving their rancho, she had stopped at the garage where Glenn had told her he had left the pickup and trailer. The owner had confirmed part of Glenn's story. Yes, he had found the two vehicles parked in front of the garage when he'd come in on Wednesday morning, with a note on the windshield explaining the problems to be fixed. But, he had no idea when they had been left there. The only thing he could say for certain was that the motor of the pickup was cold.

So, Glenn Dessaline had an alibi of sorts; but it had a number of holes in it. If he had left the house at five on Tuesday, as he claimed, there would have been plenty of time for him to drive to Organ Pipe, commit the murders, and still get back in time to leave the vehicles at the garage at least two hours before it opened. Due to the intense heat of the desert where Consuela Torres had been found, there could be no accurate fix on the time of her death. But was Glenn Dessaline a likely suspect? What about motive? He might be the black sheep of the family, but everyone already knew that. From what she had heard, his reputation couldn't get much worse, so why would he be paying a blackmailer?

With a sigh, she let herself out of her apartment and started up the street toward the dry canal bed. It was still hot, and she could feel the sweat already collecting between her breasts and in the small of her back.

She was warmed up by the time she reached the path up the side of the embankment that led to the footpath along the canal bank. There were no other runners in sight — they had more sense than she had, she thought, wondering if this had been such a good idea.

On the footpath she began to run, easily

at first, working the knots of tension out of her muscles. Gradually, she increased the pace, welcoming the feel of her feet striking the hard ground, the movement of her muscles driving the cobwebs out of her mind.

She had almost slipped into the trance-like state that she often achieved while running, when she became aware of the sound. It was an angry sound, like a motor revving. Glancing back over her shoulder, she saw that a white pickup had left the road and was coming up the sloping bank behind her. Her first thought was annoyance; what was the fool doing?

It took her precious seconds to realize that the high, steel bumper was aimed directly at her.

She looked around frantically. Not a soul in sight. She began running flat out, her feet pounding the earth. The sound of the motor increased in volume. She risked another glance. The pickup had now gained the top of the bank. There was just enough room on the running track to accommodate it. The sun reflected off the windshield, and Casey could see only the shadowy shape of a single figure behind the wheel.

Now that it was on the flat, the pickup was gaining speed, there was no way she could outrun it.

She looked to her right, into the rock-sided, weed-choked canal. She didn't think the pickup could make it down the steep bank, but it was almost upon her now. She would have to jump!

Moving toward the edge of the canal she glanced down. It looked like a long drop, and she knew that there was every chance that she could break something when she landed, but there seemed to be no choice.

As she felt the hot breath of the vehicle coming up behind her, she gathered herself and jumped.

She watched the bottom of the canal coming up at her and bent her knees to cushion her impact. She struck the hard soil with tremendous force, staggered, and was thrown forward against the hard surface of the other bank.

Stunned, for the moment she could not move. There was a loud crash to her left. She jerked her head in that direction, and pain flooded her head and neck as the pickup smashed head-on into the side of the canal about ten feet from where she lay.

Her response was panic. If the pickup caught fire and blew, she was close enough to be caught in the explosion.

Frantically, she attempted to roll to her left; but pain flared again in her skull, and she slumped back as the world went dark.

* * *

Josh was on his way home when he picked up the call on the police radio that he had had installed in his private vehicle. The operator was asking all units in the area to report to the scene of an accident, at a location only a few blocks from Casey's apartment.

Josh felt his gut grow cold. There was no reason to believe that Casey was involved, but he was convinced she was. God! He really had it bad, to let his imagination take over this way. Still, he wasn't far away, and it wouldn't hurt to check. Ever since she had become involved in this messy case, he had been apprehensive about her.

Two police cars were parked next to the canal embankment when Josh arrived. One uniform was on his radio, and the second wasn't in sight. Josh could see deep tire tracks leading from the side of the road up the embankment. What kind of nut had driven up there? But he felt better. This looked like some type of weird auto accident, nothing to do with Casey. Still, as long as he was here, he might as well see what was going on.

The unit officer hung up his radio as Josh stopped beside his car. Josh knew the patrolman, a broad-shouldered, tall man in his mid-thirties, Ted Newman.

Newman, recognizing Josh, nodded. "Sergeant!"

"What happened here, Ted?"

"A pickup went over the bank and into the canal bed."

"Is the driver dead?"

Newman nodded his head. "It looks like it. The front of the vehicle is a mess, crushed all to hell. The driver wasn't wearing his seat belt, and we're going to have to cut him out. There's no pulse. I just called for an ambulance and a wrecker with an emergency crew."

"Any one else involved?"

"Well, there's an unconscious woman lying a few feet away. She might have jumped or been thrown from the vehicle before it crashed, or she might have been a jogger. Many runners and joggers use the embankment path."

Josh was already in motion, plunging up the slope. On top, he stopped to catch his breath. He saw where the pickup's tires had made tracks along the footpath, then veered to the left, disappearing from the bank. His gaze jumped to the bottom of the canal to where the ruined vehicle was nosed in against the opposite bank. A few feet to the right of the pickup, the other patrolman knelt beside a prone figure in running clothes. His bulk hid the face of the figure. Josh went down the slope in long steps, his heels digging in to keep from falling. In seconds he was beside the patrolman, who stood as Josh approached.

Josh felt a surge of panic, like a blow to the gut. It was Casey, her face pale as milk, her eyelids faintly blue.

At the officer's questioning look, Josh said, "Sergeant Whitney, Homicide. How is she?"

"Alive but still unconscious, Sergeant. There's blood and a lump on the top of her head. She must have hit a rock."

Josh knelt, gently touching Casey's cheek. He murmured, "Casey? Babe, can you hear me?"

There was no response.

He looked up to meet the young patrolman's puzzled look. "Sergeant, why is Homicide involved in this? Isn't it just an accident?"

Josh bit his lip to keep from snapping at the boy. "I'm a personal friend of this lady, and no, I don't think it was an accident. Where is that damn ambulance?"

As he spoke, two paramedics came carefully down the bank, bearing a stretcher. As they approached, he stood and moved back. The best thing he could do for Casey right now, was to stand aside and let the medics tend to her.

As the medics began their work, Josh walked over to the ruined pickup. There was a round sticker on the lower right-hand corner of what was left of the windshield. A rental vehicle.

He returned to the medics and Casey. The taller of the two was examining her, and as his practiced hands gently probed for damage, she moaned and moved spasmodically. The medic looked up.

"I don't think she has any broken bones, but she's had a nasty whack on the head. Could be a concussion."

Casey's eyes fluttered open, and took a minute to focus. She looked dazed. "Josh?"

He knelt beside her, taking her hand. "You'll be okay, babe. Just lie still. They're taking you to the hospital. You may have a concussion."

She frowned, and for a moment panic filled her eyes. She grabbed at his sleeve. "Josh. He tried to run me down; he came right at me, up the hill. He tried to kill me!"

She struggled to sit up, but the medic gently but firmly held her down.

Josh said, "I know, Casey, but it's all right now. He can't hurt you. He's dead. Just lie still. We'll talk about it later. Let them take care of you now."

She lay back, her voice barely a whisper. "But why, Josh? Why?"

The medic said, "We're going to take her

now. You can follow us to the hospital."

Casey tried to shake her head, and winced. "No. Josh, Donnie will be home by now. Please, take care of him."

Josh nodded. "I'll pick him up and bring him along. You do what they say, babe. Hear me?"

She smiled weakly.

Josh stood back as the two medics deftly moved Casey onto the stretcher, then slowly mounted the bank with her. By the time they disappeared over the top, the wrecking crew arrived. Josh waited until the men pried open the pickup door and extricated what remained of the driver. Josh felt his stomach roll. No matter how many times he witnessed this kind of thing, he never got used to it.

Steeling himself, he went methodically through the dead man's pockets. He found two driver's licenses under separate names; and in the man's pants pocket, a large roll of bills. He whistled when he finished counting it, five thousand dollars in hundred dollar bills.

In the remains of the glove compartment he found the rental agreement for the pickup, in the same name of one of the driver's licenses. Josh was pretty sure that both licenses were phony, but that would have to be checked out. Quickly, he wrote the names and addresses in his notebook.

As he left the scene, the two wreckers were debating how best to hoist the wrecked pickup out of the canal.

Back at his own car, Josh called Dispatch, read off the names and addresses on the dead man's licenses, and asked that a record check be run on both names, and that someone be sent to check out the addresses.

That done, he drove to Casey's apartment, and picked up a worried Donnie.

By the time Josh and Donnie reached the hospital, Casey had been released from Emergency and moved into a private room. When Josh checked at the nurse's station, he was told that they did not think she was concussed; however, the doctor wished her to stay overnight for observation. Josh explained Donnie's relationship — stretching it by saying that he was Casey's son — and the nurse said that they could see Casey.

When they entered the hospital room Casey was sitting up part way, disinterestedly watching the TV set bolted onto the ceiling.

"Casey!" Donnie cried as he ran to the bed. "Are you all right?"

Casey opened her arms to him and gazed at Josh over the boy's head. "I'm fine, kiddo; the doctor just wants me to stay here overnight."

"Won't do you any harm, Casey," Josh said. "You can get a good night's rest."

She smiled at him. "Yeah, right."

She kissed Donnie on the cheek, and Josh pulled two chairs up beside the bed. Before sitting down, he kissed her lightly. "How's the noggin?"

She grimaced. "It's been better, and several body parts are going to be black and blue in the morning, but all in all, it's not too bad. I'm just happy to be here."

Josh felt a foolish grin spread over his face. "So am I, babe. So am I." He touched her hand. "You do have a penchant for getting into trouble, don't you?"

She sighed. "I guess I do. That nut came right up over the bank at me . . ." She broke off, glancing at Donnie, who was beginning to look worried.

Josh caught her look and turned to the boy. Pulling out a handful of change, he handed them to the boy. "Say, Donnie, I saw some pop machines out near the nurses' stand. Why don't you get us a couple of pops? And take your time."

Donnie jumped up eagerly. "Sure. If there's enough money, can I get a candy bar?"

Josh hesitated. "We haven't had dinner yet, kiddo, but yeah, I guess so. Don't forget the room number."

196

Taking the money, Donnie ran out of the room.

Casey reached for Josh's hand. "You spoil the kid, but thanks. No use in spooking him. Josh, that bastard was after me. If he hadn't lost control of that truck . . ." She shuddered. "And I haven't thanked you yet."

Josh squeezed her hand. "For what?"

"For being there when I woke up. It was sure nice to see your ugly face."

"Wish I could say the same." Josh's voice was husky. "You looked like hell."

He paused, and when he spoke again, his tone was serious. "I kept thinking what it would be like without you, and I found that I couldn't even consider it. It's a good thing that bastard died, because if he hadn't, I would have killed him."

Casey, touched by the feeling in his voice, was swept by a wave of affection she wasn't sure how to express. She settled for returning the pressure of his hand.

"Have they found out who he was?"

"Yeah. Got it on the radio on the way over. Had two phony IDs, but his real name was Miles Corbett. He was a small-time hood with a rap sheet several feet long. One arrest for vehicular homicide, but not prosecuted. Lack of evidence. Word on the street is that he would do somebody for a fee, and we found five thousand dollars in his pocket. What does that tell you?"

Casey frowned. "You think somebody paid him to hit me? Good Lord! I assumed he was just some wandering psycho. This puts a different face on things, doesn't it?"

Josh nodded. "It does." He could almost see Casey's mind working.

"But who could want me out of the way? Who would profit if I was out of the way?"

Josh gave a sour grin. "Well, the only one I can think of is Donnie's charming aunt; but I hardly think she has the imagination, or the money."

"Then it must be the investigation. I've gotten too close to something or somebody; and the only case I'm currently working on is the Organ Pipe case."

Josh nodded. "It's possible. Why don't you fill me in?"

She told him everything that had happened, everything she had found out. "I know it's not much, but a pattern is beginning to emerge. After talking to the Dessalines, I'm more certain than ever that they or the Hallecks are involved."

Josh sat for a moment in thought, rubbing at his chin. "Well, I agree with you on one thing, that the story the *coyote*'s girl friend told you about the twenty-five grand they got hold of does fit the pattern of a blackmail pay-off. The thing is, the blackmail victim could be anyone. You don't have anything to directly connect the *coyotes* with the Hallecks or the Dessalines."

Casey shook her head. "I know I'm on the right track. I haven't talked to all of the Dessalines, but I've talked to four of them — and got considerable over-reaction to my questions — and tomorrow I'll talk to the Hallecks, at least those of them who are at the party."

Josh straightened, a frown on his face, just as Donnie entered carrying two cans of soda and a Butterfinger bar.

"I had trouble with the machine," he said. "That's what took me so long. Here."

He handed one of the cans of pop to Josh, who set it on Casey's night stand.

"Party? What party?" Josh said.

Casey put her hand to her head. "Oh, I forgot to tell you. I meant to today but . . ."

"What party?" Josh repeated.

Casey leaned back against her pillows, her expression sheepish. "Theresa Halleck's birthday party. I've been invited."

Josh rolled his eyes. "Great. Just what you need after a bad fall and a near concussion. You must be out of your mind."

Casey's face showed her annoyance. "I'll be

fine, maybe a bit achy, but fine. I won't go otherwise."

Josh looked at her steadily. "And just how did this invitation come about?"

Casey sighed. "It 'came about' as you so quaintly put it, because I met some of the Hallecks at that charity bash."

Josh nodded. "And just which Halleck tendered this invitation?"

Casey sighed again. "Mark Halleck, if you must know. He spilled my drink, and we got into a conversation."

Josh's eyes narrowed. "Does he know that you're investigating his family?"

Casey started to shake her head, but pain made her stop with a grimace. "No, not really; although I did tell him that I work for the task force and that I'm investigating the Organ Pipe killings."

"And even though he knows that, he asked you to this party? Did you ever think, that if he or any other of the Hallecks *are* involved, he might have invited you so that he could do a little investigating of his own?"

Casey gave him a hard stare. "Did it ever occur to *you* that he might, simply, enjoy my company?"

She had to strain to hear Josh's next words, which were uttered almost under the edge of audibility: "That's what I'm afraid of."

She squeezed his hand. "Well, not to worry. It's strictly in the line of duty. Can I count on you to watch Donnie? Maybe you two could take in a movie."

"Yeah!" Donnie said, pulling the pop can from his mouth. "Batman Four is playing. Johnny says it's great!"

Josh nodded reluctantly, his eyes still on Casey, who felt a twinge of guilt. She had assured him that her interest in Mark Halleck was strictly business; but she wasn't certain that this was true.

She could tell that Josh was trying to control what he was saying, and she could tell that it was not easy.

"I don't think you should go, babe. If you're right about the Hallecks . . ."

She was touched by his hard-won restraint, and answered gently, "It will be a large party, Josh, maybe a hundred people. I don't think they will try to do me in front of so many witnesses."

Josh slapped the arm of his chair, causing Donnie to jump.

"Jesus! I wish we were married."

"Oh?" said Casey calmly. "And why is that?"

He glared at her. "Because then, dang blast it, I wouldn't let you go. If you haven't got enough sense to look after yourself, then I'd look after you."

"Well, thanks, Tarzan," she said dryly. "That's a real inducement to marriage."

He let out his breath in a gusty sigh. "I don't know why I try to talk to you. I might as well talk to the wall."

He got up reluctantly. "Well, I guess I'd better get this kid fed something wholesome before he overdoses on pop and candy. And you watch yourself at that party. I don't want somebody to finish what that guy started today. I'll take Donnie to my place, but I want you to call me when you get home, no matter how late. Okay?"

Slowly, she nodded, unable to decide if she should be annoyed by his paternalism, or pleased that he cared.

CHAPTER THIRTEEN

During the nearly two years Casey had been living in Phoenix, she had never been to Carefree or Cave Creek.

About an hour's drive north of Phoenix and at a higher altitude, the area was cooler than Phoenix. Scattered over the rise and fall of the land were huge, granite boulders, looking like great abstract sculptures. It was an attractive location, and some years ago had attracted the resort trade. More recently the population had exploded, as the wealthy had migrated to the area and constructed expensive and beautiful homes.

Casey did not go into the office the next day — it was her first day of sick leave — and by late afternoon, decided that she felt well enough to attend the party. Her head was still sore to the touch, but the headache had gone, and although she ached here and there, and had some lovely plum-colored bruises, none of them showed when she was dressed.

Mark arrived at her apartment shortly after six. Casey was amused to see his interpretation of casual. He was wearing a pair of beautifully tailored fawn-colored western pants, and shirt. The sleeves of the shirt were rolled to his forearms, and it was open at the throat. Besides an expensive-looking wafer-thin gold watch, the only jewelry he wore was a heavy gold signet ring — that is, if you didn't count the carved gold belt buckle. His boots were only a trifle darker than his pants, and were of incredibly soft leather. He could, Casey thought, easily be used as a model for one of the trendy men's magazines — what to wear to a party in the western U.S.

Casey was somewhat embarrassed by the fact that she found him so appealing. She had teased Josh last night about his being jealous; but maybe he had cause. There was no denying that she found Mark Halleck exceedingly attractive.

She was glad that she had worn the new outfit that she had picked up on sale, unable to resist the soft, flowered material — reds, golds, orange and black — of the full skirt, and the way the black halter top hugged her waist. With it she was wearing strappy, light, flat-heeled sandals.

When she answered the door, he stared at her appreciatively.

"You're a beautiful woman, Casey Farrel," were his first words, so unexpected that she found herself blushing.

"You're very kind to say so," she said with attempted lightness, "but a simple hello was all that I was expecting."

He looked at her closely. "Have I embarrassed you? I'm sorry. I have the bad habit of speaking my mind."

Casey smiled. "And I have the bad habit of not accepting compliments well. I apologize. Thank you for the kind words."

"Only the truth," he said. "I know politicians are not known for telling the truth, but I try."

At his car, he opened her door for her, and a traitorous thought invaded her mind: When was the last time that Josh had held open a car door for her?

Mark proved to be an excellent driver. He seemed at one with the car as he maneuvered the vehicle in and out of the heavy, rush-hour traffic. He drove in silence until they were out of the traffic and headed north, toward Carefree.

During those first minutes, Casey had a chance to study him. It was clear that as well as good looks, he possessed sophistication and a great deal of charm. He was articulate and laid-back, seemingly the perfect male. She was curious as to why he had never married. A wife — preferably charming and clever, and failing that, rich — was considered an asset to a politician. In fact, a politician who was not married came under a certain kind of suspicion; so why, at thirty-eight, was Mark still a bachelor? Could he be gay? She doubted it. The vibes weren't right.

She glanced at him again, and found him looking at her. He was smiling slightly, as if he could read her thoughts. As he looked back at the road, she glanced out the window and saw that they were now out of the heavy traffic. On each side of the road there were stretches of empty desert interspersed between new housing developments.

Mark said, "So, how is your investigation going?"

Casey recalled Josh's comments about Mark possibly doing some investigating of his own, and answered cautiously. "Not very well, I'm afraid. It's going to be a tough one to crack."

"I gather from what you told me that the two dead *coyotes* . . ."

"Castelar and Sanchez."

He nodded. "You said that they have, in the past, provided workers for the Halleck and Dessaline groves?"

"Yes, but evidently not recently."

"Have you talked to Bert Raskin, Father's foreman, yet?"

She shook her head. "I thought I might do that tomorrow."

"As I told you, Father is no longer active around the ranch. I don't think he's been out there more than two or three times since he built the house in Carefree. About the only time any of us visit there any more is when we want to ride."

Casey tensed. "You keep horses there then?"

He glanced over at her, then back to the road. "There's a stable there, yes. About a dozen riding horses. We all like to ride. Father started each of us when we were barely able to walk. Of course I don't have much time these days. Haven't been out to the ranch in months."

She said, "Speaking of horses, I was over at the Dessalines' ranch yesterday."

He smiled. "Did you find out anything helpful?"

"I'm not certain. I do know that they weren't too happy to see me. Mrs. Dessaline was gracious, and her husband cool but courteous; but Glenn was rude, and Jarvis was downright hostile."

Mark shook his head. "I think Jarvis was born hostile. Old man Dessaline is not all that friendly to strangers, especially those he figures are poking their noses into his business. And Glenn . . . Well, Glenn is Glenn. Was he sober?"

"Marginally."

"That's about par for the course. He's an alcoholic, but he won't try to help himself. It's cost him several jobs, and I wonder how long old Alex will put up with his running of the ranch."

They drove for a few minutes in silence. All the while Casey grew increasingly aware of the physical magnetism of this man. It made her uneasy, and she cast about for a neutral subject of conversation.

She said, "I understand that most of your law practice is devoted to corporate law."

He gave her an amused glance. "Been checking up on me, have you?"

"I must have read it some place," she said uncomfortably.

"Well, you're right. I specialize in corporate law, as do all the attorneys at Mateson, Cartier."

"Have you ever had any urge to handle criminal cases?"

"Once, yes. After I first got my degree, I was all aflame to be a criminal lawyer — to defend the innocent, of course," he said with a laugh. "Then I met the kind of people that I would be regularly dealing with — disillusioning — and found that I had little taste for the theatrics that seem to be necessary to becoming a successful trial lawyer. Corporate law looked like an intriguing area, and I have

208

found it, surprisingly, very interesting. I still have a desire to help people — if that doesn't sound too pompous. I think that's one thing propelling me into a political career."

Casey said casually, "That AZCAM scandal must have provided a lot of work for defense lawyers."

"You might say that," he said dryly. "God, what a unholy mess that was! The aftershocks are still being felt."

"The current governor wasn't in office when that first went down, so I don't suppose it will provide you with much ammunition if, and when, you campaign against him."

"That's true, but he's not doing so good handling the continuing mess over gambling on the Indian reservations. How can the government be so opposed to gambling on the reservations when it's collecting taxes on horse and dog racing in the state, and running a state lottery?"

Casey was a bit surprised by the vehemence in his tone. "Then you favor open gambling?"

He shook his head. "I didn't say that. But it's something that should be looked into. It might help the state's struggle with the budget."

"Then if you were elected governor, you'd favor casino gambling, the whole bit?"

"I didn't say that, either." He laughed uncertainly. "Sounds like the typical politician's waffling, doesn't it? All I'm saying, Casey, is that it wouldn't do any harm to look into it."

They rode a few moments in silence before Casey said, "I'm half Indian, you know." She watched carefully for his reaction.

"Oh? I wouldn't have guessed it." He flashed her that white-toothed smile, full of charm. "There's some Indian in our family, I've been told. My great-grandfather on my father's side married a full-blooded Apache."

"My mother was Hopi. The Hopis have never gone in much for gambling on the reservation, except for a little bingo."

They were nearing Carefree now, and attractive homes began to appear dotting the boulder-strewn hills. Rising up straight ahead on the flat, was a block-sized collection of beautiful buildings, looking like a modern Camelot.

Casey pointed. "What's that?"

"A mall; but we turn off before we get that far."

Even as he spoke, Mark was slowing the car for a left-hand turn. The street he turned onto climbed gently and was dotted with huge piles of giant boulders. On both sides were large houses, most built in the southwestern style. Straight ahead and up the hill, loomed a spectacular house. At the top of a huge lot covered with tamed local and imported desert flora, the house perched upon a sort of ledge composed of natural boulders and stonework. Rock surrounded it, and loomed above it, so that it looked like a cutting-edge cliff dwelling. The house was the same color as the rock, and the view from its many windows would have to be fantastic.

Casey drew in her breath. "Now that's what I call a house. It's magnificent."

Mark smiled. "Father will be glad to hear you say so. That's Castle Rock, otherwise known as 'Halleck's Folly.' "

"Oh? Why is that?"

"Because it cost a fortune to build."

"I can imagine. How did they ever get men and equipment up there? It's like an eagle's aerie."

"It wasn't easy, believe me, but it's what Father wanted, and he has the money. Oh, Theresa wanted it, too. She lives here with Father, and she loves the place. I spend most weekends here as well. It does have its attractions. You can see for miles in three directions, and it's cooler here than in Phoenix."

Mark was parking the car now in one of the few remaining places in a large, paved parking area just off the street. The lot was shielded from the road by trees and shrubs; and Casey noticed that several of the spaces had name-signs, including the one into which they had just pulled.

She smiled. "Your own parking place."

He shrugged. "It's necessary. Father has so many guests and business people here; and then there's the parties. Father gives one several times a year; and Theresa throws a bash about once a month."

As he opened the car door for her, Casey looked up at the house looming above them. It seemed enormous.

Mark seemed to read her thoughts. "Big, isn't it? And you can't really see it all from here. Up on the level, behind the house, are tennis courts, a pool, and a patio."

Casey sighed and shook her head. "It must be nice to have money."

Mark smiled. "They say money won't buy you happiness; but I must admit that it makes life comfortable while you're looking for it."

"Well, your father's money should be a help to you in your election campaign."

"Again, I won't lie to you. Yes, it will."

She looked at him curiously. "It doesn't bother you that some people may accuse you of buying the governor's office?"

He shrugged. "I can live with that, but let's not talk politics. We're here to have fun."

Casey smiled, feeling a little guilty at the thought of her hidden agenda.

Mark took her arm, and they walked toward the edge of the parking area, where a glass-enclosed elevator and shaft rose against the rock wall at one end of the house. She smiled up at Mark. "I must say I'm glad to see that. I was afraid that we were going to have to hike!"

Mark shook his head. "No way. Guests of the Hallecks travel in comfort. There's a private garage behind the house, but the drive is steep; and almost all of us prefer to park down here and ride up, unless we're carrying something heavy."

The elevator was fronted by a small foyer whose side walls accommodated two comfortable-looking padded benches. The elevator itself also had a seat along the back, and the framework holding the glass panels of the front and sides, was of polished brass.

As they began to rise, slowly and smoothly, Casey admired the view. You could see for miles.

Mark said, "All the family should be here today, including the grandchildren. Allen and Ann Marie have been reasonably fruitful, and they have five children between them. Sometimes it seems more like fifteen. I hope you like kids."

Casey smiled. "As a matter of fact, I do. I'm in the process of adopting one right now."

Mark looked surprised, but did not comment. The elevator was slowing. Casey said, "How about your younger brother, Steven? Does he have children?"

An expression of distaste flickered across Mark's features. "Steven is the Glenn of our family. Our black sheep. No children. He's living here with Father and Theresa for the moment."

There was a trace of amusement in his eyes. "But, I suppose that computer of yours has already divulged his rather checkered background for you."

Casey felt herself flush. Was she that obvious?

The elevator had stopped now, and the door in the rear slid slowly open to reveal a large entry-way lined with plants and art-work, which led to a wide pair of polished doors ornamented with beautiful brass door-knockers in the form of Claddaghs. Through the doors, Casey could hear the sounds of music and laughter.

Mark smiled down at her. "Evidently the party is already in full voice."

As they approached the doors, Casey became aware that she was exceedingly nervous. She took a deep breath, and then another, as Mark opened the door on the right, and they stepped into the house.

Casey saw that they were standing on a beautiful parquet landing. On the other side of the landing a wide curve of six steps led down to a sunken great room of magnificent proportions. The wall to the right was one huge window through which it seemed one could see forever. The wall opposite the landing was of flagstone, and contained a fireplace in which one could easily roast an ox. The wall to the left consisted of a row of patio doors behind which Casey could see the rich green of well-cared for plants.

The room was filled with handsome, well-dressed people, drinking, talking and laughing; and apparently having a wonderful time.

As Casey turned toward Mark, she saw a woman coming toward them. It was Theresa Halleck. She was wearing a short, full, white silk skirt, a matching blouse tied beneath her breasts, and flat, white sandals. She looked cool, beautiful, and completely in charge. Her cool green eyes passed over Casey without acknowledgment, and focused on Mark.

"I was beginning to think you were going to miss my birthday, Mark," she said reprovingly.

"I told you I'd be late," he said quietly. "I got away as soon as I could. I think you met Casey Farrel at Catherine's charity dinner?"

Casey was the recipient of the woman's cool gaze. "Yes. Ms. Farrel and I have met. You're a detective, I believe?" She managed to convey a world of contempt in the word "detective."

"It's nice to see you again, Ms. Halleck," Casey lied smoothly, "but I'm not a detective *per se*. I believe investigator would be more appropriate."

"Whatever." Theresa dismissed the matter with an elegant wave of her hand and hooked her arm in Mark's. "Come along, Mark. There are some people I want you to meet."

Mark turned toward Casey, and Casey saw his sister pull him back. It was a rude gesture, and Casey's surprise must have shown on her face, because Mark flushed.

"I'm sure that Ms. Farrel will excuse you for a few minutes. Family business, you know," she said to Casey, and pulled again on her brother's arm.

Mark's lips were a thin line, but he did not contradict Theresa. Instead, he gave Casey a forced smile. "Will you excuse me, Casey? Get yourself a drink; the bar is set up in the game room next door." He pointed. "I'll find you in a few minutes."

As Theresa led Mark into the crowd, Casey looked after them curiously. That had been a strange bit of by-play there. It was clear that Theresa Halleck was very close to her brother, perhaps too close. Possessive wives were bad enough, but a possessive sister? That would have to be the worst of two worlds.

And Casey was a little miffed with Mark. She had classified him as a polite and charming man; but leaving her at the door without even introducing her to someone she might talk with, was rude and thoughtless. Of course it was Theresa's idea; but why did Mark give in to her. He didn't seem like the type of man to be bullied by anyone.

Well, she was here; it was what she had wanted. She might as well put her time to good use.

Making her way through the crowd, she found the game room.

It was approximately the same size as the great room, but furnished for fun. There was a large pool table, a billiard table, and dozens of arcade machines. A huge oak bar and mirrored back-bar took up almost all of one wall. The other walls bore framed memorabilia: wanted posters, advertising posters, beer and soft drink signs, and a pegged coat and hat rack above which was posted a sign: Please Park Guns Here.

This room was, if possible, even more crowded than the great room. Above the crowd a large ceiling fan spun slowly. The big old Wurlitzer juke-box in the corner was lit, and above the cacophony, Casey could hear the voice of Clint Black.

Studying the crowd at the bar, she decided against trying to get a drink.

On one side of the room she could see another row of French doors. Pushing through the crowd she opened one of the doors, and found herself on a flagstone patio. This, she decided, was evidently the area behind the house. In the center of the area was the pool — one of those pseudo-natural numbers with rocks, waterfalls, and a built-in water slide. Donnie, she thought with a pang, would love it. To the left of the pool was the tennis court, and to the right an enormous flagstone barbecue, and barbecue pit. To the right of that, meeting the side of the house, was a low building that must be the garage Mark had mentioned. Round umbrella tables, set with bright yellow linen table-cloths and napkins and blue china to match the blue and yellow of the umbrellas, had been set up in almost every available free space; and everywhere, there were people. Kids frolicked in the pool, splashing and shrieking, as the adults sat at the tables, or stood in small groups, talking. Smoke, bearing the wonderful odor of roasting meat, drifted from the barbecue, where two men in chef's hats and white aprons bent over the barbecue pit.

She shook her head slowly. It was all a bit much — conspicuous consumption to the max.

As she inhaled the delicious odor of the cooking food, she felt a hand touch her elbow, and Mark's voice said in her ear: "Is that head-shake caused by disgust over my rudeness?"

She turned to look at him. "Not exactly. It's just that this place takes your breath away. But, you *were* rude. I was beginning to feel like an orphan among so many people I don't know."

He winced. "You're dead right, and I'm sorry. It's just that Theresa is . . ." he smiled wryly, "impetuous, even arrogant I suppose you could say. We're so used to giving in to her whims that we sometimes forget how she seems to others. We've spoiled her, I suppose. She *did* have someone that it was important that I meet, although I know that doesn't ex-cuse her. Am I forgiven?"

Casey let him wait a moment for her answer, then: "If you'll show me the rest of the house. I'm anxious to see it; it's not often I get to see a place like this."

"No problem. I'd be happy to."

He gave her his arm, and they went inside. As they threaded their way through the crowd — which appeared thicker than ever — Mark said: "The only other rooms on this floor are the kitchen, dining room, and two bedrooms for the live-in help."

He led her past the bar in the game room to a door that opened onto a hall running along the east side of the house. He closed the door behind them. "The rest of the house is off-limits to guests when we give a party of this size. There's a bathroom off the other end of the bar, another off the entry-way, and another just off the patio near the outdoor bar, besides those for the servants' quarters. Now, here's the kitchen."

He opened the wide door into a kitchen obviously designed to serve large numbers of people. The four people working there did not look up. The next room was the dining room, and Casey admired the beautiful wooden table, long and narrow, around which she counted twelve elegant chairs. Behind it was a long built-in sideboard, and over the table was a gorgeous light fixture of Spanish design.

Just past the dining room was a curved staircase curving upward.

Mark gestured down the hallway. "Down that way are the servants' quarters, and that's about all there is to see down here. The main family living quarters are upstairs."

As Mark led her up the wide, curved stairs, Casey trailed her hand along the polished wood of the banister. It must be nice to live like this, in elegance and comfort, never having to want for anything. She wondered briefly how it must feel. She suspected that people raised in such privilege must experience difficulty in relating to ordinary people with their ordinary worries.

"This is really the heart of the house," Mark said, gesturing.

Casey looked down the wide hallway with its paintings, plants, and southwestern sculpture. Magnificent.

He opened the first door onto a large room with a king-size bed, sitting area, vanity table, and fantastic view. "This is one of the guest suites. There is another next door, with twin beds, but otherwise pretty much the same."

"Theresa, Steven, Father, and I all have our own suites, and this is Father's study."

Mark opened a heavy, ornately carved door, and showed Casey into a large comfortable room. The room was furnished simply with a huge, worn, oak desk and chair; and two comfortable looking leather easy-chairs and ottomans crouched on either side of a stone fireplace.

Two walls were bookshelves, floor to ceiling. Casey took a quick glance at the titles: biographies, histories, political tomes. Another wall sported a number of mounted animal heads and game-fish. The fireplace, and its wide mantel, took up most of the fourth wall. The mantel was covered with trophies, photographs, and mementos. It was a man's room all the way.

She gestured to the mounted trophies. "Did your father kill all these animals?"

Mark grimaced. "God. I hope you're not one of those animal activists. Tell me you're not!"

Casey smiled. "No. I love animals, but I understand the hunting urge, and I know that the animal population must be kept in balance. My father used to hunt, and heaven knows my grandfather did."

Mark gave a sigh of mock relief. "Well, then, I can tell you the truth. Yes. Father brought them down, one and all. He was quite a hunter once; but he gave it up years ago. Gave away his gun collection too. Kept the trophies though. He said that he had hunted and killed them, and by God, he'd keep them."

Casey felt a twinge of disappointment. "I'm curious. Why did your father get rid of his guns and stop hunting?"

"It was the Kennedy assassinations. After John and Robert Kennedy were killed, Father said he no longer wanted to have a gun around."

"But the Kennedys were Democrats," Casey said.

Mark nodded. "I know, but I told you that Father marched to a different drummer. He said at the time that it didn't matter what their political affiliations, the killing of our political leaders could not be tolerated."

"And I got bounced out of the NRA for my stand," said a deep voice from the open doorway. "Not that I lost much sleep over that. Always did think that organization hides behind the Constitution."

Casey and Mark whirled around.

"Father!" Mark said, obviously a touch embarrassed. "We didn't hear you come in."

"That's quite obvious," Wager Halleck said dryly. "You should know by now that I'm like Tiger, our old setter; mention my name within a hundred yards, even in a whisper, and I come running."

He looked directly at Casey. "You'd be Casey Farrel, the investigator from the Governor's Task Force."

Casey, feeling like a kid with her hand caught in the cookie jar, opened her mouth to answer, but Mark broke in smoothly: "I was just showing her the house, Father. We were just going to look for you so that I might introduce her."

Wager Halleck was a big man, well over six feet, and broad in the shoulders and chest. Even at seventy-seven he was an intimidating presence, with the physique of a football player. Casey, remembering the mention of a heart attack in the run-down she had done on him, thought that it certainly didn't show. He had a thick thatch of white hair, keen brown eyes, and a florid face with a full mustache. She thought that she detected a lingering sadness in his eyes. The heart attack, the thought of impending death? Did he still mourn his dead wife?

"Here to ask questions about the Organ Pipe murders?" he asked in his deep voice.

"She's here as a guest, Father," Mark said quickly.

"Is she?" Halleck smoothed his mustache, never taking his gaze from Casey. "Well, young lady?"

"As Mark said, I'm here as a guest," she said steadily.

"Is that so?" His expression showed signs of amusement. "Well, it's been my experience that the law is the law, always nosy no matter what the situation. They never turn it off."

He shrugged massive shoulders. "I've heard through the grapevine that you think there is some kind of connection between the dead aliens and our ranch. Well, it sounds pretty thin to me, but if you've got any questions, you might as well ask them now and get it out of the way."

Casey returned his look steadily, took a deep breath, and decided to go for it.

"Since you ask," she said calmly. "I understand that you have had dealings with Victor Sanchez and Pedro Castelar. I have been told that they supplied you with workers for your grove."

A sharp light sparked in Wager Halleck's brown eyes. "If these men did, as you say, supply grove workers to my ranch, they didn't deal with me, young lady. I haven't been involved with the management of the grove for several years. You'll need to talk to my foreman."

"Who the hell is this?" said a voice from the doorway. They all turned. Filling the doorway was a large man of thirty-some years. He was wearing khaki shorts, over which a large belly spilled unattractively, and a red golf shirt. His face was ruddy, and his expression disagreeable. "What are you answering her questions for?"

"It's all right, Steven," Wager Halleck said in an annoyed tone. "Miss Farrel is only doing her job."

"Well, this is a fine time to be doing it." Steven's tone was still accusative.

"She's my guest, Steven," said Mark. "Please try to behave like a civilized human being."

"Well, it's a hell of a way for a guest to

behave, interrogating her host. But maybe she doesn't realize that it's bad manners."

Casey felt her face go hot. This son-of-a-bitch was so disagreeable that he made Jarvis Dessaline appear almost good mannered.

"That's enough, Steven," Wager Halleck said sharply. "Continue, Miss Farrel."

Casey nodded. "All right. As you say, we might as well get this over with. I need to know where all three of you were on the night in question."

Steven shook his head. His sparse red hair, cut too long, fell into his eyes. He grunted. "She's treating us like suspects. How ridiculous can you get?"

Wager silenced him with a glare.

Mark said, "Well, I was at a fund-raising dinner. At least seventy-five people can testify to that."

Casey nodded. "And you, Mr. Halleck?"

"I was here, in the house," Wager Halleck said, without hesitation.

"Were you alone?"

"Steven and Theresa were with me. We dined together at seven, and finished about eight thirty."

"And after that?"

"Steven and Theresa went to their suites. I read for several hours in my study before retiring."

226

"So you can't vouch for their whereabouts after eight thirty. I understand that their suites have private entrances."

"What the hell is this?" Steven said explosively. "What damned reason would any of us have to kill five wetbacks? And who gives a shit about five dead Mexicans? Too many of them around anyway."

Mark said, "You're hammered, Steven."

Steven glared back at Mark with red-faced belligerence. "So what if I am?"

"You'd better take a nap, Son," Wager Halleck said with surprising gentleness. He took Steven by the arm. "Come along."

Steven, shoulders slumped, allowed himself to be led away.

Mark shrugged. "What can I say? Steven is a touch prejudiced, especially when he's drinking."

Casey was embarrassed for him, didn't know what to say.

Mark took her arm. "You've seen the house now, or most of it. Let's go back downstairs, and I'll introduce you to the rest of the family."

As they left the study, they met Theresa hurrying down the hall.

"Why is Father taking Steven into his suite?" she demanded.

"Because Steven is wasted. Father thought

a short nap would do him good."

Theresa's lovely face took on an expression of willful petulance. "But we're about to start serving the food," she said angrily. "And I want them there."

"Don't sweat it, Theresa," Mark said soothingly. "Father will be down as soon as he gets Steven settled, and Steven will probably be feeling okay by the time the cake is cut. Now, come on, let's go downstairs before all the food is gone."

Putting his other arm through that of his sister, he led both women toward the staircase.

Casey, who had disliked Theresa from the moment she met her, felt her dislike mounting. Theresa had ignored her again, as if she didn't exist. Also, from her conversation, it wasn't difficult to come to the conclusion that the woman was a spoiled brat, used to having her every whim granted. Questioning *her* was probably not going to be pleasant, but it would have to be done. Not tonight — she had already presumed enough on the strength of a social invitation — however, since she was out of the closet now, there was no longer any reason not to play the role of investigator. Yes, very soon, she would confront Theresa Halleck one on one; and then let Theresa try to ignore her.

★ ★ ★

Appalled, the old man stared at his favorite child and felt the pain, like a rusty knife, in his gut.

"You say you paid *a man to kill her? My God. What were you thinking of?"*

"I told you I would do what was necessary."

He shook his head. "It wasn't necessary. This woman, this Casey Farrel, knows nothing damaging. When no evidence turns up, when they realize there are only dead ends, the interest will die down, the case will fade away. Please! No more killing. Leave that young woman alone. She can't hurt you."

"You don't know that, Father. She's very determined. If she keeps nosing around she might come across something. We can't afford to be complacent."

The old man's tone was harsh: "Complacent is hardly a word I would use to describe what I'm feeling. If you had not killed those people, there would be no problem to consider. None of this would be 'necessary.' "

"If I hadn't killed them, they would have destroyed us. I couldn't let them continue to blackmail us. They would have only become more and more greedy, and there was always the risk that they might have told someone else. No, this is the only way."

The old man sighed. "Is there any way that your connection to this dead man, this hit man, can be uncovered?"

"*Absolutely none. I never met him face to face. My only contacts were by telephone and mail. When I mailed him the five thousand dollars, I did so in a hotel envelope, and I mailed it from downtown Phoenix. I wore gloves while handling the money and the envelope.*

"*Still, you are partially right: I shouldn't have hired him: he bungled the job. I see now that the old saying is true. If you want something done right, do it yourself.*"

CHAPTER FOURTEEN

On Thursday, Casey received a surprise visitor. The task force had, at present, only a few permanent employees, and it was relatively easy for anyone to just wander in and out. The only person who had a secretary was Bob Wilson. There was a receptionist, but she spent most of her time answering the phone, and paid scant attention to anyone passing her desk.

Casey had been in her office for about an hour, absorbed in wrestling with her report for Bob Wilson, when she heard a soft cough from her open doorway.

The woman standing there was tall and striking. She was stylishly dressed in a business suit, had shoulder-length reddish-brown hair, and looked to be in her early thirties.

The woman took two steps into the office. Casey, annoyed at being interrupted, said shortly, "May I help you?"

"Are you Casey Farrel?"

Casey frowned. The woman looked vaguely familiar. "Yes. I am."

"I'm Sandra Dessaline. May I talk to you

for a few minutes?"

Casey's annoyance vanished. "Of course." Casey indicated the chair before her desk. "Please sit down."

Sandra Dessaline did so, adjusting her skirt over perfect knees. She was a handsome woman, with perfect features and dark, glittering eyes.

"I saw you at the ranch the other day when you were there talking to my father and brothers."

Casey sat back. "I think I saw you with your mother in the rose garden. What can I do for you?"

Sandra Dessaline leaned forward, her dark eyes intent.

"I don't know if you realize that my father is not a well man. He was badly upset by all of those questions the other day."

Casey thought back. Alexander Dessaline had not struck her as being particularly upset. That reaction had come from his son.

"No, I didn't know that," she said slowly. "And he certainly didn't seem upset when he talked with me. If he was, I'm sorry; but I was only doing my job."

Sandra pulled back, and crossed her legs. "I'm afraid that I'm not very sympathetic toward that excuse, Miss Farrel. That's what all bureaucrats say when they come poking their noses into other people's business. It's absolutely ridiculous for you or anyone else to imagine that any member of our family knows anything about those desert murders. I realize that you think there is some kind of connection because those *coyotes* used to supply workers for the groves; but if that's the case, why aren't you questioning other growers, like the Hallecks?"

Casey raised an eyebrow. She was rather enjoying this. "And why, in particular, the Hallecks, Miss Dessaline?"

Sandra looked at her sharply. "For the obvious reason, Miss Farrel; Pedro Castelar and Victor Sanchez supplied grove and stable workers for the Halleck ranch."

Casey nodded. "Yes. I know that, but how do you? I understood that for a number of years the Dessalines and the Hallecks have not been on speaking terms."

The woman's glance slid away. "That's true. But since Glenn has taken over the groves, I occasionally help him. Last year I was present when Castelar and Sanchez delivered workers to our ranch. Pedro happened to mention that he was also delivering workers to the Halleck Ranch that same week."

Casey stored that bit of information away. "But this year your brother decided not to pick the crop."

"Yes. It would not have been profitable."

"And that was his decision alone?"

Sandra frowned. "Why yes, but I agreed with him. It would be far more profitable to take out the groves and devote the property to raising horses."

"But your father does not seem to agree."

Sandra's frown deepened. "How do you know . . . ?" She sighed. "At any rate, you're right. He doesn't. He was born there, has spent most of his life there, and there have always been the groves. But how did we get on this subject? I came here to talk . . ."

Casey interrupted. "I know, to talk about my questioning your father. But since you are here, I'd like to ask you a few questions. For instance, can you account for your whereabouts on the night of the murders?"

The woman stiffened. "I didn't come here to be questioned." She started to rise from the chair.

Casey raised her hand. "Please, Ms. Dessaline. There is no need to make it difficult for yourself. You will have to be asked this question sooner or later."

"I deeply resent the implication that I or my family are involved in this filthy mess!" Sandra's lips were tight, and her eyes blazed; however, she sank back into the chair, back stiff, hands grasping the arms of the chair.

"The night in question, I went out to dinner and to a movie afterward. I got home about eleven."

"Was anyone with you?"

Sandra's gaze did not flinch. "No. I went alone."

"And where did you have dinner?"

"At Don Jose, on Thomas Road."

"Do the people there know you? Are you a regular customer?"

Sandra shook her head. "No, it was the first time I've gone there. Whether or not the waitress and bus-boy will remember me, I don't know."

"What movie did you see?"

Sandra sighed and rolled her eyes. "The new Mel Gibson flick."

"See anybody there you know?"

"I did not."

"Any of your family up when you came home?"

"How do I know?" Sandra said in exasperation. "It was late. My mother retires early, and my father often does also; although sometimes he sits in his office and reads. I didn't see any lights in his office, so I assume he was in bed. As for Glenn, I didn't see him, and all the servants' quarters were dark. I suppose what you're getting at is that, barring the help at the restaurant, I have no witness to show where I was that night. Well, I'm sorry; but I have nothing to hide, and I feel under no obligation to provide witnesses for every minute of my evening. I wonder if you can tell me where you were, and what were you doing for every minute of that same night!"

Casey smiled. "It would be difficult. But these things have to be asked. I'm sorry that you find it so invasive."

Sandra gave a lady-like grunt. "Well, if you're sorry, perhaps you'll leave my father alone. He's answered your questions, and there can't be any reason to bother him again. I hope you agree."

Casey bit her lip. "Ms. Dessaline, I can't make that promise. I'll be as circumspect as possible, but if I find it necessary to question any members of your family again, I will have to do so. Please try to understand."

Sandra sighed, and the tension suddenly went out of her. "Surprisingly, I do," she said, her tone softer. "I realize that you must investigate all avenues, and that you can't make exceptions. And since that's true, I'm sure that you will also question the Hallecks and talk to their foreman, Raskin."

Casey nodded. "I intend to do that tonight."

The Halleck ranch was only two miles or

so north of the Dessaline place. The road leading off into the grove was paved, and the trees on each side were in fine shape and picked clean of fruit. This grove, she soon realized, seemed to be much larger than the Dessalines' grove.

It was late now, and she had to turn on her car lights as she drove down the road to the house. She had called Bert Raskin and he had informed her that since he had to deliver horses to Flagstaff that afternoon, the only time he would be available was eight in the evening. Rather than postpone the meeting until tomorrow, Casey had agreed to the late hour.

Josh was working tonight and couldn't take Donnie, so it had been necessary to hire a sitter. She was certainly putting in long hours with this case. She hoped that Wilson appreciated it, but doubted it. It would be something he would expect of her.

About a mile or so into the grove, her car nosed into a clearing, and she could see the ranch house ahead. The building appeared much older than the Dessaline homestead, and had more of the look of a home built for practicality, a plain, two-story wooden structure, painted white, with a wide porch running the length of the front.

As she turned into what appeared to be a parking area in front of the house, her headlights illuminated a dark pickup attached to a two-horse trailer.

She could feel her pulse rate increase. Maybe, at last, she was going to get a break.

She parked her car next to the pickup, shut off the motor, and sat for a moment. Lights were burning in the front room of the house, and over the sounds of the motor cooling, she could hear the blare of a TV. A glance at her watch told her that she was about twenty minutes early. Except for the faint sounds from the television, it was almost eerily quiet, and, except for the spill of light from the living-room windows, exceedingly dark. A lonely place to live, Casey thought.

After waiting a few minutes more, she got out of the car, climbed the porch steps, and rang the bell. Three ancient rocking chairs were arranged in a neat row to her right. A strong breeze had come up, and its force set the chairs into gentle, creaking, motion.

The door opened, and a middle-aged man wearing faded denims, a stained T-shirt, and cowboy boots stood in the doorway. He was carrying a glass in his hand, and Casey caught the scent of liquor.

"Mr. Raskin?"

"Yeah. I'm Bert Raskin. You Miss Farrel?"

Casey nodded. "Yes. I called you this morning."

"Sure. Come on in."

He stepped back, and held open the screen door. As she passed him, Casey was assaulted by the odor of whiskey and horse. The heat inside the house was stifling. That combined with the smell, made her stomach roll.

She stopped, looking up at Raskin. He was dark, with a round face and deep-set black eyes, and wore a straggly, drooping mustache. He looked like he had Hispanic blood.

As the sweat popped out on her forehead, she reached for the tissue in her pocket. Wiping her forehead, she said, "I'm sorry. It's just that it's awfully hot in here."

Under her gaze he grinned widely, showing stained teeth. He drank from the glass as if toasting her. He was sweating heavily. "I've been gone all day, and the house has been closed up. No air-conditioning. The old man never had it installed. There are swamp-coolers in the bedrooms, if you want to talk there." His grin was mocking.

Casey gave him a hard look, trying to decide if he was being obnoxious, or just pulling her chain. She decided that it was the latter, and smiled primly back. "No, I don't think so. Maybe we could sit on the porch. There's a breeze out there."

He nodded slowly. "It's all right with me."

Following her outside, he gestured to the

rockers. "Have a seat."

Casey sank into the first rocker. The wood felt smooth and comforting against her buttocks and back. Automatically, she began to rock. It was a pleasant sensation.

Raskin settled his bulky frame into the next rocker, and took a long drink from his glass. "Now, what's all this about? Mr. Halleck said that it's something to do with those murders in the desert. I don't know how I can help you with that."

Casey stopped rocking and leaned toward him. "I understand that you knew the two dead *coyotes?*"

Raskin frowned. "Sure, I knew Pedro and Victor. They used to bring us workers for the grove."

"How long did they do that?"

"About five years or so."

"And this year?"

"Yeah. Sure. Back in the early summer, when the fruit was ready."

"And that's the last time you saw them?"

"That's it. June, I think it was."

"Then this group of illegals, three of whom were murdered at the same time as Castelar and Sanchez, were not being brought into the country to work here?"

Raskin shook his head. "Nope. No reason to. No work here for them."

"Can you think of any reason that anyone would want to kill Castelar and Sanchez?"

"Not a clue. Of course they probably had enemies. They were *coyotes*. There's lots of competition. And feuds too."

He shook his head. "It's terrible that they died like that. They weren't really bad men; just trying to make a buck like everybody else."

"Do you know if they were involved in drug smuggling?"

He squinted at her in the dim light from the window.

"Look, lady, I wasn't bosom buddies with either of these guys. What they're up to is anyone's guess. But I will say that it doesn't seem likely. Pedro was the boss of that pair, and I don't think old Pedro had the sand for that. Could be wrong, though." He tilted his glass and drained it.

Casey decided to switch subjects. "The pickup and horse trailer at the side of the house, they belong to the ranch?"

He nodded.

"How many people drive the truck?"

Raskin yawned. "Sorry. It's been a long day." He stretched.

"Let's see, I drive it, of course, and so do the hands. The Hallecks drive it too, when they're here. I guess probably four or five people drive it occasionally, but I'm the only one who drives it regularly."

He rocked his chair forward, and stood up. "I'm dry here. I'll just pop in and fix myself another drink. Can I make one for you too?"

Casey shook her head. "No, thanks. But I would love a soft drink."

"Coke okay?"

"That would be fine."

"Coke coming right up!"

With a slightly unsteady step, he entered the house.

Casey relaxed against the back of the chair, rocking gently, listening to the hum of insects in the warm air. She thought of a question she should ask the foreman. Who shod the horses? Did someone on the ranch do it, or did they call in a blacksmith?

In a few minutes she heard Raskin returning. She glanced toward the doorway just as he stepped into it, framed in light.

As he stepped forward, the stillness was shattered by the crack of a gunshot. Frozen, Casey watched as Raskin staggered, thrown backward by the force of the bullet, then fell.

It all happened in an instant, and yet seemed to take forever. Still frozen, Casey saw the glasses fall and break, their shards sparkling in the light, saw the red flower of blood bloom on his chest, his expression of surprise and disbelief.

Suddenly able to move, Casey leapt from her chair and took a step towards the doorway; then, realizing that she was silhouetted against the lighted window, she drew back into the shadows, glancing to the trees of the grove about fifty yards away, the direction from which the shot had come.

As she did so, there was a flash of light from the grove, and a shot whined over her head. Throwing herself down on the deck, she hugged the floor. She stared at the trees where she had seen the muzzle flash, but there was no further sound or movement. Quickly, she considered her options.

Her glance went to her car, sitting in the spill of light from the open door. The shooter would hit her before she could even get close to the vehicle.

She looked down the length of the porch. On the other end the citrus trees crowded close to the house, shrouding it in shadow. It was her only chance.

Splinters from the aged wood of the porch gouged into her flesh, ripping her trousers. She crawled on, using her elbows to pull herself along.

When she reached the edge of the porch, she saw that there were steps on this side also.

She felt a surge of relief as she slid down them on her belly. As she did so, another shot rang out, but the shooter appeared to be firing blindly, for the shot came nowhere near her.

As the sound of the shot reverberated in the darkness, she rose to a crouch, and ran for the sheltering trees. Once in the trees, she began to run, trying to figure out in what direction she was travelling. Where would the nearest road be?

Deep in the grove she stopped to rest, crouching near the trunk of a large orange tree, whose branches almost came to the ground. Straining for sounds of pursuit, she could only hear the pounding of her own heart and the rasping of her breath.

Should she stay where she was, hoping that the shooter would give up and go away, or should she keep moving?

The thought of crouching here like a hunted animal, stuck in her craw. No, better keep moving. She had passed a service station just about a mile down the road from the ranch, when she had come in. If she could make it there she could call for help.

When her breathing had slowed, she crept out from the shelter of the tree, holding her breath, the better to hear. Nothing, except for the slightest of rustles from the leaves as a sudden breeze stirred the branches.

She headed in what she hoped was the direction of the highway, and within a few hundred feet, found herself on a narrow service road, used by the trucks when the grove was picked.

Should she risk it? It didn't offer the seclusion of travelling between the trees, but her progress would be swifter, and it probably headed toward the highway. She decided to risk it, and set off at a rapid walk, keeping close to the trees.

She had been travelling for several minutes when she heard the sound, a thudding, pounding sound that at first confused her, until she realized that it was the sound of a horse, galloping swiftly. It was coming directly toward her.

Bile filled her throat as she thought of the hoofprints around the body of the dead girl in the desert.

Quickly, she darted off the road into the shadows of the nearest row of trees, and crouched behind the sheltering leaves. Her eyes had become accustomed to the darkness, and she could see the lighter area of the road. The sound of hoofbeats grew louder, primitive and powerful in the stillness of the night. Casey felt consumed with a frightening curiosity as she waited for her pursuer to appear.

And then the horse and rider were there, making one dark shadow against the light-colored soil of the roadbed. The horse seemed huge, the figure astride it simply a smaller shadow, and then they were gone, the sound fading. Dust from the roadbed filled the air, and Casey suppressed a cough.

She would have to stay off the road now, but she would travel parallel to it. Strangely, having finally seen what she had to assume was the shooter, she felt reassured. As her Hopi grandmother used to say, "It is better to know where an evil spirit is, than to have it surprise you."

Softly, under her breath, Casey began the chant against evil that the old woman had taught her. She didn't know if it would really work, but it did make her feel better.

Casey had no idea of how long she walked. Time seemed to have become frozen. She was not conscious of fatigue. She was in good condition, and the adrenaline in her system kept her energy high.

She walked briskly, but stopped frequently to listen for her pursuer, but heard nothing.

And then, at last, she did hear a sound, one that filled her with hope and relief, the sounds of speeding cars.

It took her only a few minutes more to reach the road. There was no sign of pursuit now, probably the shooter was busy making his escape.

A car passed her, travelling fast, the tires singing against the roadway. She drew back. What if the shooter was on the highway now? She would be a sitting duck. But she had to reach the service station. There was nothing for it but to set out, and be ready to jump into the ditch if anybody slowed or swerved toward her.

There were relatively few cars at this time of night, but she felt herself cringe as each one passed. By the time she reached the service station, she *was* tired, but she had made it without incident. The station was open, and the attendant, when she told him what had happened, was solicitous as he pointed her to the telephone in the office. When she dialed the number of the Maricopa County Sheriff's Department, she saw that her hands were trembling.

CHAPTER FIFTEEN

Casey stood on the porch of the old Halleck house with Paul Storey, the Phoenix homicide officer Casey had met at the last force meeting, and Walt Edwards, the investigator from the Maricopa Sheriff's Office.

After calling in, Casey remained at the service station until the first response car showed up, then rode back to the house with the officer. Bert Raskin was indeed dead. A quick search of the house had revealed that it was otherwise empty. The pickup and horse trailer were still parked beside the house. The only other vehicle on the property was a beat-up old van, parked near the bunkhouse, that probably belonged to one of the ranch hands. The hands, there were three, had been playing cards with the stereo turned up full blast, and had heard nothing.

Now, Edwards turned to Casey. "Okay, Farrel. Let me get this straight: you were in that first rocker, and Raskin was coming back to the porch with a fresh drink. He was shot just as he stepped into the lighted doorway. Right so far?"

She nodded. "That's the way it went down, Walt."

"And the shot came from over there?" He pointed.

"I'm not absolutely sure about the first shot, I was looking at Raskin. But the second shot, the one fired at me, I am sure about. When I realized that I was exposed, I threw myself down. I was facing the spot when I saw the muzzle flash. The third shot, as I was leaving the porch, came from the same location."

Paul Storey said, "Must be a hell of a shot, whoever the shooter was. Got Raskin dead center."

Casey asked, "Walt, was anything found over there?"

Edwards shook his head. "Nada."

"No footprints?"

He shook his head. "Nothing recent. The grove hasn't been watered for a few days, and the ground is dry with a good growth of grass."

"Then how about the slugs?"

"The one in the victim will have to wait for the autopsy, but we found the one fired at you on the porch. It was buried in the outside wall."

"A .45?"

"Yep, looks like it."

Paul Storey broke in, "Did you learn anything of value from Raskin?"

"Not really. We had only just started to talk when he was shot."

Edwards said, "The rider who chased you through the orchard, you think that was the shooter?"

Casey hesitated. "Who else could it be? Unless there were *two* people involved."

Storey said, "And you think the shooter was after you? Maybe Raskin was the primary target."

Casey shook her head. "No. I don't think so. I think the shooter took him out because he was with me, and because he made an easy target. This isn't the first try at me, Storey. Somebody tried to run over me Monday."

"I saw the report on that," he said with a shrug. "But that could have been an accident. There's no proof that it was connected in any way with this case."

"An accident?" she said incredulously. "A pickup climbing that steep bank, me, the only person in sight? Besides, the driver of the pickup was a professional hit man. They found five thousand dollars in cash in his pocket. Wasn't that in the report?"

"Sure," Storey said. "Still, nothing in the report proved any connection."

"Maybe not. But I'm convinced of it."

"Why?" Storey said challengingly. "Why

would you be a target?"

"Because I'm beginning to worry somebody. I'm getting close to the killer."

"Aw, come on, Farrel!" Storey said. "How can you be worrying anybody? You don't have a clue as to who the perp is. Now admit it?"

Edwards intervened quickly. "One thing puzzles me here, Casey. How did the killer know you'd be here?"

Casey looked down sheepishly. "I'm afraid that's my own fault," she said. "Several people knew that I'd be here: Mark Halleck, Wager Halleck; in fact they both suggested that I talk to Raskin. And this morning, Sandra Dessaline was in my office, and I mentioned it to her. Any of them could have mentioned it to any member of their family."

"Say that you're right," Storey said, "as far-fetched as it sounds, say that the shooter was after you because you're getting too close. The shooter was hidden in the trees. Raskin wouldn't be able to identify him. So why take out Raskin?"

"Maybe because Raskin knew something and the killer was afraid he would tell me. Or maybe it was someone that Raskin knew was on the property, and if I was killed he might become suspicious. Don't you see? It has to be someone from one or the other of the families!"

Storey made a dismissive gesture. "It doesn't mean anything, Farrel! Hell! Any number of people could have known you were coming out here tonight. You're fixated on the Hallecks and the Dessalines. I'm more inclined to believe that Raskin was deeply involved with that pair of *coyotes,* and his death ties in with their killings. You say he admitted that he knew both men well."

Casey stared. "How could he be involved?"

Storey shrugged. "Hell, I don't know. Maybe he was taking kickbacks from them — it happens all the time — and maybe they didn't pay up. So he offed them. And maybe one of their buddies, or a relative, decided to get even — happens all the time too, with the greasers. If that is the case, then you were just an afterthought." He grinned. "Because you were there."

Casey shook her head, almost too angry to speak. "You think Raskin killed those *coyotes* for a kickback that could only amount to a few hundred dollars? That's ridiculous!"

"People have been killed for less. At any rate, that theory is as good as yours, and there's just as much proof to back it up."

Casey turned away. "You're impossible," she said. "It's no use talking to you."

She turned to Edwards. "Did you find any hoofprints on the service road?"

Edwards raised his hands in a gesture of despair. "Yep, dozens of them. It would appear that the road is regularly used as a bridle path. Like I said, the ground in the grove is dry, and there is no telling what's old and what's new. If there had been fresh mud . . ." He smiled sympathetically.

Casey's attention was distracted as two men came out of the house carrying a stretcher bearing the mortal remains of Bert Raskin.

She said, "You need me for anything else, Walt?"

"Nothing I can think of."

"You'll call me in the morning when you get the results of the ballistics test?"

"I'll call."

It was near midnight when Casey got back to her apartment. Donnie was already in bed, and the baby sitter was waiting impatiently.

Casey apologized to the girl, who lived in the same apartment building, let her out, and locked the door behind her.

Then she went quietly down the hall and peeked into Donnie's room. A dim light burned by his bed. Donnie was sleeping soundly, the covers thrown off, as was his habit. Smiling fondly, Casey tucked the covers up under his chin. Donnie didn't stir.

In the kitchen, she debated whether to fix

a pot of tea or have a drink. She finally decided that, after the night she had had, a drink was in order. She mixed a strong gin and tonic, and took it down the hall to her bedroom. She took a swallow of the drink, sat down at the small corner table she used for a desk, picked up the phone, and punched in Josh's number.

The phone rang several times, and she was about to hang up when the phone was picked up.

"If this is the station, my name is Clark Kent," he said grumpily. "If it's anybody else, you shouldn't be calling at this time of night."

Laughing, Casey said, "Does that apply to me, too, Josh?"

"Hey, Casey!" he said, his tone changing completely. "Babe, is anything wrong?"

"I woke you, didn't I? I'm sorry. I didn't know how late you'd be working. I thought you might not even be home yet."

"Hey, it's okay. You know I'm always home to you. Besides, I'm not in bed. I got home, had a couple of drinks, started watching an old flick, then dozed off. But you didn't answer my question. Is anything wrong?"

"Maybe I just wanted to hear your voice."

"Yeah, right. Don't bullshit a bullshitter, babe. Something's bothering you. I can tell."

"You're right, Josh," she said with a sigh.

"I've had quite a day — or I should really say night."

"Okay. Let's hear it."

Quickly, she sketched in the story of the evening.

"Goddammit, Casey, it's not safe to let you out alone," he growled. "That's twice in one week that someone has tried to nail you. The next time you may not be so lucky. Are you carrying that piece I gave you last year?"

"You know I don't like guns."

"I guess that's a no, huh? Well, *liking* guns is not necessary. You just have to be able to use one, and as I recall you were getting pretty good with that automatic. You certainly scared the hell out of Ray Tibbets when he tried to break into my house after you. Besides, do you want to give the bad guys more of an edge than they already have? You have a right to protect yourself."

Casey sighed. "All right. All right. But Josh, don't you think that these attacks mean that I'm on the right track?"

"I'd say that's a pretty safe assumption, yes. But the thing is, you still don't have any hard evidence. Casey . . ." He hesitated. "Maybe you should consider backing off a little; let Storey and Walt Edwards carry the ball for a while. I know that you think Storey's something of an asshole, but he's a fair homicide investigator, and from what I know of Edwards, he's a damned good man."

"Walt is, yes. At least I can work with him. But Storey is a different matter. He clearly doesn't think women should be doing police work, and he balks me at every turn."

"But I'm sure that won't prevent him from doing a good job."

"Well, it sure doesn't help me do mine! I was assigned to this case, Josh; and I have no intention of backing off just because there may be some danger. Would you let that stop you from doing your job?"

"No, but . . ." He stopped abruptly.

Casey let out a sigh of exasperation. "But you're not a woman, right? And a man's gotta do, what a man's gotta do. Right?"

"Come on, Casey. I didn't say that."

"But you were thinking it. You're so transparent, Josh."

She heard his deep sigh in her ear. "I should know better, stubborn woman like you. All I have to do is say don't, and you're hell-bent for doing."

"Well, maybe you should stop telling me what to do and not do. You knew going in that I'm not the barefoot and pregnant type. Just try treating me like an equal. Okay?"

He sighed again. "Okay. I do try, you know."

Casey smiled into the mouthpiece, and her voice was soft when she answered. "I know you do, tiger."

"It's just that I care about you. And honest to God, I don't know what I'd do if something happened to you. At least promise me that you'll be careful. Okay?"

"Depend on it, Detective."

"Okay, now that that's settled, maybe I should come over, cheer you up a little."

"Now Josh," she said quickly. "We have an agreement, remember? No hanky-panky in my apartment, with Donnie here."

"I was thinking along the lines of something more serious than hanky-panky," he said with a smile in his voice. "You sound like you need some comforting."

She was strongly tempted. The warmth and strength of his arms would indeed be comforting. Unbidden, like a sneak thief, the thought of Mark Halleck came into her mind. Feeling guilty, she pushed the thought away.

"Thanks for the offer, Josh. It's very tempting, but what I need most of all right now is sleep. And it sounds like what you need too, falling asleep in front of the TV like that."

"I'm never *that* tired."

"Good night, Josh," she said firmly, and hung up.

She was smiling as she turned away from

the desk. Just talking to Josh had lightened her spirits considerably. It always did. What life would be like without Josh around, even if only on the telephone, she didn't wish to consider.

She drained her drink, performed her bathroom chores, put on her pajamas, and got into bed. She had been afraid the turmoil and horror of the night would replay in her mind and keep her awake, but sleep claimed her weary body within minutes.

The next morning, Casey was at her desk, doing her report on the events of the past evening, when Walt Edwards called.

"I just got the results of the ballistics test on the slugs we found last night, Casey. They're .45s, and they match the ones found in the victims down at Organ Pipe."

Casey's hand tensed on the telephone. She had been right!

"So we have our tie-in with the killings in the desert."

"It looks that way. And, considering what happened last night at the Halleck ranch, it looks to me as if you might be right about *that* tie-in too."

Casey smiled into the phone. "Thanks, Walt. I needed that. Everybody else seems to think I'm crazy."

He chuckled. "Don't mention it. I'll call you as soon as there is anything else."

That was the good news. The bad news came with Bob Wilson, who came to her office a few minutes after Edwards called. Wilson's visit was an unusual occurrence. Usually, when he wanted to speak with her, he summoned her to his office.

"Good morning, Farrel."

"Good morning, Bob."

He sank into the chair before her desk with a sigh. "I heard about what happened last night. That makes two attempts on your life."

Casey nodded, biting back a comment on his ability to count.

"I want you to back off, Farrel."

Casey's hands tensed on the arms of her chair. "Back off! Why?"

He frowned. "I think that should be obvious. I'd like to keep you alive."

Casey took a deep breath, and tried to keep her cool, hearing the unspoken comment; it wouldn't be good for the task force if one of their operatives was killed.

She leaned forward. "Last night's attack must mean that I'm on the right track, Bob. Also, since the same gun used in the Organ Pipe killings was used to kill Raskin, it would seem to give credence to my theory that the Hallecks or the Dessalines, or at least somebody on one of their ranches, is involved in some way. Why would you want me to quit now?"

He sighed. "Because I don't want you killed, dammit. For some reason I've grown sort of fond of you, even though you are a pain in the ass."

Casey almost smiled. This was the nicest thing Wilson had ever said to her.

"And there is something else. Some of the others involved in the investigation think that you're getting in their way."

Casey felt herself flush. "Others? What others? Not Walt Edwards. I don't believe that. Storey! It's Paul Storey, isn't it? And that guy from Tucson, what's his name, Ben Thornton, from the Pima County Sheriff's Department."

"Doesn't matter who." Wilson shifted uneasily in the chair. "It's not our job to antagonize local law enforcement officers. We're supposed to work with them, not against them."

"And they aren't supposed to work with us?" Casey said disgustedly.

Wilson raised a placating hand. "We're supposed, mainly, to act as coordinators."

"Coordinating what? There will be nothing to coordinate if it's left to Storey and some of the others. Walt Edwards is okay, but . . ." She broke off, staring intently at him. "It's pressure from above, isn't it? You've gotten word to go easy on the Hallecks and the Dessalines, they're untouchable! That's it, isn't it?"

Wilson shrugged. "They *are* important people, Farrel, and they *do* have powerful friends."

Casey sank back in her chair, angry to the core. "And what about your brave statements? You told me that no matter how important the perp was, you wanted me to nail him. As I recall, you said you'd back me up all the way!"

Wilson had the grace to looked embarrassed. "That was then. This is now. The situation has changed. If we press ahead, without any hard evidence to back us up, we could both be out on our asses. I'm only asking you to slow down, ease off a little. Let the other agencies do some work. When they come up with something definite, we'll get this guy, and it'll all be behind us."

"Never happen." She stared at him narrowly. "Why don't you just take me off the case? Or would that look too fishy, too much like you were bowing to political pressure?"

Wilson slapped his hand down on the desk. "Look, Farrel, all you need to know is that you're to stay the hell away from the Hallecks and the Dessalines, and that's a goddamn order, understand?"

"Oh, yes, Mr. Wilson. I understand completely," she said softly.

Seething, she watched him leave the office. Damn him to hell! He had gotten her into this investigation, and now that the heat was coming down, he was reneging on his support.

Almost by reflex, she reached for the phone, to call Josh. Then, after punching in the first digit of his number, she slammed the receiver back down.

Josh was her mentor, her tower of support, and she had become used to turning to him for advice; but not this time. This time she knew she must make her own decision. She could imagine what he'd say, anyway: "Unless you have firm ground to stand on, don't fight City Hall; you'll only get ground into hamburger."

But she also knew that there were times, even when your position wasn't strong, that you had to fight; and this was one of those times. At the moment, there might not be enough evidence to prove her case; but there was too much evidence to let it go. She might lose her job in the end, but she'd rather do that than play stooge for the likes of Paul Storey and Thornton. She was definitely going to keep on with the case; she was just going to have to do it on the quiet.

★ ★ ★

The old man watched his child pace back and forth. He turned his eyes away. The pain was too much. How could he let this go on? He could stop it with a word in the right place; but it would mean betraying his flesh and his blood; and would bring shame and destruction to the rest of the family. No. No matter how monstrous, he could not betray his favorite child.

"So you have killed again?" he said, the pain showing in his voice.

His remark was greeted with a curl of mocking laughter. "Father, Bert Raskin was born a victim! Who is going to mourn such a nonentity?"

"He was a man, a human being. And why? How could he have hurt you?"

"He saw me, Father. He knew that I was on the property. If I had killed her *and left him alive, he would have told that to the police. No, it was necessary. The only mistake I made was to miss the woman. I should have taken her out first."*

The old man's voice rose to a cry. "Is there nothing human left in you at all?"

"Oh, I'm human, Father. It's just that I've learned at last how the world really works. Only the strong, and the selfish, survive. These 'victims' as you call them, were all little, unimportant people. They lead miserable, mean lives. Perhaps I did them a favor in eliminating them."

263

"*You are mad,*" the old man whispered. "*Quite mad.*"

"*Am I, Father? By whose criteria? Not mine. But I am curious as to why you should think so.*"

The old man lifted eyes dimmed by pain. "*Because none of this was necessary. None of it.*"

"*It will stop soon. When the Farrel woman is eliminated.*"

The old man raised his hand. "*No. It will stop now. I have taken care of matters. She will no longer be actively involved in the case. I told you that I would be able to take care of this, given enough time.*"

"*She has been removed from the case?*"

"*No. That would be too obvious; however, she has been removed from active participation.*"

His words were greeted by an unbelieving laugh. "*So you say, Father; but Farrel is a pushy, nosy, woman. Perhaps she should be named Ferret? It would suit her. I doubt that she will give up so easily. If the situation was different, I could almost admire her for that. But we shall see, won't we?*"

CHAPTER SIXTEEN

The next morning, Friday, Casey received two more surprise visitors, Mark Halleck and his sister, Theresa.

They arrived about nine, looking beautiful, perfectly groomed, and sure of themselves. Casey felt scruffy in comparison.

Theresa stood back, looking bored, as Mark leaned over Casey's desk, an expression of concern on his handsome face. "Casey, are you all right? I was out of town yesterday, and didn't get back until late last night. I didn't hear about what happened out at the ranch until Theresa told me this morning. It's almost unbelievable!"

Casey nodded. "I know what you mean. But I'm okay. Thanks for the concern."

He shook his head. "I hope that you're going to take proper precautions from now on."

Casey shrugged. "Maybe I won't need to. It seems that I've been taken off the case, or at least removed from active participation. The word has come down from on high.

"Look, I'm glad you're here. Mark, do you

remember mentioning to anyone the fact that I was going to the Hallecks' last night?"

Mark looked thoughtful. "I'm sure I didn't."

"What about your father, I mentioned it in front of him too?"

Mark shook his head. "I have no way of knowing, but I doubt it. Did he mention it to you, Theresa?"

Theresa looked down at her nails, then up at Casey, her eyes cool. "No. He didn't mention anything to me."

Mark leaned forward, bracing his hands on the desk. "Do you want me to ask him?"

Casey sighed. "No, don't bother. I suppose it really isn't that important. There were any number of people who knew that I was going to visit Raskin."

Mark removed one hand from the desk and placed it over Casey's. It felt good.

"Then you think that the gunman was after you too, and not just Raskin?"

Casey, very conscious of the warmth of his hand, felt self-conscious, but did not pull away. "Everything points to it."

Mark removed his hand and stood up. "Well, seeing that this is the second attempt on your life, perhaps it's just as well that you will no longer be actively involved."

Casey narrowed her eyes. "How did you

know about the other attempt?"

He ran a well-manicured hand over his smooth julienne, frowning. "Didn't you tell me?"

She shook her head.

Theresa put her hand on her brother's arm. "I told you, Mark. Don't you remember?"

Casey thought she saw a flicker of something that might have been relief flash briefly in Mark's eyes. "You're right. That's it."

Casey looked at Theresa, who met her gaze with a hint of mockery in her eyes.

"But, how did *you* know?" Casey said softly.

Theresa shrugged slim, well-tailored shoulders. "From Father. When Mark told him that he was asking you to the party, Father checked you out."

She smiled slightly. "Father has a habit of doing that; it goes back to the days when he was still active in politics. He has always said that he likes to know who he is associating with."

"I see," said Casey slowly, thinking it looked like Josh had been right; only it was Wager Halleck, not Mark, who had been doing some investigating of his own. She was surprised to find that she felt violated; then felt chagrined when she realized that turnabout was supposed to be fair play.

"Well, it sounds fair to me," she said finally,

with a rueful shake of her head, smiling at Mark.

"Well," he said cheerfully, "as I said a minute ago, it may be for the best. You'll have a better chance at staying safe riding a desk instead of the range."

"Yes. I suppose so; but I'm really not fond of desk jobs, and I enjoy investigative work. Moreover, I think I'm pretty good at it."

A frown darkened his handsome features. "Do you know why you were taken off the case so suddenly?"

Casey shrugged. She didn't want to express, in front of these people, her thought that power had been brought to bear. It would hit too close to home, and if repeated to members of the Halleck or Dessaline families, might put her in further danger.

Theresa, a narrow smile on her perfect lips, leaned forward. "Was it because you're a woman? I can imagine that the male investigators objected to having a woman in charge."

Casey seized upon the excuse gratefully. Besides, there was enough truth in the remark to make the statement legitimate.

She smiled at Theresa, feeling for the first time, that the woman might not be as snotty as she had thought. "You've got it," she said warmly, knowing that she was trying to make points, and doing it shamelessly. "You're very perceptive. Law enforcement officers have not always admitted women into their ranks gracefully, and — being a native Zonie I can say this — Arizona men can be a wee bit old-fashioned."

Suddenly Theresa's half-smile changed to an expression of bitter contempt. "Macho bullshit!" She spat out the words loudly. "That's all it is."

Casey tried not to show her surprise. From what she had seen of Theresa Halleck, this outburst was entirely out of character. She had pegged Theresa as a sheltered china doll, interested in only herself and her own pleasure. Was it possible that she had read her wrong?

Casey sneaked a look at Mark, and found him seemingly undisturbed by Theresa's statement; in fact, he seemed not to have heard it.

Meeting Casey's gaze, he smiled his charming smile. "Casey, Theresa and I are attending a horse auction tomorrow down near Casa Grande. Bert was going to handle it, but now . . ." His expression darkened, and he gestured emptily.

Casey had trouble concealing a shudder, as the image of the huge, dark horse and shadowy rider, pursuing her through the grove, thundered through her mind. She said inanely, "A horse auction?"

"Ever been to one?"

Casey shook her head.

"I think you might find it interesting." He flashed his winning smile. "Would you like to go with me?"

Casey's glance jumped to Theresa. As if reading her thoughts, he continued. "Theresa will be driving down by herself and taking the horse trailer, in case we make a purchase. I thought that you and I might have dinner afterward, if you like. Does that appeal to you?"

Casey took her time answering, stealing another glance at Theresa. The other woman's face gave away nothing. Finally, Casey said: "That sounds like fun, Mark."

His smile widened. "It certainly will be for me, now that I don't have to worry any longer that you might be in my company only because you want to investigate me."

Casey felt herself flush.

He gestured, "Wear something cool, and a wide-brimmed hat, it will be hot."

Casey saw another side of Mark when he came to pick her up on Saturday afternoon. Dressed in Levis, a faded blue western shirt, boots and sweat-stained Stetson, all showing signs of wear; he looked like any hand you might find on any ranch in the Southwest — almost. Country clothes couldn't quite hide the assurance, or the movie-star good looks.

He evidently noticed her look of surprise, for he grinned widely, sweeping off his hat to hold it over his heart. "I do declare, ma'am, you look plumb startled. Was you expecting someone else maybe?"

Casey had to laugh. "Well, you must admit that this is a change of image."

He shook his head. "Not really. I *do* know how to do *real* work you know. Ever since I was so high," he gestured at about waist level, "I've been working on the ranch. Father always believed that a kid who was working, was staying out of trouble."

Casey nodded. "Sounds logical to me. Well, I'm ready to go."

He eyed her up and down with evident approval. She had opted for fitted jeans — which showed her bottom and legs to good advantage — and a long-sleeved white shirt for protection against the sun. She had decided that boots would be too hot, and settled instead for comfortable denim sneakers. A blue-grey leather fanny-pack held her necessities. She looked, in her own estimation, fresh, perky, and pretty. She was glad to see that Mark shared her opinion. It did wonders for the ego.

★ ★ ★

As they headed out of town, Casey said: "So, are you a good horse trader?"

He shot her a knowing grin. "What politician isn't? But seriously, I'm not bad."

"Well, it's great that you can do it. Step in like that. I imagine that your father appreciates it."

"Father? I don't know if he appreciates it, but he expects it. And there are some advantages to being the dutiful son. Most of the people attending these auctions are property owners, and some are *large* property owners, and all of them are the kind of people who take the trouble to vote."

Casey shook her head. "And just when I was beginning to think of you as noble. So you're going to work the crowd, right?"

He grinned. "Of course. My father also taught us that when opportunity knocks, you answer the door. You know, you'd make a good politician's wife, my girl. You catch on quickly."

Casey knew that she was blushing, but Mark looked away then, concentrating on his driving as he turned onto 117, heading south.

As they sat in the not uncomfortable silence, Casey's thoughts turned to Donnie. Josh had agreed to take the boy for the afternoon and evening. She knew that he really enjoyed spending time with Donnie, and the feeling was reciprocated; but still she felt guilty. She had told Josh she was working on the case today, which was only partly true. She *did* hope to learn more about the Hallecks from Mark and Theresa, but that wasn't the only reason she had agreed to the outing. She had wanted to see Mark again; and she was enjoying his company far too much for her own comfort.

Also, she had not told Josh about being taken off direct participation in the case, partly because she had wanted to make her own decision about how to handle it, and partly because she felt a certain shame about what was, in effect, her demotion. She also felt that she was letting Josh down. He had been instrumental in getting her the position, and she had wanted to show him she could handle it. A fine job she was doing! And to put a final cap on her guilt, she knew how Josh would react if he found out that she was seeing Mark Halleck socially.

With an effort of will, she put these thoughts out of her mind, and turned to study Mark's patrician profile. Was he the upright, politically concerned citizen he appeared to be? Or did he have a darker side? His relationship with his sister struck her as a little odd; but she knew that members of large families were often very close, and that the relationships were often, also, very complicated. It didn't seem possible that Mark could be the killer — people in his situation seldom did their own dirty work — but could he have hired the killings done? And if so, for what reason?

She mentally ran down the list of members of both families. None of them, she had to admit, even the black sheep, seemed a likely candidate for the role of murderer, yet the connection to the families grew stronger all the time. But, best not to worry the subject just now.

She shook her head and broke the silence. "Mark, I asked you this once before, and I know it is none of my business, but why have you never married? Let's face it, your position makes you a real matrimonial prize. Dozens of women must have been spreading their nets for you, and you know that the voters prefer family men, so why are you still a bachelor?"

"I could give you the pat answer, that I haven't met the right woman yet, but I'll tell you the same thing I told you the night of the Dessaline benefit — I'm not sure. I like the idea of a wife and family, but at the same time, I suppose, I'm a little reluctant to be tied down. I could make a practical marriage, do it for the image; but I've watched the men who do that. They usually seem to get along all right, because they are the kind of men who can compartmentalize their lives. They have their work, and a woman or two on the side, and they're doing fine; but the families, their wives and kids, never seem very happy. The women have a drawn look, and some of them start drinking or over-medicating themselves; and the kids turn out insecure or turn into bastards like their fathers. I wouldn't want to wish that on a woman."

His serious expression suddenly turned playful. "I won't try to tell you that I've been celibate, you might think I'm gay, but I guess, to put it simply, I've never really been in love, and until I am, I won't marry."

Casey's cheeks grew hot. "I never thought you were gay," she said crossly. "You don't give off those kind of vibes."

"Not all gay men do," he said, laughingly. "But why this concern over my marital status, Casey? Are you applying for the job?"

Casey felt her face grow hotter. "Of course not. What a stupid question!"

He continued to smile. "Oh, I don't know. I don't think it's stupid at all. In fact, I've been giving the idea considerable thought."

Casey stared at him through narrowed eyes. "You can't be serious."

"Quite serious. I think it would be very easy to fall in love with you, Casey Farrel."

Casey, unsure whether he was joking or not, found herself flabbergasted. "You hardly know me, for heaven's sake."

"From everything I've ever heard or read about love, that's not important." He began to sing "Some Enchanted Evening" in a pleasant baritone.

Casey decided that he was putting her on, and relaxed a bit, knowing that because of her nosiness, she deserved a certain amount of teasing.

"Besides," he said. "I have a talent for sizing up people."

She laughed lightly, "And you're never proved wrong?"

"Rarely." He looked over at her. "I know you're not married, Casey, but are you seeing someone? You must be, an attractive woman like you."

"I'm seeing someone, yes."

"How serious is it?"

Casey felt uncomfortable, but she had started this conversation. "I . . ." She hesitated. "He's asked me to marry him."

"And what was your answer?"

"I told him that I'm not ready for marriage. It's too soon. I need more time."

Mark nodded thoughtfully. "Then I guess I'm a little premature here. I apologize for mentioning this so soon. But just think about it, okay?" He reached across and touched her hand lightly. "Promise?"

She moved uneasily. She couldn't say what she was really thinking, that this was pretty strong talk considering that they had never kissed, never made love. If she voiced these thoughts he might think she wanted him to make love to her. Maybe she did. No, she didn't really know what she felt, except confused.

Finally she said: "I don't know how to answer that, Mark. Now that you've brought it up, I don't know how I can *not* think of it."

He smiled easily. "Maybe that's what I had in mind all along." He laughed. "Politicians are sly, cunning bastards, as I'm sure you know."

He fell silent as they took an exit ramp and drove west away from the freeway, leaving Casey awash in a boiling mixture of emotions.

She had to admit that she was flattered by his prelude to a proposal, or whatever it was. Marriage to this man would almost have to be exciting; and being the wife of the governor of Arizona held a certain appeal. There was also the strong possibility that the governor's office would be only the first step toward a brilliant political career.

She gave herself a sharp mental shake. How

could she entertain such thoughts? She was in love with Josh, and in any case, as she had said often enough, she wasn't ready for marriage.

The site of the auction was a working horse ranch well out in the country. Mark found a place to park the car among the other vehicles parked haphazardly around a large roofed arena. As they walked toward the arena, Casey could see a collection of sturdy wooden bleachers huddled on the west side of the show ring — many of the seats already filled.

Most of the attendees were clad in well-worn western gear, the badge of working horsemen and horsewomen. The atmosphere was no-nonsense, and Casey could tell that these people took their horses seriously.

Mark led her toward the bleachers, and as they climbed in search of seats, hands were waved in recognition:

"How are you, Mark?"

"Mark Halleck! Ain't seen you in a coon's age."

"Whatcha doing, Mark? Slumming?"

Smiling widely, Mark returned all greetings, calling most people by name, pausing now and then to shake hands. He was, Casey thought, in his element.

At last Mark found them two seats on the aisle, and as they sat down, Casey glanced around casually. Three rows up, she spotted three familiar faces — Alexander, Glenn, and Sandra Dessaline. Sandra met Casey's eyes, but her gaze passed over her with no acknowledgment.

When Casey turned back, she found Mark shaking hands with the man seated next to him, a scrawny, twig-brown individual in faded Levis and scuffed boots, who looked to be anywhere between fifty and seventy.

"Casey . . ." Mark turned to her. "Meet Jake Jenkins, an old friend. Jake, this is Casey Farrel."

The man leaned forward to peer at Casey with shrewd brown eyes shaded by the wide brim of a rolled Stetson.

He held out a weathered hand. "How do, Miss Farrel. Or is it Ms.?" He gave a cackle of laughter. "Never can tell in these touchy days."

Casey reached across Mark to shake his weathered hand. It felt dry, like old leather. "Glad to meet you, Mr. Jenkins. Why don't we compromise on Casey?"

"Fine with me, as long as you call me Jake. What you doing out here with this old boy, helping him with his politicking?"

Mark grinned lazily. "Nope. Same as you,

Jake, looking for a horse or two to buy. Lost one of our best riding horses recently. Broke a leg."

Casey's antenna went up. Jenkins gave another cackle of laughter. "Yeah, sure! I'll bet you don't go to the public restroom lately without politicking the guy next to you at the urinal."

"Well, there's nothing wrong with taking advantage of an opportunity," Mark said. "But I am here to buy a horse."

"If you say so," Jake grunted. "Have you seen anything you like?"

Mark gestured toward the stables on the other side of the arena. "I haven't looked them over, Theresa is taking care of that. When she gives me the signal, I'll do the bidding."

The older man nodded. "Well, your sister knows her horseflesh, I'll say that for her. Say, I see you two didn't come prepared. How about a couple of cold ones?" He gestured to the small ice chest upon which he was resting his feet.

Mark turned to Casey. "Want a beer?"

Casey, who was beginning to feel the heat, nodded. "Yes. That would be nice."

Jenkins removed his feet from the ice chest and lifted out three cold, sweaty bottles of beer. He handed two of them to Mark along with a bottle opener. "Never did come to like canned beer. Doesn't taste the same."

Mark popped the caps on the bottles and handed one to Casey. She took it gratefully, and turned her attention to the area in front of the bleachers where the auction was evidently beginning. A number of horses, wearing numbers, were being led or ridden around the track. She knew a little about horses, but not enough to tell one breed from another.

Noting the direction of her attention, Mark said, "Beautiful animals, aren't they?"

Casey nodded. "What breed are they?"

"Morgans. That's what they breed here. Most of the ranches around here breed quarter horses, but father has always had a weakness for Morgans, and I guess he passed it on to us."

Casey grinned. "Yeah. Just like some families are Chevy families, and some are partial to Fords — western version."

He laughed. "That's one of the things I like best about you, Casey, you always seem to make me laugh."

Casey shrugged, but felt a glow of gratification.

"Looks like they're starting," Jenkins said.

Mark leaned forward. "I wonder where Theresa is. I don't want to bid without her input. She's the family horse expert, and she's damned particular; been known to attend a half dozen auctions a year, without making a buy."

At that moment, Casey's attention was distracted by Sandra Dessaline who was going down the steps past her.

"Excuse me a moment, Mark," she whispered as she stood and left her seat, hurrying to catch up to the other woman.

She touched Sandra's shoulder, "Miss Dessaline?"

Sandra tensed, whirling around. "What . . . ?" Her eyes narrowed. "I know you."

Casey nodded. "Yes. I'm Casey Farrel. You came to my office the other day."

Sandra stared at her for a moment. "Yes. You looked different. What do you want? I'm rather in a hurry . . ."

"This will just take a moment. When you were in my office, I told you that I was going to see Bert Raskin, the Halleck foreman, that same evening. Do you remember?"

Slowly, Sandra nodded. "Yes, I suppose so. But what has that got to do with . . . ?"

"Did you tell anyone else about it? Think, it's important."

Sandra frowned. "I may have, I don't recall. Why does it matter?"

"Haven't you heard about Raskin's murder?"

"Why, yes. But I still don't see . . ."

Casey had to fight to keep exasperation out of her voice. "The killer attempted to kill me, also; and I have reason to believe that I was the primary target. Ergo, the killer knew that I would be there at the Halleck ranch. Do you understand now?"

Sandra flushed. "Yes, I can see where you're coming from. But I resent the implication that anyone I might have told could be involved in such a thing. As far as I'm concerned, this conversation is over." Turning away, Sandra continued down the last few steps and turned in the direction of the stables.

Slowly, Casey faced about and returned to her seat. Mark was turned away from her, deep in low-voiced conversation with Jake Jenkins; as their voices rose, she tuned in.

"Jake, you know very well that I can't take a public stance in favor. Not with the climate the way it is right now. People still remember ASCAM, and the uproar about gambling on the Indian reservations."

"But you've always been in favor of legalized gambling. I still remember that long talk we had. You said that in your opinion legalized gambling was a way to raise money painlessly, a way out of the budget mess without raising taxes."

"The situation is different now," Mark said

with a sigh. "Now it would be political suicide."

"Just like all politicians," Jenkins said angrily, "weaseling, bending with the wind."

"Jake, to accomplish anything, I have to get elected. That's the first priority. After that, we'll have to see."

"You saying that if you're elected governor, you'll pump for legalized gambling?"

"I didn't say that, did I?"

"Damned politicians; can never get a straight answer from you!" Jenkins subsided, grumbling.

Mark turned to Casey. "Sorry. Just a bit of a friendly disagreement here. I saw you corner Sandra. What was that all about?"

"I just wanted to ask her something; nothing to do with the case, really." She avoided his eyes, looking instead at the arena. "Oh, look!" She pointed. "There's your sister."

Down below, Theresa Halleck, in riding clothes, was cantering a beautifully proportioned black gelding in front of the viewing stand. Despite her dislike of the woman, Casey had to admire her skill. Theresa and the horse moved as one.

After riding the animal back and forth several times — the animal seemed feisty — she stopped it in front of the stands, and lifted and raised her white hat twice, before returning it to her head.

Mark leaned forward. "That's the signal. I've got to go to work."

He sat forward as the auctioneer began his, to Casey, incomprehensible spiel. The crowd was quiet and intent, as one after another of the viewers raised and lowered their programs to make their bids.

It was, Casey had to admit, exciting. The price kept mounting steadily until it approached eight thousand, and most of the bidders had dropped out. The auctioneer slowed his chant, "I'm bid seventy-five hundred. Who'll bid eight? Do I hear eight?"

Beside her, Mark raised his program.

"I have eight. Who'll bid eight five for this fine animal?"

The one remaining bidder raised his program.

"I have eight five! Who'll bid nine?"

Again Mark raised his program.

"Nine. I have nine. Who'll go nine five? I have nine. Going once. Going twice. Sold for nine thousand to Mr. Halleck!"

Casey glanced over at Mark. His eyes were on Theresa and the black stallion as she rode the animal out of the arena.

Casey said, "Well, it looks like you bought a fine animal. He's beautiful."

Mark, his eyes still on Theresa, nodded.

"Looks like it. Theresa really knows her animals."

His expression was soft and fond, almost paternal in its affection; and Casey felt a sneaky prick of jealousy. Having no siblings, she had never known the closeness of a brother or sister.

She said softly, "You love her very much, don't you?"

He gave her a startled look. "Of course I do. She's my sister, isn't she?"

How nice, Casey thought, that that was all that it took to be loved; not because you were good, not because you were smart, not because you were beautiful, but simply because you were part of the family.

CHAPTER SEVENTEEN

"Do you know your trouble, Farrel?"

Casey looked up from the papers she had been working on, to see Bob Wilson scowling down at her. She had just gotten into the office, and could not imagine what had set him off this early on a Monday morning. His narrow face looked pinched and tired, and she wondered if he had gotten any sleep, so she softened her reply.

"I suppose many things; but what, specifically, did you have in mind?"

"You never listen! Didn't I tell you to keep your distance from the Hallecks and the Dessalines?"

Casey raised a hand placatingly. "Look, Bob, I haven't been . . ."

He ranted on. "So what were you doing on Saturday with Mark Halleck? And you questioned Sandra Dessaline right in front of God and everybody!"

So much for the soft answer. Casey leaned forward. "My engagement with Mark Halleck was purely social," she said firmly. "He happens to enjoy my company, and, I must admit,

I enjoy his. And as for Sandra, I wasn't questioning her, not *per se*. I only asked her if she had told anyone about my plans to see Bert Raskin the night he was killed. Dammit, my life is at stake here, Bob, and I have a normal concern about trying to protect it. The question was put on a personal level!"

Wilson shook his head, but she could see that some of the wind had gone out of his sails.

"You say your connection with Mark Halleck is social, so I'll buy that; but you'd better not use it to get around my directive. You have the makings of a damned good investigator, Farrel, but you've got to learn to take orders. I don't like what's coming down any more than you do, but that's the way it is. Now this is your last warning. If I get any more complaints about you, you're out of here. Understood?"

"Understood," she said tightly.

He nodded curtly, turned on his heel, and strode out.

Casey looked down and saw the fists that her hands had made. Her knuckles were white with pressure. She could not remember when she had been so angry. She felt strongly tempted to tell Bob to take his job and shove it; but that would mean admitting defeat. Also, she needed this job. The court certainly wasn't going to give Donnie into the custody of a woman who was unemployed.

There seemed to be nothing to do but give in as gracefully as possible, no matter how she felt. But she was so close! Maybe, just maybe, if she was very careful, she could keep on with her investigation on the sly.

If she could bring about a quick resolution to the case, get enough evidence to go to trial, she knew that all would be forgiven. No matter how much power and influence they possessed, not even the Dessalines and Hallecks could get away with murder.

The buzz of the telephone interrupted her thoughts. Impatiently, she picked it up. "Yes?"

"Casey," Josh said without preamble, "I just had an interesting chat with Paul Storey."

She said dryly, "A hello would be nice."

"Don't screw around with me here, babe. I'm not happy with you. Why didn't you tell me that you'd been pulled off the case?"

"Because I have not been pulled off the case, pulled back maybe, but not off."

"Don't split hairs, babe. Why did Bob do it?"

"Why do you think? Evidently I've been stepping on some important toes, and pressure has been brought to bear. Bob says there is nothing he can do."

"Did he tell you where the pressure is coming from?"

"No, but I can guess. I think it's the Dessalines, probably Alexander Dessaline. I evidently flouted orders by asking Sandra Dessaline a question — personal really — on Saturday, at the horse auction, and she evidently tattled to papa. When I came in to work today, Bob really reamed me out. He said that I've had my final warning, and that if I don't back off from active participation, I'm out."

"Are you backing off?"

"I'm not sure. I'm so close, Josh, I can taste it. If I give up now, and the case just fades away, I don't think I'll be able to forgive myself. Tell me, if you were me, would you give up?"

There was a pause before Josh answered. "I'm not you, babe, that's the thing. I've been on the force a long time, and have a certain amount of clout of my own; you're the new kid on the block. I think maybe you should consider backing off."

"I don't think I can, Josh. I think that I'm going to be very careful, and very sneaky; but I think that I'm going to keep on it. If I'm fired, I'm fired." She added vehemently, "It's personal now, Josh. Twice someone has tried to kill me, and that pisses me off!"

Josh gave a little laugh that did not quite

sound convincing. "You've got sand, Casey; that's one of the things I like about you, but don't let it get you killed. Think about this, okay?"

Dear Josh, she could tell that she had him really worried. "I will," she said softly, "and don't be upset. I can take care of myself."

"Yeah," he said with a deep sigh. "So you tell me; but I can't help being upset when you're in danger, and it chaps my hide that somebody is pushing you around. Maybe I should have a little talk with Bob, the asshole."

"No, Josh, you stay out of it. I can't come running to you every time I have a problem. If I'm going to make it in this business, I have to do it on my own. Don't you see?"

Another heavy sigh. "Yeah. I see, but what about this Mark Halleck? It seems to me that you're seeing an awful lot of him."

"He's a suspect, Josh."

"Is he now? The reading I'm getting is that he's a little more than that, and it doesn't do much for my peace of mind to know that you're dating another man. You know how much I love you, Casey."

Casey started a sharp retort, then checked herself. She was behaving like a tease, and the last thing she wanted to do was to hurt Josh.

She said softly, "I know, Josh; but I hardly

think you need worry. Mark and I are from two different worlds."

There was a moment of silence before Josh said: "I wish you had given me a different reason, babe. Anyway, be careful out there."

Casey, thinking of what he had just said, took a second to realize that Josh had hung up. A great sadness welled in her as she realized that she had just as much as admitted to Josh her attraction to Mark Halleck. He was hurt, she knew.

As she replaced the receiver, she gave a deep sigh. Why were human relationships so difficult? She cared for Josh, loved him, was grateful to him; but she could not deny the fact that she was excited by Mark Halleck. His good looks and position were a given; but he was also charming, kind, and fun to be with.

After the auction Saturday, Mark had taken her to dinner at Bobby McGee's, where they had enjoyed an excellent steak. It had been a relaxed, leisurely dinner. Their talk had ranged over many subjects, but as though by unspoken assent neither of them mentioned the murders, and Mark did not again mention his rather strange proposal. He was a witty, even brilliant conversationalist, keeping her entertained by slightly wicked stories about the rich and powerful citizens of Phoenix.

After dinner, he drove her home and left her at the door. She had been surprised when he did not try to kiss her, or invite himself in. He simply expressed his appreciation for a wonderful day and evening, and left with a promise to call her soon.

She had to admit to herself that she had experienced a pang of disappointment that he had not at least *tried* to push it further. She was pretty sure he was attracted to her, and she knew she was to him, so what had held him back?

Several times lately, waking in the late hours of the night, she had found her thoughts moving to him; wondering how it would be to wake up next to him in the morning.

She had also wondered, rather guiltily, to what degree it was his wealth and position that attracted her. Casey had never had money; not the kind of money that would allow her to go out and buy anything she wanted. Her parents had been solidly middle class; but she had seen the stark poverty on the Hopi Mesa where her grandparents lived; and after her parents died she had been left almost penniless. Since then she had struggled to make ends meet. It would be nice never to have to do that again.

And what about Josh? He had asked her to marry him a dozen times; and once or twice she had seriously considered it, then backed off at the last moment, afraid of making the commitment. Josh was stable, strong, secure in himself, and he loved her very much; but he was a cop, and so was she. Everyone knew about the divorce rate of cops.

She sighed again and pushed the phone and the thoughts away. At any rate, she couldn't waste her time thinking of personal relationships until this case was solved, one way or another.

As she pushed the phone away, it rang again. She picked it up. "Hello?"

A crisp female voice said, "Ms. Farrel?"

"Yes."

"This is Judge Pritchard."

Casey straightened in alarm. Had the judge reached a decision about Donnie? "Yes, Your Honor."

"I wish to see you in my chambers today, Ms. Farrel."

"Certainly, Judge Pritchard. Is this about Donnie?"

"I am going to be tied up in court all morning and early afternoon. But unless something comes up, I shall be free between four and five. Is that hour convenient for you?"

"Yes, of course."

"Then I'll expect to see you in my chambers at four o'clock."

Again, Casey was surprised by the click of a hang-up. She frowned, thinking that the woman might at least have said good-bye, and she had never answered Casey's question.

What was this all about? Apprehension nibbled at her mind. The judge's voice had not been at all friendly. Of course she was, evidently by nature, rather brusque; but she had sounded more so than usual. Had she decided to give Donnie back into the custody of his aunt? In the face of what his aunt was like, that did not seem possible; but who knew which way a judge would rule. She only knew that she had grown to think of Donnie as her son, and to lose him would devastate her.

Instinctively she started to punch out Josh's number at the station, but halfway through the process she hung up abruptly. Very likely he would be out on the street, and the judge hadn't asked for him. It would be better if she found out what this was all about before she contacted him.

The phone rang again. She jumped, staring at it like it was a coiled snake. Was it more bad news? She'd had just about enough for one day.

Slowly she picked up the receiver, said cautiously, "Hello?"

A small voice said, "Miss Casey Farrel, please."

"This is Miss Farrel."

"Miss Farrel, this is Rita Valera. Do you remember me?"

Casey felt a tingle of excitement. "Indeed I do, Miss Valera. Victor Sanchez's girl friend, right?"

"Yes. The thing is," Rita said hesitatingly, "you told me to call you if I found anything or learned anything about Victor's death."

Casey's tingle of excitement became a surge. "You've found something. What is it?"

"Well, I don't know if it means anything or not. I found it last week, but I couldn't make up my mind to call you or not. Then I thought, if it helps catch the man who killed Victor . . ."

"You're doing the right thing, Rita. What did you find?"

"I don't know if it *is* anything, Miss Farrel. You'll have to see for yourself."

"That's fine. Can you come to my office?"

"Oh no! Someone might see me down there. You'll have to come here."

"Where is here, Victor's apartment?"

"Yes. The rent is paid till the end of the month."

"Then you stay right there. I'll see you in about thirty minutes."

She made it in twenty-five. Rita opened the

door before Casey could ring the bell, and closed it quickly behind her. The girl looked pale, and tired.

She said in a rush, "I almost changed my mind and left before you could get here. I keep thinking that if this tape I found had anything to do with Victor's death, then maybe whoever killed Victor might come after me too."

"You found a tape?"

The girl nodded.

"And the police missed it?"

Rita nodded again and looked away. "Victor had a place in the bathroom where he hid things sometimes. A piece of wallboard in the shower that can be taken out. You can't tell unless you know where to look. The cops, when they search, they look in the usual places — you know, like the toilet tank and behind the medicine cabinet. They don't think of the shower. The other ones missed it too."

Casey froze. "What other ones? What are you talking about?"

Rita's pale cheeks grew red. "I didn't tell you, but when I came to the apartment, just after Victor was killed, it was all torn up like somebody had been looking for something. I cleaned it up so the landlord wouldn't be mad."

Casey shivered with a mixture of anger and

excitement. "Why didn't you tell me that when I first talked to you?"

The girl hung her head. "I didn't think it was important. Victor, he had some wild friends. I thought maybe they had heard about him being killed, and had come looking for . . ."

"Looking for dope," Casey said.

Rita nodded. "It wasn't till later that I thought about Victor's secret place, and that's when I found this."

She reached for her purse which lay on the table, and removed a video cassette.

Casey took it from her with trembling hands, and inserted it into the VCR. "You've watched this?" she asked the girl.

Rita nodded and seated herself on the couch. She looked relieved now that the tape was out of her possession. "I don't understand why it's important, but if it wasn't, Victor wouldn't have hidden it."

"Let's hope you're right," Casey said as she turned on the VCR and came to sit beside the younger girl. Silently she watched as the screen flickered and flashed, mentally praying that this was the break she had been waiting for.

Three men. Three men standing close together talking in what appeared to be a horse barn. The picture was poor, the lighting bad, and although the camera microphone had picked up the sound of the horses, the men's conversation was only a distant mumble.

Then the images of the three men grew clearer as the camera operator zoomed in, and Casey gasped. One of the men was Mark Halleck!

She leaned forward. There was light enough to see his face quite clearly. He was facing the camera, speaking rapidly. The second man was half-facing the camera. He was a big man in rumpled clothing, his face and body bloated and soft looking. The third man was slender, nattily dressed, and had the look of a man familiar with unsavory company.

Casey's belly felt cold. Neither man had the look or the manner of upright citizens.

The men seemed to be arguing now. The big man occasionally interrupted Mark, even placing a hand familiarly on Mark's shoulder. The third man talked very little, but once he turned to face the camera, taking a big cigar out of his mouth to spit on the ground. His face was smooth, unlined, his eyes cold and lifeless. Casey had seen men with faces like that before. What had Mark been doing with men like these?

The argument seemed to be growing more violent. The big man seemed to be urging Mark, the rumble of voices rose, and Mark was shaking his head angrily.

Casey wished that she could hear what they were saying, but the photographer was probably hidden in one of the horse stalls, and the camera microphone was picking up the nearest sounds, those made by the horses.

The picture faded to black, and Casey reached for the remote control.

"No," said Rita, touching her arm. "There's more."

Casey sat back, then leaned forward as another picture came on the screen. At first she wasn't sure what she was seeing, and then it became all too clear. Two people, a man and a woman, were making love, writhing in the throes of evident passion on hay-strewn ground.

As their naked bodies heaved and thrashed, Casey wanted to look away, feeling like a voyeur. The sounds, the panting and the sound of flesh on flesh made it even more embarrassing. The light was dim, and the color washed out; but there was enough to see that the people were young, with good bodies.

Then the woman's face came clearly into view, eyes closed, features contorted in ecstasy. It took Casey a moment to realize that the face belonged to Theresa Halleck.

She felt astonished and shocked. It did not

seem possible that the cold, aloof Theresa could ever experience such feelings. And why had someone taken the trouble to film this intimate moment? Was it because of the man? Was he someone prominent? Someone else's husband, perhaps? Casey got up and moved closer to the screen, but because of the bad lighting, and the position of the man's body, it was impossible to see his face. The film was so dark, that she couldn't even tell the color of his hair. There was, however, one distinctive feature about his back. On his right shoulder, like a spreading stain, she could see what appeared to be a large birthmark.

On the screen, Theresa's nails clawed at the man's naked shoulders, her long legs locked around his plunging hips. Now Theresa's mouth opened, and she moaned, an animal sound that made the hair on Casey's neck raise. Then the picture faded to black, and Casey sat staring at the flickering screen.

What did she have here? Obviously Victor had thought that the tape was important, or he wouldn't have hidden it. The only thing that made sense was that the tape was the blackmail instrument that had gotten Victor and Pedro their "money tree" and had also gotten them killed. But what was on that tape that could trigger blackmail and the deaths of six people? So Mark had been taped talking to two men in a stable somewhere. If that was important, then it had to be because of who the men were. The same thing applied to the tape of Theresa; it was the man who was the crux of the matter. She had to find out who these men were. Then perhaps, she would begin to find some answers.

She put the tape on rewind and turned to Rita. "Rita, do you recognize any of the people on that tape?"

Rita shook her head. "Nobody I've ever seen."

"Do you mind if I take the tape with me?"

Rita shrugged. "No. I'm just glad to get rid of it. You take it. I hope it helps you find out who killed Victor. He wasn't the best man in the world, maybe, but I loved him." Tears welled in her eyes.

Casey put her hand on the girl's arm. "Thanks. I think that this may be a great help. And one more thing. Don't tell anyone else about the tape, or that I have it. Okay?"

Blinking back tears, Rita nodded.

"And do yourself a favor and go home. It won't make you feel any better hanging around here. Too many memories. You go home to your parents."

Rita nodded again. "I will. And thanks for being so nice; for not treating me like . . . You know."

Casey squeezed the girl's hand. "I know," she said.

"She hasn't stopped, Father! I can't wait any longer. I'm going to have to deal with her once and for all; I have no choice now."

The old man's face twisted with a mixture of love and anger. "You will do nothing, hear me? Nothing. For God's sake, a little patience!"

He watched as his child paced back and forth, back and forth. He could not help but think of a tiger in a cage, so handsome and so dangerous. You could not let it out to roam free, and yet, such a pity to hold it. He said: "I have taken further steps. I hired a private investigator to dig into her past. Everyone has secrets, and he has found hers."

This earned him a look of alarm. "A private investigator? They're scum, you know that. He'll know the family is involved, and we'll be right back where we started, being blackmailed. That was stupid, Father!"

The old man flushed and felt the urge to strike out. He had never let anyone talk to him like this, but his love made him weak.

"Still," he said angrily, "do you think that I am a fool? I was taking care of family scandals and other . . . more dangerous and complicated matters, since before you were born. Don't push me too far. My own patience has a limit.

"Now, this Casey Farrel is not entirely a saint. My man found out that she is trying to adopt a child, that boy that was a witness in the Dumpster Killer case. She evidently is very fond of the child, and he is important to her. The judge in the case is very straight-laced — a woman who goes by the book. A copy of my man's report is now on her desk. I believe that it will give the Farrel woman something to concern her more than the task force investigation."

There was a pause during which the old man watched his child's face closely. When had it become so closed? Had it always been this way? Had he simply not noticed?

An angry sigh. "All right, Father, but this had better work. If it doesn't, I'm going to end her interference. No mistakes this time."

CHAPTER EIGHTEEN

Casey was five minutes late for her appointment with Judge Pritchard. She had stopped off on her way to the courthouse to have several copies made of the tape Rita had found. She did not want to risk losing her one piece of evidence.

When Casey was ushered into the judge's office, she was greeted by a cool, "Hello, Miss Farrel," and a measuring look.

Casey felt the urge to apologize, then decided that she'd be darned if she would. Who did the judge think she was, anyway, issuing orders to arrive at "exactly four o'clock"? Casey's time was valuable too, and she was just a little bit tired of being pushed around.

She settled for a hello and nod as cool as the judge's own, and, not waiting to be asked, settled herself into the seat in front of the desk.

Judge Pritchard was tapping the eraser end of her pencil against a thin sheaf of papers on her desk. In her usual abrupt manner she said: "In the morning mail I received what is evidently a private investigator's report." She looked at Casey sternly. "In it are some rather disturbing allegations."

Casey stiffened. Was the bad news never going to end? She forced herself to speak calmly. "I presume that these allegations concern me. May I ask what they are?"

The judge's gaze seemed, for a moment, almost sympathetic. "I fear so, Miss Farrel."

"Somebody is investigating me? May I ask who, and why?"

"That I can't tell you. The report was sent anonymously."

Casey felt a flood of anger. "I should think that I have a right to . . ."

The judge held up her hand. "Your rights are not at issue here. It is the rights of Donnie Patterson that concern me at the moment, and to make the best decision for the boy, I need to know everything possible about you and the boy's aunt. I do not, as you seem to think, automatically believe what is in this report. However, it is my duty to find out if these allegations are true. That's why I've asked you here. Now," she looked down at the papers, "it says here that two years ago, in Los Angeles, you had an abortion. Is that true?"

Casey took a deep breath. "Yes. But that's not a crime."

The judge sighed. "Look, Miss Farrel, I am not enjoying this any more than you are. I am not a rabid anti-abortionist; however, I do not believe that any woman should resort to abortion on a whim. In the matter of the Patterson boy's adoption, your character is important, and this matter has to do with character; therefore, I must ask you about the circumstances under which you made this decision."

Casey forced herself to relax, settling back into her chair.

"While I was in California, I became involved in a short but messy affair with my employer. It ended badly; and shortly after that I found out that I was pregnant. I was without a job, I had little money, no prospects and no husband. I saw no solution except to have an abortion. Perhaps I was wrong. Perhaps I would not make the same decision today; and I confess that what I did has always bothered me. But it was done, and I can't change that."

"I see." The judge tapped her pencil on the papers. "It also says here that you lived for a time with Sergeant Josh Whitney."

"That's true, but only in the literal sense. It was during the Dumpster Killer case, and the killer had made threats to kill me as well as Donnie. I had no place to stay, and Donnie's aunt was afraid that the boy's presence in her apartment would put her in danger, so Sergeant Whitney took us in. He did it for our protection, out of his own kindness, and I will always be grateful to him. He's been a good friend."

The judge looked at Casey, her eyes thoughtful. "You and Sergeant Whitney seem very close. Are you going to marry him?"

Casey hesitated, then answered honestly, "I won't lie to you, Judge Pritchard. I don't know. He's asked me, and I care about him, and I know that it would be good for Donnie; but I just don't know. However, Sergeant Whitney is very fond of Donnie, and the two are very close. Josh spends almost as much time with the boy as I do, and I feel certain that whatever happens between him and me, he and Donnie will remain friends. I would like to add that Sergeant Whitney is a considerably better influence on Donnie than Edith Black's live-in lover would be; and I believe that my character, warts and all, is a great deal better than Miss Black's."

The judge's lips tightened. "That may well be, Miss Farrel, but I am the one who must make the decision, and there is one thing in here," she tapped the papers, "that seriously troubles me. I know, of course, what line of work you are in; however, I had no idea that it was so dangerous. Is it true that there have been, in the last week, two attempts upon your life?"

Casey felt a sinking feeling in her stomach. She said slowly, "That, I'm afraid, is also true. You must know that police work of any kind carries some danger with it; but you also must know that this is not the norm, particularly when working for an agency like the task force."

"It says that one attempt occurred within a few blocks of your apartment. It occurs to me that the boy could be in some danger here."

Casey shook her head. "I'm sure that Donnie is in no danger; why should he be? I would never place him at risk."

"I'm sure you wouldn't, knowingly; but it seems to me that you may, all the same."

Casey sat forward. "Look, I hope to tie up this case very soon. I got a break on it today. But meanwhile, if it will ease your worries, I'll have Donnie stay with Sergeant Whitney. He's certainly safe there."

Judge Pritchard sat back with a sigh. "I am thinking of the long-term situation, Miss Farrel. You will have other cases, and, no doubt, find yourself in other dangerous situations. However, we will leave things as they are until I make my decision."

Casey held the judge's eyes with her own. "I just ask that you remember that people with dangerous jobs, law enforcement officers included, have children all the time, and in most cases raise them very well. Donnie is so much a part of my life now that I don't know what I'd do without him, and what he would do without me. I love him as much as if he were my own child. I hope that you will see your way clear to grant the adoption."

The judge did not answer, and Casey turned to leave the room, conscious of the judge's eyes on her back, hoping that she had said, and done, the right things, and bolstered by the fact that she had been as honest as she knew how.

As she reached the doorway, she turned back, as an idea occurred to her. "Judge Pritchard," she said, "in your time on the bench, have you ever tried a case in which an expert in lip reading testified as an expert witness?"

The judge frowned thoughtfully. "Why, yes, I have. Why?"

"It's important to my case. Do you recall a name, someone I can contact?"

The judge's frown changed to an expression of impatience, and for a moment Casey was certain that she was going to say that she didn't have time for this sort of thing. Then the judge turned to a large Rolodex, her slender fingers flicking efficiently through the cards, until she found what she sought. "Here!" she said, holding out a card.

Casey, notebook and pen already in hand, quickly jotted down the name, address and phone number.

Handing the card back, she said, "Thank you very much. If I'm right, and if I'm lucky, this may help me wrap up my case."

At the pay phone downstairs she punched out the number of Josh's station, and caught him just as he was leaving.

"Josh, are you doing anything tonight?"

"Well, I do have this tentative date with Elizabeth Taylor, but then she'll probably cancel at the last minute," he said amusedly. "Why, do you have something better in mind?"

"How about coming over for dinner tonight, around six?"

"What's the occasion?"

"Isn't the fact that I want to see you occasion enough?"

"It certainly is. I'll take that over a date with Liz any day. See you at six, babe."

At a few minutes after six, Casey was still in her kitchen, putting the finishing touches on dinner. Josh and Donnie were seated on the sofa before the television, watching "Monday Night Football." The Cardinals were playing out of town, and losing, as usual. Despite this fact, Donnie, who was an ardent Cardinals fan, cheered loudly every time they made a good play. Josh, working on a martini, played devil's advocate, grumbling about what a lousy team they were, winking at Casey whenever she peeked out of the kitchen to check on them.

At last the meal was ready, and she called them to the table: "Dinner's ready, guys. Come and get it."

Donnie bounced up and down, overexcited as always when he was with Casey and Josh together. "But Casey, the Cardinals are about to score!"

Josh hooted. "No way, Jose! They'll fumble just short of the goal line. Depend on it."

"You can watch from the dining room, kiddo," Casey said. "Now come on and eat while it's still hot."

Casey had prepared Josh's favorite dinner — lettuce and tomato salad, steak, baked potatoes, and corn on the cob. When she and Donnie ate alone, she tried to fix a larger selection of vegetables; but knowing that Josh wouldn't eat most of them, she had kept it simple.

Both Josh and Donnie sat where they could keep an eye on the game through the archway that separated the small dining room from the living room. The game was becoming more

312

and more of a disaster for the Cardinals, but with the confidence of the very young, Donnie kept rooting them on.

After the main course was pretty well destroyed, Casey brought out the Rocky Road ice cream, without which, for both Josh and Donnie, the meal would have been incomplete.

After the ice cream she joined the "men" while they watched the game to its bitter end, and listened to Donnie tell them why the Cardinals would win next time.

"Time for bed, kiddo," she said, ruffling his hair.

"Ah, Casey. Do I hafta?"

"Yes, Donnie, you know the rules for school nights."

Resignedly the boy got up and went around to Josh for a hug, then trudged after Casey into his bedroom. In his room, she turned down his bed, and bent to give him a kiss. "Now don't forget to brush your teeth; and good, not just a lick and a promise. Okay?"

He hung his head. "Okay. But I wish I could stay up until Josh goes."

She hugged his thin shoulders. "You know you can't stay up that late. Besides, I have a feeling that you're going to be seeing quite a lot of Josh, real soon."

His face brightened. "That would be great."

She looked at him sternly. "Hey there, you trying to make me feel unloved?"

He threw his arms around her legs. "Course not. You know that you're my favorite person, for a girl."

She bent down and pulled him close. "Yes, I know that, kiddo, and it makes me proud. Now," she gave his rump a gentle smack, "get into your pajamas, and don't forget the teeth."

When Casey returned to the dining room, she found Josh awkwardly clearing the table. She watched him for a moment from the doorway, smiling. He really was sweet. He lifted the plates as if he was afraid that they would crumble in his grasp, and seemed to have no clue that you could stack the dishes and carry them that way; but he was trying.

She stepped into the dining room. "Leave those till later, Josh. We have to talk, and there's something I want to ask you."

He put down the plate he was holding. "Sure, babe. What's up? I poured you some coffee." He pointed to two mugs sitting on the table.

"Great. Let's take it into the living room."

In the living room, she turned off the TV and they settled themselves on the couch.

"First," she said, "I need to know if you can take Donnie for the rest of the week. It

314

would help me a lot."

For a second he sipped coffee and looked thoughtful. "I don't see why not. I'm working nights, but Mrs. Lawson — that nice older lady who lives across the street who baby sits Donnie — she says she is quite agreeable to sleeping over. She says her husband's snoring keeps her awake at home, anyway. But why? What's going on?"

It took Casey a moment to get started, but once she did, it all came pouring out: the meeting with Judge Pritchard, the woman's comments about Donnie's safety, and, finally, the matter of her abortion, which she had not mentioned to Josh before. When the flow was spent, she was relieved but very weary, and she was not at all certain of how Josh would take her confession.

Slowly she raised her eyes to his. She let out her breath softly as she realized that she saw no condemnation there.

"It must have been rough on you, babe," he said gently.

She nodded, and let him draw her into his arms. "Why didn't you tell me this before, Casey? Were you afraid I would disapprove?"

She shrugged. "I don't know. I suppose so. I guess, in a way, I disapprove myself. But I feel better now that I've told you."

He nuzzled her hair. "Well, that's in the

past. Let's leave it there and forget it."

"But what about the judge, will she forget it? She's a straight-laced sort, with pretty strong views. I feel that she's already marked this down as a black mark on my balance sheet."

Josh pushed her back so that he could see into her eyes. "Worrying about it won't do any good. Judge Pritchard has the reputation of being scrupulously fair. And as far as your balance sheet goes, well, I can't imagine that your black marks could stack up against those of Ms. Black, if you'll excuse the pun! Of course you know that report was sent to the judge just to scare you off your case, don't you?"

"Of course."

"And did it work?"

Casey, shaking her head, had to smile. "No. So long as Donnie is safe, I'm going to keep at it until I'm fired, or solve the damned thing."

Josh nodded. "That's what I thought. Now, what is it that you wanted to show me?"

"Oh!" Casey jumped up and turned the TV back on, slipped the unlabeled tape into the VCR, then returned to the couch, remote control in hand.

"A tape?" Josh's eyebrows climbed.

Casey nodded. "It's just a couple of scenes,

but I think it's very important. I got it from Victor Sanchez's girl friend. He had it well hidden, and the police didn't find it. Evidently, from what she told me about finding Sanchez's apartment wrecked, someone else was looking for it too."

The screen flickered, and came alive, and Casey watched again, intently, looking for anything she might have missed. They watched in silence. When the first scene ended, Josh stirred.

Casey held up her hand. "Wait. There's more."

Once again Casey watched Theresa Halleck and her unknown lover in the throes of sexual ecstasy, and once again found it terribly embarrassing.

As she thumbed the remote, turning off the film, Josh stretched. "Whew. That last part is a bit steamy. Who took this bit of film?"

"I figure that it was either Sanchez or Castelar."

Josh nodded. "Then if your blackmail theory is correct, this could be the material used."

"I'm almost certain of it."

"The tall man in the first scene, that's Mark Halleck, right?"

"Yes. Do you recognize either of the other men?"

"Afraid not, but they don't look like boy

scouts. How about the woman in the sex bit?"

Casey took a deep breath. "That, my detective friend, is none other than Theresa Halleck!"

Josh whistled. "Mark's sister?"

"Mark's sister. You can't really see the man — his back is to the camera the whole time — but I'm willing to bet that he is either very important, very married, or both. How's that for a blackmail motive?"

He gave her a grin. "Pretty good. And the first clip?"

"I figure that those men with Mark Halleck are people that he didn't want to be seen with, people that it might be bad for him to be seen with."

"The meeting in a dark horse barn gave you the clue, did it?" Josh said dryly.

Casey narrowed her eyes, and showed her teeth. "Yes, and the fact that both men look like something out of a Mafia movie. But seriously, what do you think?"

"I don't know, babe. If only the camera mike had picked up the sound."

"I have a way around that," she said excitedly. "At least I hope so, an expert in lip reading, I got his name from Judge Pritchard when we had finished our little chat. I've got an appointment to see him tomorrow morning."

Josh sighed gustily. "I just hope to hell you know what you're doing. If Wilson finds out you're still working the case, you'll be hip deep in excrement before you know it."

"Excrement?" she elevated her eyebrows. "Is this the Josh Whitney I thought I knew so well?"

He grinned. "Could be I'm becoming more delicate as I age."

"Yeah, right. But if I bust this thing, if I get the killer, I'll be the hero, all will be forgiven."

"Probably. That's the way the world works. But I want you to promise me something, Casey. Whatever you learn from this film, I want you to check in with me before you go charging ahead, and maybe get your tit in a wringer."

She rolled her eyes in mock exasperation. "Now *that's* the Sergeant Whitney I know."

The name of the man who was to lip read the piece of film was Thomas Haynes. He and his wife, Martha — through whom Casey had made the appointment — lived in Mesa. Mrs. Haynes had informed Casey that Thomas could neither hear nor speak, and that he earned his living teaching lip reading and signing to hearing or speech impaired children.

Casey's appointment was for ten o'clock, and she arrived a few minutes early, eager to get on with it. Thomas and Martha Haynes lived in a small stucco house on a palm-tree-lined street in a quiet neighborhood. The house and yard were well-maintained, and fronted by a small, green, recently mowed lawn, bordered with bedding plants and rose bushes.

Going up the walk, Casey crossed her fingers behind her back. If all this came to nothing, she was up that well-known creek.

The door was opened by a small, plump, pleasant-faced woman in her mid-to-late fifties.

"Mrs. Haynes?"

"Yes, I'm Martha Haynes."

"I'm Casey Farrel. We talked on the phone yesterday."

"Yes, of course." The woman moved back from the door. "Come in. Thomas is waiting in his study. Our TV and VCR are back there."

Casey stepped inside, and the woman closed the door behind her. The interior of the house was pleasantly cool, and Casey heard the hum of the air-conditioner.

She followed the woman through the living room — which was simply and tastefully furnished — past a so-called Arizona room, walled with windows, and abloom with potted flowers and plants, to a modest but comfortable-looking room lined with bookshelves which held dozens of video tapes as well as books and memorabilia.

A man sat in a brown leather recliner, reading. He looked up as they entered, and rose to his feet. He was tall and thin, with receding gray hair and a pleasant, craggy face.

He looked at his wife, who signed to him, and then, fixing Casey with piercing blue eyes, he stepped closer, and took her hand in a firm grip.

"Miss Farrel, this is my husband, Thomas."

Casey returned the man's handshake and said distinctly, "How do you do, Mr. Haynes? I really appreciate your doing this."

Releasing Casey's hand, he signed swiftly.

"He says that he is happy to be able to help," Mrs. Haynes said. "Do you have the tape?"

Casey reached into her bag, removed the tape, but hesitated before handing it to Mrs. Haynes. "I'm afraid the second segment is rather . . . explicit, but the woman in the scene says something, and it might be important. Perhaps you'd rather not watch it, Mrs. Haynes."

Martha Haynes smiled. "Oh, I think I can handle it, but thanks for the warning." She handed the tape to her husband, then signed to him briefly. Thomas Haynes seemed amused. Casey, feeling that she had done her duty, watched as he inserted the tape in the VCR, while Martha pulled the shades on the windows, and motioned Casey to a small sofa that faced the television.

Casey could feel her heart pounding in her chest. She hadn't prayed for a long time, but she did so now, first addressing the old gods of her grandmother's people, then calling upon any god who would listen.

As the picture came onto the screen, Thomas Haynes leaned forward, watching intently. After the first segment had run its course he ran it again, this time making quick notes on the large yellow pad balanced on his knees.

During a third watching, he enlarged upon his notes, while Casey and Martha Haynes watched silently.

At last, seeming satisfied, he handed the pad to Casey, then began signing to his wife.

Casey, by an effort of will, did not look down at the notes until he had finished.

Martha Haynes turned to her with a smile. "He says that the picture is dark, but he thinks that he got most of what was said. He has numbered the speakers: the one in the center, the big man is number one, the tall man number two, and the small man number three."

"Thank you," Casey said, and turned eager eyes to the yellow pad.

"1. . . . need all the support we can get.

2. I agree that legalized gambling would be of great benefit to the state; but it's not politically expedient for me to openly support your cause at this time. Opposition to gambling is strong among a great many voters.

1. We've recruited close to a dozen legislators, and all have agreed to vote yes when our bill comes before the legislature.

2. But they are already in office. They run no risk of losing votes until they run again; and by that time it will probably have been forgotten.

1. We are willing to spend a great deal of money to get legalized gambling into Arizona, Mr. Halleck. We have already contributed generously to those legislators who have promised to cooperate.

2. You mean you've bribed these people?

1. We don't consider it bribery. We're no different from many other state lobbyists. We have simply contributed generously to certain campaign funds.

2. I have a question. I've never met Mr. Venezia here; but his name is familiar to me. He's been linked with organized crime, and is prominently known for being connected with the casinos in Las Vegas.

1. (Laughing) Don't believe everything you read, Governor.

2. Let's not get carried away. I'm not Governor yet.

1. But you will be. With our help you'll be a shoo-in. As for Johnny here, the media always exaggerates. Johnny has never been convicted of anything, not even a traffic ticket. He's a legitimate businessman. Check it out.

2. I may just do that.

1. And you'll find it's just like I said. Now, can we count on your support. If we can, we'll contribute a neat hundred grand to your campaign fund.

2. I have no need of your financial support, and I want it fully understood that I am not soliciting it.

1. Anyone running for office can use financial support, Governor, even one who has a wealthy father. I don't have to tell you how expensive it is to run now. And we have ways of doing it so that it's clean as a whistle. No paper on it anywhere.

2. *If* I am elected Governor, and if there is no hint that organized crime will be involved in the proposed casinos, I will lend my support to the bill's passage . . ."

Thoughtfully, Casey put down the pad. What was transcribed here could do Mark some damage politically if it became general knowledge. If the second clip, as Casey suspected, showed Theresa with a married man, particularly one in a prominent position, put together, the two clips could cause the Halleck family considerable embarrassment, and possibly cost Mark the election. To some people this, indeed, might seem cause for murder. People had certainly been killed for less.

She turned to Mrs. Haynes. "The second scene?"

Mrs. Haynes signed to her husband, and he started the tape again.

Theresa and her mysterious lover again in passionate embrace. Casey concentrated her gaze on the mark on the man's left shoulder. She had the mark memorized now and would recognize it if she ever saw it.

Again and again the couple embraced, the woman mouthed words, the picture faded.

When Haynes at last turned off the tape, he began signing to his wife.

Martha Haynes turned to Casey. "He says that this bit is more difficult. It is darker, and harder to see the woman's mouth. He is fairly certain of most of the words, which seem to be: 'Yes. Yes. Now. (something) Now!' but the first syllable of the fourth word is unreadable. He thinks it may be a proper name, perhaps Arthur, or Luther, but he can't be absolutely sure. He's sorry."

Casey sighed. It wasn't as much as she had hoped for, but it was something. She smiled. "Tell him thank you so much. I really appreciate it. I'd also appreciate it if he, and you, would not tell anyone else about what you saw. I'm certain that you realize what it could mean."

Martha Haynes nodded. "We've done this kind of work before, for the prosecutor's office, and for the Phoenix Police Department. You can count on our discretion."

Casey shook hands with them both, tucked the yellow papers from the scratch pad into her purse and returned to her car. All the way back to Phoenix she kept going over the last words Haynes had written. "Yes. Yes. Now, Arthur, now!" Who was Arthur, or Luther, what was his last name, and how could she find him?

CHAPTER NINETEEN

The first thing Casey did when she got back to her office was to run John Venezia's name through the computer. She came up with a long record of arrests: assault with a deadly weapon; drug peddling; operating a house of prostitution; a manslaughter charge, second degree. But the big man on the tape had been right about one thing — Venezia had been convicted of none of the charges. She noted that Venezia's last arrest had been five years back, so either he had gotten smarter, or had cleaned up his act. However, he still carried the reputation of mob connections, and his association with any political figure was bound to tarnish that politician's image.

She stared at the computer, trying to think of some way to find out who the other man was. If she showed the tape to the other members of the task force, it was very possible that someone might recognize him; particularly if he was a known criminal. However, as soon as she showed the film, she would be permanently out of a job. No, she had chosen her way to go, and she would play it out.

Turning away from the computer, she punched out the telephone number of Mark's law firm. No, Mr. Halleck wasn't in today. Was there any message?

Casey said no, and put down the receiver, not knowing whether she was glad or disappointed. It wasn't going to be easy to confront Mark with the tape. While not entirely incriminating, it made him look bad. The last part of the dialogue had the big man telling Mark how they could contribute to his campaign without it being known; and Mark stating that if elected he would support legalized gambling. The segment had ended there. Casey could think of several things that might have occurred after that. Perhaps Mark flatly refused their money and told them to get lost; but what the tape seemed to show was a slippery politician accepting a bribe.

Even knowing this, Casey realized that she felt disappointed in Mark. The shine was off his image. If she felt that way, others would feel the same. It raised too many questions: one of which was why he had gone to meet these men in the first place?

But that wasn't the point now. Now she had to concentrate on putting these two pieces of the puzzle together. She was so close — she knew it — and yet so far. If she couldn't tie up the case within the next twenty-four hours she might as well turn over the tape and the dialogue sheet to Paul Storey or one of the others. She couldn't, in all conscience, delay any longer; and that would mean the end of her job with the task force. The situation was drastic, and drastic times called for drastic measures. She could see nothing to do but to go for a direct confrontation. Wager Halleck was the patriarch, the power of the family; it was quite possible that he had ordered the killings to protect his children. If she told him of the tape, even showed it to him if that's what it took, would he break down? And if he wasn't involved, wouldn't he have a good guess as to who was?

It would be dangerous; but if she told him that there were other copies of the tape in the hands of other law enforcement officers, wouldn't that protect her? It wasn't entirely true; but Josh had a copy. And for all Halleck might know, she might have given out several copies, all marked to be turned over to the police if anything happened to her.

So it would be foolish to kill her, for it would only add to the scandal. Of course if Halleck didn't break, or give her something she could use, she was out of a job, but that seemed to be true in any case. Taking a deep breath, she thought, The hell with it. It was something she had to do.

There was another precaution she could take. It would be good to have someone with her. Reaching again for the phone, she called Josh's home number. Since he had the night shift, he should still be at home.

The number rang four times before connecting her with his answering machine. She left a message: "Josh, this is Casey. I talked to the lip reader and now have a copy of the dialogue. I promised to tell you before I did anything, but can't reach you. It's now 2 p.m. In a few minutes I'm leaving to drive up to Carefree to see Wager Halleck. I'll call you when I get back."

She then called the station, thinking that she should leave word there for Josh. Not wanting to announce the fact that she was going to the Hallecks', she told the desk sergeant to ask Josh to call his home answering machine, if he had not already done so.

Feeling that she had done what she could to protect herself, Casey left the office.

By the time she reached the parking area at the base of Castle Rock, her breathing had slowed to normal, but she still felt keyed up and tense.

There were no other cars in the parking lot, and the door to the elevator lobby was locked. Seeing the intercom to the right of the elevator door, she pressed the button. In a moment a tinny, male voice said, "Yes?"

"This is Casey Farrel. I'd like to see Wager Halleck, please."

"Señor Halleck is not receiving callers."

"Just tell him who it is. I think he'll see me."

Casey waited for several minutes, impatiently, until the speaker finally announced: "Señor Halleck will see you."

Something clicked behind the closed door, and Casey reached out and turned the knob. As the door closed behind her, it clicked again. For an instant she seemed to feel chilly fingers along her backbone. It was just normal security, of course. Halleck couldn't have just anybody popping into his elevator and up to his house. Still, under the present circumstances, it made her somewhat uneasy.

When she got out of the elevator and knocked on the door of the house, it was opened by a tall, dark-haired man, with broad shoulders. He was young, but his face was stern and his eyes sharp. He said, "Señor Halleck is in his study. I will take you there."

Following the tall man, Casey again felt those phantom fingers touch her spine. The man was obviously a bodyguard, or at least security of some kind. Position and notoriety might have their perks; but it must be depressing to be in a situation where you had to constantly be worried about being harmed. Casey knew that she certainly wouldn't like having someone hovering over her all the time. Even then, would you ever feel safe?

As the tall man showed Casey into Halleck's study, Wager Halleck rose from behind his desk. He looked tired, Casey thought, and older. His brown eyes settled upon her disapprovingly. "Why are you here, Miss Farrel? I thought you were through with us. I debated with myself about turning you away, but . . ." He sighed, running blunt fingers through his gray hair. "I remembered your fabled persistence, and yielded to the inevitable."

Casey frowned. "Fabled persistence? I don't think that I've been at this job long enough to have become a legend, Mr. Halleck."

Something flickered in Halleck's eyes. "Well, word gets around you know. You have been rather insistent in your harassment of my family, and the Dessalines also, I understand. You must see it from our point of view, Miss Farrel. We know that we have done nothing; we have told you all we know; and still your questions persist. What is it this time?"

He motioned to the chair across from his desk. "Sit down, we might as well be comfortable."

Casey seated herself gingerly on the edge

of the chair. Her nerves were singing like wires. He was so poised, so sure of himself. He wasn't a man who would rattle easily. She would have to be direct. She leaned forward.

"So you were surprised that I came here, Mr. Halleck. Could it be because you thought I was off the case?"

She thought his eyes flickered. "Why should I think that, Miss Farrel? You're being off or on the case does not concern me in the least."

"Oh, I think it does. It has become very clear that someone with considerable power has been pressuring the higher-ups to hold back on this case. I think that someone is you."

Halleck's neutral expression suddenly slipped; and as Casey looked into the face suddenly exposed, she felt, as many before her had felt, the sheer indomitable will and power of the man. The expression was only there for an instant, but she was glad when it had passed.

Mask firmly in place again, he said, "Where did you ever get such a crazy notion? Even if I was interested in your investigation, you are badly informed about my influence. At one time perhaps, when I was U.S. Senator; but those days are long past."

Casey's stomach felt tight, but she kept on. "I don't think so. I think you still have enormous political clout, besides the influence that your wealth brings. As to why you should concern yourself, I think it was because I was getting too close to the truth."

"And just what is this truth?" he demanded icily.

Casey took a deep breath. "The truth is that a member of your family is involved in these murders."

He leaned across the desk, the mask gone again. Casey had to exert an effort of will to keep from flinching. Her heart was hammering.

"You have just crossed the line, Miss Farrel. My family is very important to me, and I will not let you insult or libel the Halleck name. I must ask you to leave, at once!"

"Does the name Johnny Venezia mean anything to you, Mr. Halleck?"

"The name means nothing to me. Now, I want you to get out."

He stood, and Casey stood also. "Look, Mr. Halleck, I know that you can have your goon — who I am sure is outside the door right this minute — throw me out; but I would advise against it. I have some evidence in my possession that . . ."

Halleck turned his gaze to the door as it opened, and Mark stepped into the room and stopped suddenly at the sight of Casey.

"Casey? What are you doing here?"

"I needed to talk to your father, and to you," she said. "I called your office, and they said you were out."

"What is it? What's the problem?" He appeared shaken, Casey noticed, lacking his usual self-assurance and poise. Quelling her own mixed feelings at his appearance, she focused on her choice of words.

"Mark, I've come across a piece of film that could be harmful to you. If it was made public, it might very well ruin your chance at the governorship. I believe that this film was used to blackmail your family."

Mark's face showed confusion, and as his glance went to his father, Casey's did also. The elder Halleck's face was white, and his expression one of terrible pain.

"Do you have this tape with you?"

Casey nodded. "A copy, yes. I left the original with a close friend, with instructions to release it to the task force, and the media, if I should, for any reason, not get home tonight. And there are other copies as well."

Mark stepped nearer to his father. "Father, do you know what this is all about?"

The elder Halleck would not meet his son's eyes, nor did he answer. Mark turned to Casey.

"Casey, what's on that tape? I think I have a right to know."

Casey nodded. It wasn't easy, but she met his eyes directly. "There is a segment showing you and two men in what appears to be a horse barn. One of the men is Johnny Venezia. The segment closes with you agreeing to support legalized gambling if you are elected. It looks as if you are accepting a bribe."

Mark's face whitened. "Someone filmed that meeting? But it was nothing. I didn't initiate that meeting, or the place where it was held, and I don't really know either of those men. Perhaps it was unwise of me to meet with them at all; but I assure you that I didn't accept, or agree to accept their money. I told them what I believe; that legalized gambling would be good for the state, but there was no agreement. No deal. No payoff! If it appears otherwise, then they must not have taped the entire meeting."

Casey nodded. "The tape cuts off right after your statement about your position. But the important thing is that it *could* hurt you, and cause you and your family embarrassment, and that it *was*, I'm quite certain, used to blackmail your family. What I want to know is, who paid the blackmail?"

Mark's expression tightened. "And to whom was this alleged blackmail paid?"

"Castelar and Sanchez."

He looked at her steadily. "And you think the person being blackmailed was the one who killed them and the others. Are you accusing me of murder, Casey? Can you really think that I would kill six people so that I can win the election?"

"It's possible. I am sure that it was someone in your family. You could have hired it done."

Mark's shoulders slumped. "My God. Do you really think I'm capable of something like that?"

His father reached out a hand and placed it on Mark's shoulder. Casey saw that the hand trembled. "Son. Mark, I . . ."

Both men looked shaken to the core. Casey, feeling a painful mixture of sorrow and inevitability, pushed on. "There is more on the tape than the scene with Mark in the barn," she said to the older man.

Wager Halleck looked up, his eyes filled with pain. "What?"

"There is another scene on the tape. It shows two people making love."

An expression of puzzlement passed over the old man's face.

"Making love?"

"Yes. And one of them is Theresa."

The blood returned to Wager Halleck's face, suffusing it with darkness.

Casey looked at Mark. He appeared as shocked as the old man.

"What kind of filth . . . ?" the old man said. "Why would anyone film something like that?"

"It had to be because it would incriminate Theresa in some way. It could only be because of the man involved."

"And the man?" Wager said in a hoarse whisper. "Who is the man?"

Casey was opening her mouth to admit that she didn't know, when a voice said coolly from the doorway, "Don't bother to answer, Ms. Farrel. You've said all that you're going to say."

Casey whirled around to see Theresa Halleck standing just inside the room. She held an ancient .45 revolver in both hands. The gun was aimed directly at Casey.

Casey felt the shock of pure fear and sudden realization.

Wager Halleck was speaking in a hoarse voice, "Theresa, put that gun down. This won't solve anything."

Casey's gut grew colder as Theresa smiled. It was a smile of serene confidence, a cold smile, a smile that flirted with madness. "Oh, I think it will, Father," Theresa said calmly. "I think that once Miss Nosey here is permanently taken care of, everything will be fine."

"She has the tape, Theresa," Wager Halleck said, "and she has left copies with other people."

The serene expression left Theresa's face with shocking quickness, and the dark look that replaced it was frightening in its intensity.

"Copies of the tape? Then there is nothing to lose. It will take a little while for them to know she's missing. By then," she gave a sudden, shocking giggle, "we'll be far away. Won't we, brother?"

She turned her gaze quickly to Mark, and Casey, for a moment, felt lightheaded. Mark's face was frozen, his eyes blank.

Casey felt a wave of sickness rising in her belly like an evil tide. It all made a dreadful kind of sense. It was ugly, almost unbearably ugly, but it made sense. The name that Theresa had called her lover was not Arthur, or Luther, or any variation thereof. The name she had spoken was "brother."

Theresa, holding the gun unwaveringly on Casey, moved, smiling now, toward her brother, who seemed to shrink as she approached.

Casey shot a look at Wager Halleck who was staring at his children in confusion.

"Yes, brother," Theresa was saying. "Maybe it's for the best. I know that you wanted to be governor, but now we can go where no one knows us. Where we can be who we are. I tried to save you. To protect you. But it will be all right, when she's gone."

Wager Halleck's voice was only a hoarse whisper. "Theresa. What are you saying?"

Casey felt her own voice strained by the muscles of her throat. "Mr. Halleck," she said. "Mr. Halleck, the man in the picture with your daughter, with Theresa, he has a large birthmark on his back, on his right shoulder?"

As Casey's words hung in the air like an evil spell, Wager Halleck's face seemed to collapse. His hand went to his chest and he staggered. Mark, ignoring his sister's restraining hand, moved toward the old man. His father reached for him, as if to support himself; but at the last moment he grabbed the fabric of Mark's shirt at the shoulder, and, with sudden strength, tore it away.

For a moment they all stood frozen as if in tableau, everyone's gaze centered on one spot, Mark's shoulder, where the dark birthmark bloomed.

"The two of you," the old man said. "Brother and sister, the two of you . . . How could you? How could you?" All the strength seemed to drain from him, and he sank weakly into the chair behind his desk.

Theresa shot Casey a look of pure hatred. "I didn't want Father to know. I wanted to spare him that, at least," she spat out, raising the heavy gun.

Casey could only stand dumbly, knowing that she had found the truth, and waiting for the bullet that would kill her.

Slowly, Mark turned toward his sister. "You killed them? You killed those people? For God's sake, why?"

"Not for God's sake, brother. For yours, and mine, and for the family. When those two slimy *coyotes* showed me the first part of the tape I laughed at them. It didn't prove anything, really. I wouldn't have paid them for that, or killed them for it either. But the second part; that was *our* secret. If it got out, you would never be governor, and the family would be shamed. I had to do it, don't you see? They had no right. They deserved to die!"

She turned her gaze to her father. "I'm sorry, Father. But Mark is the only man in this world that I have ever truly loved. I would do anything for him. *Anything!*"

Mark groaned and put his hands to his face. Theresa smiled and began to tighten her finger on the trigger of the .45. "And you, *Ms.* Farrel, you thought you could take him away from me. Do you know how ridiculous that is? Mark is mine. He has been mine since I was old enough to seduce him. He doesn't need anyone else, doesn't *want* anyone else. Oh, sometimes he thought he did," she smiled her cold smile, "but I always made him see he was wrong." The finger was still moving. Casey closed her eyes and thought of her dead grandmother.

The roar of a .45 rocked the room like a crack of thunder, and Casey's heart stopped. Then started again with a painful thud, as she realized that she was still alive. Slowly, she opened her eyes.

In front of her, Theresa lay upon the floor, her chest a red stain, her gun on the floor beside her.

With a cry of anguish, Mark ran to her and fell on his knees beside her body, cradling her head in his arms.

"May God in his infinite mercy forgive me," Wager Halleck said in a ragged whisper. A .45 revolver, apparently the mate to the one by Theresa's body, hung limply from his hand. "I could not allow another death. I loved her, but she could not be allowed to go on. You may call the police now, Miss Farrel."

As he spoke, the wail of police sirens could be heard, sounding like the cries of the souls of the damned, growing in volume until they filled the terrible silence of the room.

CHAPTER TWENTY

Casey and Josh stood side by side at the edge of the pool behind the Halleck house. Almost an hour had passed since Wager Halleck had killed his daughter, Theresa. A handful of policemen were still in the study, securing the crime scene.

Theresa's body had been taken away, and Wager Halleck had been taken to the station. Mark had accompanied him, and the old man had clung to him as if to a life raft. Casey watched them go with very mixed feelings. The case was solved, justice had been served; but she could feel no triumph as she watched the two broken men get into the police car. Theresa Halleck had destroyed more lives than those of her victims, and the damage to the other members of her family would continue, like ripples spreading outward from a central agitation. The one positive thing was that Theresa had been stopped before she could destroy more lives.

Casey turned to Josh, and he put one long arm around her shoulders. His face was drawn, and he looked as tired as she felt. Although the day was still hot, she felt cold to the bone. Leaning against Josh, she drew in his strength.

"You shouldn't have come out here alone, babe. It was a foolish thing to do. When I think of what might have . . ."

She looked up at him. "It seemed the right thing to do at the time," she said. "I didn't think Wager Halleck would harm me in his own home; but I'll admit that I didn't expect Theresa, and I had no clue that she was a psychopath."

He shook his head. "Psychos don't play by the normal rules, Casey. It was a close call."

Casey shivered. "I know. And thanks. You took quite a chance yourself, sending out the cavalry on the off chance I might be in trouble. They wouldn't have been very happy if it had proved to be a false alarm."

"It wasn't exactly an off chance. I'd take a lot of risks for you, you know that; but I had a pretty good reason for assuming you might need some help. Donnie and I were over at the Y, using the pool. They have a big trophy case in the entrance hall. It was full of trophy cups and photos, and one of the photos caught my eye. It was a picture of Mark Halleck, when he was younger, performing at an exhibition swim meet. He was in bathing trunks and his body was turned so that you could see the back of his right shoulder."

Casey let out her breath. Josh held her closer. "Yeah. For a minute I couldn't believe it, but that mark is very recognizable. I called your office right away, but they said you had gone out. Then I called *my* office to see if you had left any word for me, and got the message to call home. As soon as I heard where you were headed, I knew there was going to be trouble."

"Your gut told you," said Casey, with a shaky laugh.

He squeezed her closer still.

"Do you think they'll bring charges against the old man? If he hadn't shot her, she would have killed me."

Josh shook his head. "I don't think so. God, what a terrible thing, to have to kill your own kid."

"I think he knew," Casey said. "I mean before this. I think he knew what she had done. Why else would he have brought out his big guns to stop me, and the investigation? I think he protected her as long as he could, but in the end, he knew that she had to be stopped."

"Very possibly. But I don't think he knew about Theresa and Mark. That must have been the final straw."

"Theresa made it pretty clear that she was the one who started that." Casey shivered.

"She was like a jungle cat, beautiful, dangerous, and completely amoral. Why didn't her family notice long ago that there was something wrong with her? There must have been signs."

Josh sighed. "Probably because they didn't want to know. She was the youngest child, and from what you've told me, pampered and spoiled. They probably started making allowances for her when she was a kid, and just kept on. Family dynamics can be pretty strange."

"I didn't see it either," Casey said thoughtfully. "I thought she was cold, and too attached to Mark; but I never really considered her as a suspect. I considered the fact that a woman might have hired the murders done; but I never really thought that a woman might have committed the crimes herself. A .45 is not usually a woman's weapon; and the other factors — the truck and horse trailer, the use of the horse, the way the murders were committed — all seemed to point to a man. I guess it shows that I'm not as open-minded as I thought. I went for the stereotype, just like a man. I'll know better, after this."

Josh kissed the top of her head. "Well, nobody's perfect."

"Casey? Sergeant Whitney?"

They faced around as Walt Edwards for the

Maricopa Sheriff's Department came toward them. "We've wrapped everything up here, Casey. And congratulations for a job well done. You showed us that you were right all along."

"Will you need me for anything else, Walt?"

He shook his head. "No, you can leave any time. Of course I'll need an official statement for my files; but as it stands now, it's tied up as far as I'm concerned."

With a wave of his hand, Walt Edwards turned back toward the house.

Josh offered Casey his arm. "Shall we go?"

She took his arm, and they headed toward the house and the elevator.

"Oh, by the way, babe, I did something else today."

She looked up at him suspiciously. "What?"

"I went to see Edith Black. To make a long story short, I reasoned with her, and got a letter from her, signed and sealed, agreeing that Donnie would be better off with you, and withdrawing her claim to him. I think, that with this, Judge Pritchard will grant you custody."

Casey stopped dead in her tracks. "Josh! How wonderful. But you and I both know that you don't *reason* with Edith Black. What did you use, a rubber hose and hot lights?"

Josh laughed. "Nope. Something better,

something close to Ms. Black's heart, money!"

"Oh, Josh, you didn't! How much?"

He shrugged, "Enough, obviously."

"But your money, your savings. I can't let you use that."

He held her close. "Shhh. It's already done; besides, I told you, since my divorce I have had no one to spend my money on, and I've made a couple of good investments. And I consider this the best investment of all, helping the two people I care about most in the world."

For a moment Casey was speechless. She searched Josh's eyes and found only love shining there. Many men, she knew, would have imposed conditions, but Josh was demanding nothing.

She threw her arms around him, hugged him fiercely, then stood back with shining eyes. "Detective, you are a good man!"

"Of course," he said gravely. "Haven't I been telling you that all along? And I want to tell you something else. Despite my scolding, I'm proud of you. You stuck by your guns, and you carried it through. You're a hell of a law enforcement officer."

Standing on tiptoe, she kissed his cheek. "Thanks, Detective, I've waited a long time for that. Now, let's go home."

"Your place or mine?"

Without hesitation Casey said, "Yours."

The employees of THORNDIKE PRESS hope you have enjoyed this Large Print book. All our Large Print books are designed for easy reading — and they're made to last.

Other Thorndike Large Print books are available at your library, through selected bookstores, or directly from us. Suggestions for books you would like to see in Large Print are always welcome.

For more information about current and upcoming titles, please call or mail your name and address to:

THORNDIKE PRESS
PO Box 159
Thorndike, Maine 04986
800/223-6121
207/948-2962